The Fish ain't Biting

K. Mitchell Thomas

K. Mitchell Thomas

SHUNU PUBLISHING

First printing
December 2004

Editing
Taylor Editorial Service
www.chandrasparkstaylor.com

Cover illustration and book design
Stacy Luecker
www.essexgraphix.com

Published by
SHUNU PUBLISHING
P.O. Box 2636
Stafford, TX 77497
www.kmitchellthomas.com

ISBN 0-9742329-6-3

Printed in the United States of America

This is a work of fiction. It is not meant to depict, portray, or represent any particular gender, real persons or group of people. All the characters, incidents, and dialogues are products of the author's imagination and are not to be construed as real. Any resemblance to actual events or persons, living or dead, is purely coincidental.

"A woman's gotta have it."
—Bobby Womack

For Steven: You brought me joy every single day.

Acknowledgments

I am thankful for Michael David Carr, a quiet spirited, young man; whom I only got to know briefly some years ago, but touched me in so many ways, (introduced me to country music, too) and was my inspiration for the character, Jazz Rollins. I guess it's true that the length of time a person is with us isn't nearly as important as the difference they make while they are. In loving memory of you, Boo.

As always, I am grateful to my family; my brothers and sisters, and many nieces and nephews, XOX to all.

In loving memory of my parents and Shu, I'm still missing you.

Thanks again, Chandra Sparks Taylor, for bringing me through.

Stacy Luecker, I owe you loads of thanks. And yes, I know that Fort Worth isn't in Georgia.

And to everyone who supported me with my first novel and promised to stick around for this one. Your encouraging words meant more than you could possibly imagine.

God's blessings to all!

Flight

1

"Nothing remains constant."

Dr. Jocelyn had used those words to reassure the troubled caller. Dr. J. was the relationship guru for *"Let's Talk Love,"* a radio talk show I listened to after hours—the graveyard shift's Oprah. Her therapeutic voice always made the self-help junkie in me lay hand on the radio to absorb the words intravenously. I had been listening vigilantly as the disheartened caller confessed between sobs that her ten-year marriage had finally hit the skids.

That's when the truth about my marriage to Edmond Ross suddenly stared me in the face and winked. I thought about the low-sex diet I was on. Five years and that was the one thing to remain constant. And the odds of it ever changing were pretty slim. Realism gripped my frazzle thoughts and blended with the clarity of Ella Fitzgerald's "Solitude" drifting softly through my headset. The jazz sounded sultry and smooth but hadn't done much to curb my insomnia. Nothing had; including the cup of chamomile tea or the few dozen sheep I'd counted twice trying to doze off. My conscience fought my callous side, tampered with my plans to hurt Edmond—dearly, a razor-sharp dagger through his heart nothing could soften.

I stretched. Strangely, I felt a bit wired despite my edgy night. I cracked my eyes, welcoming the daylight as it sauntered in and painted pale amber across my spacious bedroom. I thought of the typical Monday morning that lay ahead. I needed some calmness and so did Edmond's routine; otherwise, he wouldn't notice what hit him. Not that I didn't give the brother props for being shrewd. That he was.

In fact, as the quintessential businessman, he was the toast of Jackson, Mississippi. Either the clock had him jumping for some board meeting down at the bank where he was president or he had a breakfast commitment with his young Jay-Cees, Chamber or Kiwanis Club. His morning "coteries" he called business, often left me neglected. Twisted me into fearing the ridiculous—like another woman or him living on the down low—things my heart knew better of, but my ego wouldn't accept any blame for my failing marriage.

I guess we both juggled double lives at times, it seemed. I'd purposely jetted on him lately for no apparent reason. Or I stayed up way past midnight surfing the satellite from Showtime to the Cartoon Network until I fell asleep. Petty things in the a.m.—lost keys or a run in my new Hanes—made me belligerent. I filtered my real emotions that way. My personal life was in shambles and all I thought about was escape!

Edmond thought I needed a crash course in time management. "Set some priorities, too, and stick with them," he'd suggested, like he actually cared about what had me so wound up. Then, in the same breath, he asked whether his Hilfiger striped tie and Burberry striped shirt kept him in the right color zone. That was his real concern. And his shoes—never wore the same pair two times in a row. He said a man's success was measured by the condition of his shoes. Edmond was Mr. Confident in a good navy suit, but clueless to what made me happy. He thought having money in the bank (one he nearly owned), and eating out once a week automatically made our relationship solid, but money didn't twirl my world, and it certainly couldn't buy the truth. That being, Edmond wasn't giving what our marriage most desperately needed: romance. Good sex, period.

• • •

Edmond stood inside our designer-lit, terra-cotta-tiled bathroom. He was naked. His body was the opposite of what someone with his pecuniary profession should look like. Not the overly buffed, prison-type physique either, but that of a star-quality athlete. His healthy penis hung limply between his pale thighs. The iron-tight muscles in his buttocks flexed up and down like cords when he moisturized his skin. I ogled at him like a stalker, I knew, but all else to spice up my marriage had failed. I'd tried kama sutra books, massage oils and sexy lingerie only to have Edmond scoff at me for coming on too strong. He said I was acting a bit whorish.

Harry Connick, Jr., crooned from the built-in, surround-sound speakers in our bedroom. Edmond whistled along, upbeat and blasé. The music had definitely mellowed his mood from its normal uptightness. He bobbed his head while he leisurely slipped on thin, silk socks—right foot first, always—then his matching silk boxers before his T-shirt. That was the compulsive way he dressed. And he liked listening to jazz while he did. He was tuned into the same station I had on for most of the night. The finger-snapping, contemporary stuff played now—Dave Koz, Simply Red, and Incognito. A few of Marvin Gaye's classics squeezed in as tribute on the anniversary of his death. Jazz was one of the few things Edmond and I had in common. Hazelnut coffee in the morning—iced in the summer, piping hot in winter—and a Krispy Krème while he signed onto the Web for stock tips after we played catch-up were all his habits. Mine were just the opposite: a hot cup of tea outside in the morning air and a marathon of the wild kingdom at night on Animal Planet and I was satisfied. I loved watching nature and my wild animals.

Edmond started to chatter. "There's been a change in our vacation this year," he said.

"Let me guess," I stated, sarcastically, "we're not going."

"Sorry," he went on, hardly paying any attention to my tone, "but between shareholders meetings and federal inspectors, I just can't take a lot of time away from the bank. I didn't want you to be disappointed, so I rebooked."

It wasn't that I would be disappointed. I wasn't feeling a two-week trip to the far side of the ocean with him anyway. Our weekly causeries just took a lot out of me. Like fatigued troops must feel fighting an uphill battle. My thoughts slowly drifted past all the vacation drama, back to my shoes and the fact that my three-inch suede slings versus my two-and-a-half-inch leather pumps gave me more of a butt-lift.

"So how does a weekend getaway to Biloxi sound instead?" he asked.

That grabbed my attention like radar. What about the romantic trip to Fiji we talked about? I asked sotto voce. Biloxi? Then I got genuinely pissed—about the trip, that workaholic style of his, even that southern twang in his voice, which he tended to drift back into when he got excited. I cut his thrill short.

"Edmond?" I turned slightly toward our roomy walk-in closet that he was now in. It was big enough for a dressing table, chaise, and a revolving shelf. One side was designed for his tailored suits and endless coordinated shirts; the other was for my two-piece Gucci and Ellen Tracy types and enough shoes and purses to start my own fashion site on eBay. I had settled comfortably into my morning routine. Having skipped my start of two miles on my foldaway treadmill and the few dozen arm reps with my five-pound weights, I tidied up the bedroom. I smoothed out the folds on a new set of Egyptian cotton sheets that didn't want to fit the mattress. They were lovely nonetheless—floral detail and satin trim around the edges with a soft, expensive feel. They cost far more than what I would have paid except Edmond's mother had given them as last year's anniversary gift.

"Edmond, I'm leaving," I said casually. I had given up on the bed, undecided whether to try another set of sheets.

He didn't respond. The tense-filled moment before he did, threw everything off. The timing, the mood, even the way the sun reflected off my white European silk nightie to make me look the least of how I felt—angelic. The ambience wasn't right either. We should have been on neutral ground, down at Trends, a local coffeehouse near Jackson Memorial, the hospital where I worked, seated near the window opposite each other and downing steaming cups of vanilla latté. Perhaps the night out at Copeland's while he waited for his after-dinner drink and I picked at some calorie-induced, cinnamon-spiced dessert. Then again, maybe there wasn't any right circumstance to tell him what I had planned to do.

"Ed—"

"I heard you the first time," he said abruptly. The warm sands and the crystal-blue waters of Biloxi had evaded his mind temporarily. He rolled his almond-shaped eyes at me

like what I'd said finally registered. He looked confused as
he wrinkled his forehead and raised an inquisitive brow.
"You're leaving?" he asked then exhaled, still skimming
me over. "For work? Honey, you're not even dressed yet."
He chuckled and sounded relieved.

He had taken me lightly, so I intensified my tone.
"No, not for work, Edmond. *You. I'm leaving you,*" I
snapped, irritated.

"What the hell are you talking about, Celia?" he asked,
slowly replacing his crisp, white cotton shirt back with the
rest that were still in plastic from the laundry. He came
and stood in the doorway of the closet, propped himself
against the inside frame, then crossed one leg loosely over
the other. He was still only half-dressed. His middle finger
slowly began to trace the outline of his abs through his
white silk tee. His other hand was slipped casually inside
his pants pocket. I thought he would have smiled had I
not looked so serious.

"Oh, I'm sure you understood me, Edmond," I
continued. My right thigh quivered as I tried to balance my
weight on rubbery legs. My short nightgown fluxed from
the sudden rush of brisk air through the open window.
"But...but, if you want me to repeat it, fine. I'm not afraid
to repeat it," I lashed out.

"Go ahead then. Repeat it, Celia," he said, looking
around like he was expecting backup.

"I'm leaving you, Edmond. You hear me? Today."

His expression morphed into surprise, hurt, angry
all in a matter of seconds. It was like watching Michael
Jackson's "Black or White" video. Edmond grunted and
lifted his right leg in place, then stomped the heel of
his Bally firmly against the floor. The deafening sound
of genuine leather hitting waxed hardwood ricocheted
through the quiet room. Traces of crimson crept through

his pallid complexion. He looked close to Anglo despite living under the Delta's sweltering heat. His cold, steel-blue eyes peered viciously through me. I swallowed the roughness in my throat as he walked toward me.

Mint-scented Listerine escaped his breath when he came and stood close enough to make it uncomfortable. I honed in on a small, fresh razor nick just above the cleft in his chin. Anxiety mushroomed through my chest and I weakened. The bed broke my stumble as I put necessary distance between us, eyeing his clenched fist. He relaxed it before looking back to me then ran his hand through his tussled dark curls and massaged the back of his neck. His hair made him look malicious, but a few brush strokes and a little styling gel would easily bring it under control.

His face went solemn. If he did something desperate like…I couldn't handle it if Edmond cried. Or if he did anything else I would expect when one lover felt betrayed by the other. He turned to walk away then reeled and caught me off guard with a backhand against my left cheek. I was hurled across our king-size bed, and landed, crumbled in the fetal position beneath a potted Areca palm. Shattering glass spewing across bare hardwood echoed through the air. A crystal Waterford vase filled with fresh daylilies and our silver-framed wedding picture, both kept neatly beside the bed had toppled to the floor. The room teetered. My head ached like it hadn't barely missed the end of the nightstand. Tears filled my eyes, and I tasted something warm and salty.

Edmond moved swiftly around the bed and stood over me. He sneered down; nostrils flared with both hands bunched into tight fists at his side with his legs spread apart. I sat upright and daubed at the bloody stickiness that collected in the corner of my stinging, pulsating lips.

He cocked his head to one side as his left eye twitched uncontrollably. That meant...well, that he was pissed to say the least. He exhaled heavily then spoke to me in a sinister whisper. The fear mixed with ringing in my head made him sound more British than Mississippian.

"Now come again darling. What was that you were saying about leaving me?" he asked politely, and offered me his smooth hand.

2

Geezus!

I was trying hard to shake that word. Mom hated
it. Even when I insisted it wasn't really blasphemy, she
said no matter how much I changed the phonetics, it was
blasphemous nonetheless.

I switched off the radio. My nerves were frayed with
the image of Edmond hitting me still fresh as I placed my
headset gently on the nightstand beside the bed. Thank
God I had been dreaming. Even if the scenes were as
vivid and detailed as when Victoria Principal dreamt of
Bobby Ewing's demise for that entire season on *Dallas*. I
prayed that things between Edmond and me wouldn't go
down violent that way if I left. When I left, I corrected
my weary thoughts. Leaving was the part I was sure of.
I had decided April Fool's Day was appropriate. What
else could I be for remaining five years in a marriage that
wasn't working?

My head throbbed and felt close to exploding. The rest
of my body felt just as rotten. I shifted as far to the edge
on my side of the bed as possible without falling off, then
released a somnolent sigh. It came out louder than I had

meant it to, and I wondered if I had wakened Edmond. I quickly glanced back at him over my right shoulder. He was still sleeping soundly on his back, his snores quick, soft whispers now. I squeezed the spare pillow cradled against my stomach. My thoughts faded to black like the ending to a bad B movie without a clue about how things would go down when I exited.

Edmond stirred, just as restless as I was. He had no way of knowing it could be the last time we slept in the same bed, but his mood seemed to reciprocate my thoughts anyway. I peeked again to make sure he was still sleeping. The sunlight draped across his bare chest, making his looks commanding. He moaned, then twisted his six-two, two-hundred-pound frame until he found a comfortable spot on the mattress.

He rolled over on his side, pulling the sheet completely off me only to settle on his back again. He would be rising soon for his normal routine. Sex, shave, and shower were his big three, though sex didn't happen that often and only on the day that began with the letter "T" when it did. Then it was quick and businesslike before he went off to his job down at the bank. A job he loved more than he loved me. He never took a sick day and was always there earlier than he had to be. I'd learned to accept his compulsive ways out of obligation for our five years of marriage. Like that pretentious drive-to-succeed-at-every-cost phase he went through. I pretended that was cool too.

He had succeeded. He was now president/CEO at the bank where we first met seven years ago. It was my last year at Jackson State at the time. I had gotten a summer job and stopped in to open a savings account. Edmond was executive VP/Chief Lending Officer then, but had given me a tranquil smile and his personal platinum status treatment anyway. Then he asked me out. We had a couple of years of comfortable dating and got married when Edmond felt the time was right. He said I should finish college.

"Celia," he whispered. His voice fast-forwarded my thoughts back to my dilemma on that particular morning.

Edmond said my name once more, then wheezed. Springtime was the worst for his allergies. I should have thought to close the window. I watched as his uncannily smooth hand fluttered and rested on his chest. The gold ascetic symbol on his finger intended to bond us for eternity flashed brilliantly against the sunlight. It was a larger twin version of the ring I contemplated leaving on the shelf inside the armoire. He suddenly moved his hand down below his waist and grabbed the tent his erection made under the sheet, making my quixotic side spike. I would've soothed the tension building there had it been Tuesday or Thursday.

Regardless of what day it was, Edmond and I had other unresolved issues. We had argued the night before. I had discovered papers for a loan that he had taken out from the bank to start his own restaurant business. Papers that had been signed and sealed three months ago, and he had failed to mention them just as long. Had he not accidentally left his key in his rolltop desk drawer—a careless habit when he rushed—and I had been searching for stationery…needless to say, I had confronted him with my ill-gotten evidence. Accusations were yelled, fingers pointed, blame placed; that entire scene had us cornered in bed like two heavyweights in a boxing ring. He had struck his desk, but that look of pure exasperation in his eyes when he raised his hand and it quivered, said he had come close to hitting me. At least that's what I'd feared when my common sense told me the pressure of his work had finally pushed him closer to the edge. Edmond's explosive behavior had only added to my decision to exit.

A sudden commotion near the window refocused my attention. Whatever it was had our dog, Pepper, barking erratically out on the patio. Her loud yelps sounded distressed and made me uneasy about having left the window open all night. I did that quite often in the spring. I preferred its natural feel over the bone-chilling, artificial air. I just hoped it wasn't an open invitation for some piney-woods creature to walk through.

I was relieved when a mockingbird fluttered by and perched on the window ledge. I blinked past Mississippi's dainty state bird and the set of swaying alabaster silk curtains, then out across my sizeable backyard. The lawn needed trimming again. Too soon. It had only been a little more than a week. Already the plush, green grass resembled retro shag carpet. Maybe I should have reminded Edmond to tell the gardener to adjust the blade, but Edmond had probably thought way ahead of me. The thick turf had perturbed him only two days before by throwing off his measurements as he finished the Shorea wood deck for my Bistro-styled mosaic-top table and two matching chairs. He had built it where I could sit in the center of nature's kitchen and sip my herbal tea. Have a tête-à-tête with my soul when I wanted.

The deck was cater-corner to the covered patio, near the stone privacy fence and two large magnolias that held my white nylon clothesline. Sometimes I still hung my laundry outside to dry in the crisp, fresh air, just like Mom used to do. Like her mother did before her. Geezus. I was actually going to miss living in Jackson and experiencing all that idyllic stimulation.

Edmond almost bolted upright when the alarm went off, then he slapped the snooze button with his long, slender fingers, and silenced it just seconds after six o'clock. I closed my eyes and decided to fake sleep until he left for work. My short nightgown was tousled high above my waist, leaving my body vulnerable half-exposed that way, but hadn't bothered to cover myself.

"Celia?"

I didn't answer.

He reached toward his nightstand again and switched his clock radio to the Wave, a local jazz station. Was he setting some kind of mood? The tip of his finger started to trace the length of my spine; delicately at first, sensuous like the rhythm of the saxophone. Then his touch intensified and made me squirm away. I panicked when his hand followed.

Edmond expected sex. I hadn't thought that far ahead. I was so sure of his routine until I hadn't counted on him switching it up.

"You still angry, Celia?" he asked and scooted his hips closer. He kept his hand on my back. I felt his raw heat rise from the front of his thighs. He cased his hand around and cupped one of my breasts. Nervousness stirred in my stomach. It was hard to keep down the previous night's dinner of creamy chicken Alfredo and steamed broccoli.

His foreplay was awkward, the passion rushed. Edmond's carnal knowledge had always dulled in comparison to most of the guys I dated. With them, it was a wrestling match as early as the second date. Edmond held my hand until the fifth. I chalked that up to his ten-year age difference. I wrenched in pain as he squeezed my breast like he was testing fruit in the bin down at the local Winn Dixie.

"So, you're giving me the silent treatment, huh?" His words warmed the back of my neck. The start of another bland lovemaking session, I thought. I knew the drill. Edmond hovered over me, staring down with just enough expression to say sex with me was routine. Then his quick panting followed by stiff hip gyrations; short and animated like he was in the early stage of cardiac arrest. He treated sex like work. And sex shouldn't be work.

His soft kisses roved my shoulder. My mind ran double-time. I imagined what color eroticism would be if I actually experienced it. Then I lay motionless, waited for some big, miraculous moment to finally take over. Like him going for broke and surprising me with some unique lovemaking skills. Those enticing thoughts made my pulse quicken. I felt a warm, tingling sensation between my thighs that trickled down and made my toes curl. That feeling he wasn't able to satisfy. Still, the vision of him doing to me what made the women down at Melva's Hair Affair blush just thinking about it charged my senses even more. "Going down south" is how they described it. Maybe Edmond was going to love me down to my southern comfort too. All the way to the Ozarks in my Arkansas just beneath the murky bayou in my Louisiana cross the hot delta in my Mississippi until he was deep inside my erogenous zone—Alabama deep. "Are we going to put last night behind us and make up?" Edmond's velvety smooth voice brought me back from lala land. "You know how much I hate it when we fight."

"Mmmm," I moaned, hoping to put him off.

"I take that as a yes," he said eagerly.

He pressed his broad chest against my warm back; his pecks were cool and erect. He buried his face deep into the groove of my neck. My shallow breaths were interludes to his rapid heartbeats while the tip of his manhood prodded intrusively against the back of my clamped thighs. I needed to think of something fast—stall him.

"Why do you do that?" I asked and cleared my throat of phony sleep. I kept my legs tightly intertwined.

"Do what?" he asked.

"Interpret my feelings to suit your selfish needs," I responded.

"Are we rehashing the argument from last night?"

"We never quite finished it, remember?"

"For the love of peace, Celia. Will you let it go? It's only a business loan. Diminutive at that. You act as though I've gambled away our entire life savings."

"Small? You think a one hundred and fifty thousand dollar loan is small?"

"Money is not the issue. On the other hand, a good business venture and a hell of an investment opportunity are."

"One you failed to even tell me about for three months, Edmond. What if you lose everything? And you don't know the first thing about managing a restaurant."

"That's the intelligence of having an equal partner who does."

"What equal partner? You didn't say anything about a partner." I glanced back at him.

"Why should I bother you with the trivial details of my business? We both know you're not financially sophisticated anyway." He chuckled with a hint of arrogance, then he leaned over and kissed me lightly on the cheek, making me feel even more insignificant. "Now, sweetie, I have about fifteen minutes to spare," he said, turning me over on my back, "and I don't want to spend them fighting with my beautiful wife." He rested on his elbow with his head in his hand and smiled down at me. Then he stroked the side of my face with the back of his free hand. His perfect white teeth made his smile all the more inviting.

Sexy even. His features reminded me of Collins Spencer, that handsome CNN anchorman in Atlanta I watched late at night. Edmond hated it when I compared his looks to anyone else's.

Collins was just one of the men I didn't mind substituting for my husband. But Edmond was desirable in his own right. He had smooth, olive skin, a narrow nose, and thin lips—looks that sprang up once in a while in the South, stood out like a rose in the midst of wildflowers. What my granny called "creepin' looks" after meeting Edmond a few months before we were married. The way she put it, "Somewhere in Edmond's family tree, some light, bright, or white man must've been creepin' with some dark-skinned woman."

Edmond's deceivingly good looks made me delusional. It added to the fact that I thought my marriage, if not perfect, came in a close second. Blended flawlessly like my bright, eggshell-painted bedroom did with the eggshell-and-olive duvet, linens, pillows and the hand-painted pictures hanging on the walls. I had a spacious country home on a couple of acres plus, an optional nine-to-five public relations job. My prominent, financially savvy husband adored me. So why did I deserve any more than that?

I'd been the epitome of the southern wife to Edmond, that's why. I made myself into what he needed, down to ensuring that my looks equally matched his. I wore my hair conservative—natural, black, and shoulder-length. I'd never gotten restless or rebellious enough to even cut it, let alone color it some fiery auburn or streaked blond like the Mrs. Joneses. But it looked sophisticated against my flawless, rich caramel skin tone. My oval face had delicate features like my mother's, same catlike eyes we could take a liner to and define to downright flirtatious. I didn't use much makeup; I kept it basic. At thirty-one, I could pass for ten years younger if I wanted to. In fact, my youthfulness made women either love to hate me or befriend me just to know *my* secret.

"Celia," Edmond went on, "you have to know how much you mean to me. I keep financial matters from you because I don't need a business partner at home. I need a wife. I'm selfish that way when it comes to you, chocolate drop," he said, then flicked the end of my nose playfully. He hadn't used that nickname for me since we were dating and we had dubbed ourselves the swirl team. He was my vanilla; I was his chocolate. We withstood the eye assaults from both sides—brothas who thought I had betrayed them and blond, blue-eyed honeys who thought Edmond had lost his Mississippi marbles to publicly display his taste for the fever that way.

When Edmond pressed his mouth against mine, his moist kisses brought me back to his attempt at love-making. He was eager to feed on what little emotions I had left inside me. His weight seemed unbearable on top of me. I couldn't fake my feelings any longer. What he considered erotic and satisfying sex left me empty and unfulfilled. Maybe it would be easier to tell him now that I didn't have to face him again.

"Edmond?"

He froze above me, his heartbeat strumming against my breasts. He lifted his head and looked attentively into my eyes. "Yes? What is it?"

His boyish, innocent face expressed all the reasons why it was hard to hurt him. I couldn't treat him bad—even if I was leaving him. And with the thought of how angry he had become the night before, I didn't want to rile him, either.

"Nothing," I mumbled.

Situation sticky. Things hadn't felt so grim for me since I had waited for the cutest guy in eighth grade to say hello; only when he finally did, I got a blast of his bad case of halitosis.

I slipped into my great pretender mode that I was so good at. I distanced myself from what Edmond was doing to me by staring up at the vaulted-ceiling of our elaborately decorated bedroom and counted the patterns in the paint design. I listened as time ticked away on the clock and birds sang praises for spring, while Pepper demanded some routine of her own from the patio. Lee Ritenour's rendition of "Inner City Blues" played softly in the background. I moved to its rhythm and imagined I was with Taye Diggs, the way I had done many times. Either Taye or some other chiseled glossy-brown statue, or I thought about my first love Malachi Douglas, fingered his locks and bit my bottom lip to stifle my fantasies. After Edmond finished his ride, I took a long, deep breath, rolled my eyes, and pretended to fall back asleep.

Edmond had left me unsatisfied. Again. Regardless of his deception, I had to wonder why he had chosen that morning to break his obsessive routine for once in the five years we'd lived together as man and wife. Maybe even for my happiness. I couldn't deny that. But one change in habit didn't necessarily mean that our marriage could be saved. Or did it? The last thing I needed was to feel unsure about my decision now that I was down to the wire.

By the time Edmond's aqua-scented misty fog drifted from the bathroom, settled over the bed, and rained down on me, I had already decided my next move.

• • •

I pulled into the lot of Gulf Coastal Bank & Trust three hours after Edmond left for work. One hundred and eighty sauntering minutes after I thought he would never leave. I parked next to his black Mercedes, C-Class. His reserved spot, designated "President" in big gold letters etched on a gold-trimmed black granite-stone background, stood well within sight. A few months' shy of his forty-first birthday, Edmond was in charge of the biggest and most prestigious financial institution in downtown Jackson.

The newly renovated historical building that housed the bank sat on the corner of Lynch and Washington streets. It was in a thriving section of downtown Jackson, but still a distance from the shopping malls and upscale houses of North Jackson—a stone's throw from Jackson State University—center stage to a blustering, high-traffic area where to either side a shopping center or a multiplex cinema had sprung up within a few months' span. A Mercedes dealership had recently opened across the street.

I adjusted the hem of my cotton shirt and glanced at an azure skyline. April felt more like July. I scratched a slow itch from a drop of sweat that slid down the center of my back, then smoothed my bra strap back in place with two fingers before walking calmly inside.

High, ornate walls aligned with decorative paintings and portraits of presidents past greeted me from the lobby. Of all those glaring, pasty elderly faces, Edmond's would be the youngest and by far the most handsome in dead center. Dark green carpet freckled with mint complemented the deep mahogany wood trimming on the walls. A huge crystal chandelier hung overhead, and shining brass sconces throughout gave a touch of eloquence.

I passed up the several tellers strategically facing the entrance. I wasn't really in a socializing mood had they decided to strike up conversation. I was relieved that a steady line of middle-to-upper-class African-Americans waited to conduct their business.

I was headed toward Edmond's office when one of the senior loan officers exited his office. His name was Darnell something, one of Edmond's protégés.

"Well, good morning, Mrs. Ross," he said. "It's always a pleasure seeing you."

He was just one example of what Edmond had done to enhance the reputation of his bank. Savvy business practices had quadrupled his customer base over the years. His was also the first bank in Mississippi to incorporate management level trainee jobs for minority students. Edmond brought them in from Jackson State then groomed and schooled them for future placement in bank branches statewide.

"You, too, Darnell." I smiled. He was smooth-talking, deeply bronzed, and good-looking. Very professional and well dressed as he checked paperwork from a legal-sized manila folder. *An Edmond in training,* I thought.

"Are you taking the day off?" he asked.

"Taking care of a little business, that's all."

"I ain't mad atcha." He spoke in his undercover street lingo and shot me a flirtatious smile and a wink to remind me of the secret the two of us shared. Darnell had hit on me a few times at office gatherings, and I had to admit I was flattered. Besides, why would he risk such behavior with the boss's wife unless he had read the unhappiness in my eyes? He had no idea what he had stirred inside of me, the second thoughts I had given his advances. Perhaps I would have been leaving Edmond for an entirely different reason.

Edmond's would-be-cute-if-she-wasn't-so-bland administrative assistant, Ja'Nell, sat just outside the doorway to his office. She didn't like me. That was apparent by the way she always managed to say as little to me as possible when she saw me. Then again, maybe mousy girls weren't talkative by nature, I thought as she looked up from her computer. She brushed a few strands of overly processed black hair from her face but didn't speak. She wore hardly any makeup, only a thin coat of peach gloss over her full lips. Her warm wintry outfit set her fashion sense back at least two seasons though. I thought there must be more to Edmond's choice for a secretary—that's what she really was, forget being politically correct—than her *Sarah, Plain and Tall* image. It was probably because she was always at his beck and call. So much that he used her as the example of someone who never doubted his potential, but neither had I—until the night before.

Ja'Nell puckered her lips and smoothed out her lip gloss, then wrinkled her forehead and squinted like my presence had suddenly annoyed her. We did eye assaults for a few seconds before I managed a half-ass smile, the sarcastic kind that one woman uses to taunt another. She ran her tongue across her teeth, then reluctantly gave me a smile. I walked into Edmond's office without being announced.

Edmond sat hunched over, studying a stack of computer printouts intently. His executive-style desk was made of the same rich dark wood as the rest of his office furniture and the wall trim outside in the lobby area. He pushed up on his frameless lightweight glasses which looked almost invisible against his light skin, and sniffled. He had probably forgotten to take his allergy medicine before he left home. He reached down and pulled on a shiny brass ring to open his side desk drawer without looking up.

I cleared my throat to get his attention. He stared up like I might be some misguided customer. Recognition soon put a quick smile on his face.

"Hey, sweetheart. You bring me lunch?" he asked, glancing down at his black-dial, Movado that I'd given him for our fifth wedding anniversary back in February. He rolled his winged-back leather chair away from the desk, leaned back and stretched. Then slipped his thumbs underneath his woven leather suspenders and rubbed those up and down while he fanned his leg seductively. A wide grin gave away his amorous thoughts. Like us getting risqué in his corporate office on that expensive Italian leather couch with the nailhead trim. That made me a bit joie de vivre, though I knew that wasn't his style.

"No, Edmond, I didn't bring you lunch." I spoke up, a little flushed. "We need to talk."

"Okay," he said, sounding uneasy. "Are you ill? You don't look dressed for work. What's with the ethnic hairdo?" He straightened up in his chair again and removed his glasses, looking me over with the skepticism of a fashion critic. I looked down at myself also, like it would surprise me to know I wasn't making a fashion statement in my Capri pants, sleeveless white shirt, and a pair of comfortable Skechers. I ran my hand over my freshly permed hair, which had been pulled up in several large plaits.

"No, I'm not ill. I'm not going in to work today. There's something we need to discuss."

The keen, urgent tone in my voice made him jump up and come around his desk, striking his leg on the open drawer in the process. He swore under his breath and limped over to offer me his masculine arm. I suddenly wished we were home. At least we would have the deck in our favor, a cup of tea, and the April breeze to dictate the flow of the conversation. The corporate furnishings, potted palm trees, and shiny brass-and-glass fixtures in his office made my being there seem like business. But I knew his office would be the safest place to confront him. He was too caught up on image to react violently.

"Come and sit, darling," he said and escorted me over to a soft leather chair. My hand was sweating as I wiped moisture from my upper lip and dabbed at my forehead.

"Can I get you a glass of something cold?" he asked and gestured toward a huge polished conference table. There, a couple of silver trays filled with pastries and fresh fruit remained untouched. A sweating pitcher of cranberry juice and another of orange juice were nearby. A few bottles of water close to that. No doubt, the things Ja'Nell made available for him every morning.

He went over and closed the door, blocking out the noise of the Monday morning business, but not before informing Ja'Nell to hold his calls. The sudden quietness depleted my thoughts prematurely, and I had to quickly rethink the speech I made up during the fifteen-minute drive over.

"Please, baby, sit down." He gestured toward the chair again.

"No, thanks. I'm fine. I'll stand. This won't take long."

"You look tense," he said nervously. "I thought I took care of that this morning." He stepped up behind me, close enough that his crotch brushed lightly against my backside. His fresh, clean scent engulfed me as he started to massage my shoulders. "Want a kiss?"

"Edmond," I said, stepping out of his reach. I turned back to face him. "This is serious."

"What is it?" That worried look from the night before reappeared.

"Things are not good between us," I explained.

"Oh? Except for the slight misunderstanding about the loan last night, I thought we were doing perfectly fine." He looked uneasy as he tinkered with his gold cufflinks, then he nervously adjusted his wedding ring. I placed my hands behind my back so he wouldn't notice I wasn't wearing mine. I had left it in the same armoire where I thought about leaving it when I made my plans.

"I'm afraid we're not fine," I returned, glancing at the floor.

"So what do we do? How do we fix it?" He was asking those therapeutic questions like Dr. Jocelyn, the radio talk show host would have asked, like I already had the answer to our problem.

"We can't. Not this."

"What do you mean exactly?" Another therapeutic question.

"It's not just about the loan, Edmond. You're not committed to this marriage. What little there is of our marriage. You don't treat me as your wife."

"What are you talking about, Celia?"

"I'm just not happy with the way things are between us Edmond. There are too many secrets. You call it business but I never know what to expect from one day to the next. Then when I question, I get a side of you that scares me. Do you realize how close you came to hitting me last night?" I wrung my hands and paced a small circle in front of him. Tension crept in my tone, but I felt relieved. I was about to release a small portion of the world I carried on my shoulder.

"Don't be ridiculous Celia. You know I would never lay a hand on you."

"How can I be sure? You're becoming a stranger to me and I can't be sure of anything with you right now."

"Now hold on a minute. I have always been completely honest with you."

"Do you love me, Edmond?" I asked abruptly, not real sure if I wanted to hear the answer.

"Where is all this coming from, dear?"

"I need to know."

"You even have to ask. Of course I do, don't be naïve."

"Then what about sex?"

"What?"

"Why isn't there any passion between us, Edmond?"

"What, are you doing taking notes now?" he asked, trying to force a smile.

"Why is it always under your terms? Why do you make love to me on a fixed schedule?" I asked.

He looked shaken. I had caught him off guard with no answer. Cool and collected, Edmond looked like he wanted to hide.

"Celia, honey, look. You are making a big deal out of nothing."

"Edmond, we've been here before and that's always the response I get from you. You try and make me feel like I have the problem."

"Quite seriously Celia, you can't expect me to join you in your beauty shop politics about what our marriage should be. You're imagining things."

"Am I? If this is all my imagination, then why won't you do what's best to save our marriage?"

"I wouldn't do therapy."

"Not even for the sake of our marriage?"

"I didn't need a shrink."

"You are just too afraid to face your problem. You didn't want to think that anything might be wrong with you sexually. Edmond Cornell Ross always has to be in control, doesn't he?"

"You know how I feel about bringing outsiders into my private business. I told you I don't—"

"Alright, fine. I didn't come here to argue with you." I held out my hand. "Here are the keys to the house. The bills are paid at least a month in advance, and I've submitted a resignation from my job. I'm taking the SUV, you can keep the Merce—"

"Wait a minute." He stopped me. He raised his hands

and shook his head slowly, refusing to take in what I was feeding him. "What are you saying, Celia?" He finally managed in a dry, weak voice.

I walked around him without answering and gently placed the set of keys attached to a gold keychain, on the end of his desk. I turned back to face him. My speech resumed where he'd interrupted. "You can keep the Mercedes. I took half of the money from our joint account at the credit union; I didn't take anything from here to guard your privacy. I think that's fair—"

"Fair?" He cut off my rhythm again. His tone was raised, his patience thin. "What in the hell are you talking about? Are you on crack? Have you been popping pills at that hospital you work for?"

"Edmond, you haven't been listening to what I'm saying. I'm leaving you."

"What did you just say? You mean you're actually going to leave me over this?"

"Yes," I said, nodding my head. "I'm really leaving you. I won't live like this anymore."

"Live like what? You have anything you can ask for. You act as if living like a damn queen in Buckingham Palace isn't enough for you."

"It's always money with you, isn't it? Well, Edmond, money won't even get you out of this."

"Is it someone else?"

"No."

"Yes, it is. And you're using this as an excuse to be with him, aren't you?"

"No. This is about you and me, and the fact that our marriage is falling apart and I don't know how to save it. I need time to think about the future of it and whether or not I'm a part of that future. I'm sure you can understand that."

"Understand what? You come in here laying out a case against me with little or no time to defend myself, and you expect me to understand. Work with you? We made love this morning, Celia. If you felt this way all along, why did you make love with me?"

Damn. That had been a mistake. What could I say? That I didn't have feelings for him when I did. And if making love with him could satisfy me just once, I wouldn't be leaving.

"Because Edmond, no matter what, I still love you that much. This has nothing to do with how I feel about you. This is about you shutting me out of your life. If it was about the sex I would have been gone a long time ago."

"Don't think you did me any damn favors by staying, Celia. And why are you choosing to tell me this now? On your way out, damn it." He struck the air with his fist and bit his bottom lip, then paused with his hand on his waist, realizing he had shouted louder than he meant to. He glanced around me at the glass panel on the door. He seemed thankful it was at least spy-proof. "Look, this isn't the place to discuss this." He inched toward me and grabbed on to my shoulders. "Go home, and I'll take the rest of the day off. We can take our time. So...so we can talk about this." He stammered on his words, which he did when he was stressed.

"Edmond, there's nothing to go home to," I said, shaking his hand off. "Everything of value to me is outside in the SUV. My mind is already made up. I have to get out of here." I turned to leave.

"Wait a minute, Celia," he yelled at my back, then moved in and grabbed me roughly about my arms. He swung me around. My neck strained to catch up with the rest of my body. I felt the heat from his breath on my face.

He cocked his head to one side, and his left eye twitched. "Look, sweetheart...Celia." He exhaled, then released my arms before rubbing his chin, then the back of his neck. "You haven't even told me where it is you're going."

"CeCe," I said, looking him dead in his face.

"What?" he asked confused.

"I like to be called CeCe. I've always preferred CeCe, but you've always ignored it."

"Okay," he said, giving me a questioning look. "So all of this is about the name that I call you?"

"No. I just wanted you to understand that much about me before I left."

"Alright. CeCe then. Can we at least talk about this before you go running off?"

"No, Edmond. It's been decided."

"Then at least tell me where you're going?"

"I'll call you in a couple of days, after I get settled in. I'll let you know where to forward my mail." I headed for the door.

"This is not over, Celia—ah, CeCe. Whatever." He was close at my back. "You can't just walk out on me. You're my wife. Ce—"

"Good-bye, Edmond," I murmured without looking back. Tears welled up in my eyes as I squeezed the doorknob before turning it.

I walked out the door just as Ja'Nell scurried back to her desk. She had undoubtedly been eavesdropping. I gave her a disapproving look and should have really given her an ear full but I didn't see the point. I closed Edmond's door briskly behind me and raced out of the bank.

3

"Why would you make love to me and then leave?"

Edmond's piercing words burnt guilt on my conscience like any one of my father's Sunday morning sermons could. Edmond had been so naïve to think that our problem could also be the solution.

Making love with Edmond then leaving had been the toughest part that morning; the easiest had been to jump out of bed the minute he'd backed his car out of the driveway and to pack everything I could get inside of a seven-piece luggage set. I had no clock to punch since I had resigned from my public relations job at Jackson Memorial three days earlier. I loaded the SUV with my portable memories, including my delicate doll collection. I hadn't been able to pack them all. The ones that I was taking weren't even wrapped properly in that padded packing material. Luckily, I didn't collect them for the value but for their appeal. I could only hope they made the transition.

I was a speed demon on I-20, chasing thin white lines and switching lanes like my life depended on it. I was headed to Houston, hoping to reach my designation before the sun bowed for the day. It was a six-hour drive;

maybe a little less if I continued to ignore black-and-white speed signs jumping out at me like pop-up videos. I counted another brown-and-beige state police car rushing past me, headed in the opposite direction. I'd counted ten so far. I was half-expecting any one of them to swerve around and pull me over. Edmond might have reported my car stolen to get me to come back. It was what I least expected of him, but who could second-guess the actions of a desperate man?

I couldn't get my mind off Edmond. I hated myself for worrying, but hoped that he was all right. I didn't think I would even miss him that much so soon. Not officially, just the early pings of separation. Maybe it was because we had never been apart without knowing whether we might not see each other again. I thought leaving would change my feelings.

I noted the time. I did a mental tracking of his where-abouts. He was probably already home, sitting in his favorite chair, hurting, and watching Peter Jennings wrap up the evening news.

Edmond's routine changed when he was bothered. I hoped he wouldn't start to drink more than he normally would either. I pictured him half-crazed, searching our bedroom for clues, trying to calculate the things about me he'd never taken time to notice before—the pairs of shoes I actually owned or how many clothes I had taken, whether spring, summer, winter, or fall—knowing the personal effects a person left behind determined their thoughts of returning. Then he would drink some more of that instant courage to help him explain my absence.

He would have his parents to answer to in Jackson, as I knew I had mine in Atlanta. We were both probably already too late. Gossip usually followed its own version of the truth in small towns. It wouldn't take long for my leaving him to spread through the hangouts and alleyways of Jackson like thick maple syrup. Drinking and gossip were interchangeable.

I hadn't taken much. There hadn't been a lot of time and not a lot of space in my brand-new Lexus 330X. Edmond bought it for my birthday and our fifth wedding anniversary. It was one of the many status symbols he'd given me, including my Norwich terrier, Pepper, which he surprised me with last Christmas; twenty-five thousand dollars' worth of new furniture that I hadn't really wanted but he special ordered from overseas; a seasonal shopping spree in a different city; and a lot of promises he made in between.

"You read too many self-help books is all. Have you been listening to Dr. Jocelyn again? Girl, you're married to the best man in Jackson, and you still ain't satisfied. And, sweetheart, a good man is hard to find these days," was the most consolation I had gotten from the sharp tongue of Melva Brown, my friend and *friseur*. It had been my last appointment two days earlier. She was giving me a dose of counseling while she tossed and teased my well-conditioned mane. If she didn't give the best organic deep-root stimulator treatment, which still had my scalp tingling, I would have shirked her by walking out, but I had stayed put in her swivel styling chair long after she had finished my hair and dished out her bad advice, even after she'd begun sweeping up the last clipped hair from the floor around me. The shop was quiet and lifeless as she listened patiently to my plan of escape. She was the only person I had told of my decision. Something that I knew she would harbor along with some of the best-kept secrets in Jackson.

"That's just it, Melva. Maybe he's the best man in Jackson, not necessarily the world," I had replied.

Hearing my remark, she had slowed the steady strokes

of her Easy Sweeper to a complete halt, then turned around to face me, placing a plump, oily hand on her round hip. "Honey, this is your world."

"I don't think so. At least that's not what my conscience has been saying for a while now." I found it hard to believe that what I was doing wasn't what half the women in Jackson or any place else would do if they weren't so afraid. I blinked at her, disappointed that she wasn't more understanding; thinking how sometimes women couldn't even understand women, so why would men.

"Regardless, CeCe, you don't book every time there's a problem. So you have that premature seven-year itch? It happens to couples all the time. Believe me, it'll pass," Melva stated optimistically.

"Premature seven-year itch? If I believed that for one minute, Melva, I wouldn't be leaving. Honestly, I don't think this itch can be scratched that easily."

She had no idea living with Edmond was as bad as it got when I still counted myself alone sleeping right next to him. That was just months after we married. There was only so much that I could tell him about what I needed and not have him look at me in a different light because I was a minister's daughter and in Edmond's eyes that came with some degree of responsibility. He still thought he was my first. Edmond never knew about that special weekend, two months before I met him that Malachi Douglas and I secretly spent in Biloxi during our spring break from Jackson State. Edmond never asked about past relationships, so I didn't tell. If I had, then he would have known where Malachi's kisses had been. How could Edmond ever compete with what Malachi did for me? Malachi had given me orgasms that seemed to last for hours on end. What I affectionately called his "ripple effect." How could I push Edmond for that?

I turned my cell phone back on. I had planned to leave it off until I reached Houston, mainly because I knew Edmond would be blowing it up until I answered, begging me to come back home. Bet he was pissed out of his mind when I didn't answer. It rang almost simultaneously with my thoughts.

"Celia, it's me. Please don't hang up."

"Edmond, don't do this," I pleaded.

"I want you to come home."

"Don't ask me to come back now."

"When?"

"I need time."

"I need you home."

"Not possible."

"Then tell me where you are. Let me come to you. Let's work this out," he begged.

"No."

"At least tell me how long you'll be gone."

"Can't."

"That's nonsense. You don't walk out and not know whether you're coming back. Why can't you at least tell me that much?"

"Because."

"Would you stop answering me like a damn preschooler and talk to me like an adult."

"Go to hell, Edmond."

"Ce—"

Click!

I waited for him to call again. When he didn't, I panicked. If I knew him well, he had one card left to play. He would contact the one person who could pull a guilt trip on me, and tell her all kinds of untruths—like me losing my mind as well as respect for my marriage. I needed to talk with her before he did.

"Hi, Mom."

"CeCe, baby. How are you?"

"I'm fine, Mom. And you?"

"I'm good, dear."

"Daddy?"

"As well as to be expected, I guess. He's at a religious retreat today. He's teaching. Can you believe that? Well, so much for being a retired minister. He just doesn't know what to do with himself these days."

"Daddy will never settle down because he'll always be a minister. He loves giving advice too much. Retirement will never be that permanent vacation for him like you thought." I gave her a dry laugh then cleared my throat. "Look, Mom, did Edmond call you today?"

"No. Should he?"

"I just thought he had called, that's all."

"Are you okay, honey? How's everything in Jackson?"

"Fine. But I'm on my way to Texas at the moment."

"Texas?"

"Yes. Houston."

"What on earth are you doing in Houston?"

"I'm thinking of moving there."

"Oh, so you finally talked Edmond into leaving Mississippi? I remember when he wouldn't even hear of the two of you moving here to Atlanta with us."

"Well, Mom, Edmond's not with me."

"Well, that's smart—you know holding on to his job while you check things out, just in case. I'm glad you thought that through before you decide."

"Yeah. Well—"

"Honey?"

"Yes."

"Do you know anyone there in Houston? I don't like the idea of you going there alone."

"You remember Tracee, right?"

"Yes. Clint Ledbetter's daughter?"

"Well, she's there."

"That's a relief. I feel a little better now. But, baby?"

"Yes, Mom."

"Look for a good church. Meet some good people."

"Okay, I will. Listen, Mom, I have to go now," I said abruptly without telling her I had actually left Edmond. "My phone needs charging. I'll call you later and fill you in on everything."

"Just be careful, will you, CeCe?"

"I will. And I love you."

"Love you too."

That would hold her for the moment. I knew I would have to tell her the whole truth sooner or later, but later sounded much better for the present. Besides, I had no idea what that truth might be.

• • •

Judging from the break in the tree line, I must have been completely out of the Delta. The jolly green pines of Mississippi had suddenly turned into dry white weeping willow branches dripping with furry moss. There were more license plates for Louisiana than for the Magnolia State of Mississippi. A few cars with Texas plates passed me up, which meant I was a little closer.

I switched off the static-filled radio that had started to make that frying noise. I slipped in my *Seal IV* CD. I knew it was a switch from what I normally listened to, but I thought the music would take my mind off my problems. Help justify my decisions. Seal's smooth and precise voice quickly faded my memory of the Yazoo River. I had pierced Louisiana's state line. Driving across fifteen miles of stone bridge with nothing in view except Lake Ponchartrain's murky, thick waters made me think about fishing when I would visit Greenwood, Mississippi, during those particularly long, hot summers. One especially, when I was no older than six, Grampy Cecil, my daddy's dad, my namesake, had taken me fishing at his favorite spot near his farm. Not that there was a lot of "catch" at Mills Creek, but he said fishing was suppose to teach me the facts of life. At least that was Grampy's excuse to do both of what he enjoyed—fishing and dishing out his wisdom. He said that was the way he had been taught.

"Sssshh," he had warned softly, careful not to scold me. He said we needed to be silent, that noise frightened the fish away. I barely remembered moving, sitting in the same spot hours at a time. The wooden tackle box he made from vanished hard plywood had become a makeshift seat for me. Grampy Cecil was seated nearby in a foldaway nylon lawn chair. When we had gotten no action, he gathered our belongings—fishing rods, tackle box, bait, our sandwiches—mustard and fried bologna burned on one side the way he liked, and chilled RC colas in tow—and move farther down the bank.

"What are we doing now, Grampy?" I had asked, wrinkling my nose up at him in that curious way I had of doing.

"Moving."

"Where to?" I had continued to question him, using my hand to shield the blaring sun from my eyes.

"Oh, down a ways."

"Why?"

"Fish ain't bitin' here, baby girl."

Fishing? Maybe that's what I was doing in my own selfish, faux pas kind of way, tossing Edmond back for something better. I tried to think of any advice Grampy Cecil would have given me at such a point in my life, right when the fish had stopped swimming upstream. Should I have stayed a while longer, or was I right to move on to fresher water like we had done that warm summer day in Greenwood?

Wrong or right, leaving Jackson felt good for the moment. Like old layers of me had unzipped from my body, flown out the window, and discarded themselves along the highway, contrary to the green-and-white litter signs warning "Don't Mess with Texas" as I crossed the state line. "Just don't cross Celia Ross, CeCe for short," I retorted, before glancing in my rearview mirror and pressing the accelerator firmly to the floor.

4

I pressed Tracee Ledbetter's number, which I had programmed by one-digit touch on my cellular. Tracee was my best friend from high school. Though we had barely seen each other since graduation, we had tried to remain close, but the distance had kept pieces of our private lives an even bigger secret.

A year ago when she had returned to Jackson for her mother's funeral, I'd confessed just how unhappy I was in my marriage. I thought she might halfway understand since she was divorced herself. Right then and there, she had insisted that I pack my bags and return to Houston with her. And I would have, too, if only I had been ready to leave Edmond.

I exited 610 South to Cullen Street like Tracee had instructed. From there, I had no directions. In my haste to leave Jackson, I had left those on the kitchen counter. Edmond would probably think I'd pulled some Hansel and Gretel antic in order for him to follow me.

I found the Texaco station Tracee told me about and waited. I glanced at the clock on my dashboard. It read 4:15. I had made it to Houston in six hours, right on schedule. Tracee's car was broken, so a neighbor was bringing her to meet me. I suddenly felt like a vagabond. Not only was I in a big, strange city, but I also had no place to live. Starting over from scratch was going to be rough. Tracee had offered to put me up, but it would only be two weeks maximum, I was sure of that.

I crossed my legs, then uncrossed them impatiently. I had to pee like crazy. It had been almost three hours since my last stop, and I hated going inside of a gas station. The place did look fairly new and clean, and I didn't think I could wait until I got to Tracee's. I could do this, I thought. I just needed to get past the homeless-looking man standing outside the entrance holding a tattered ICEE cup and begging for spare change. He adjusted the waist of his too-short khakis splattered with grease and oil stains and tipped his worn John Deere cap at me as I approached. My plaits were hanging loosely and bouncing about my face, and I walked with my thighs held tightly together to help control my bladder.

" 'Scuse me, young lady," he said and pulled down on the front of his grimy Texas Lotto T-shirt, which boasted in big blue letters I'M A WINNER.

"I'm sorry, sir, but I'm really in a hurry." I refused eye contact. It never took much for my wallet to give in to my heart.

"Wait a minute, baby. Slow down." He gestured at me with his free hand.

"No. Here, I only have these five ones in change." I dug in my front pocket and thrust the folded bills at him. A cashier's receipt and some loose change were mixed in. A few coins hit the sidewalk.

"Hold on a minute, boo. First, let me ax you sum'um," he said, groaning as he beat me in retrieving the change from the ground. He let it jangle with the few coins already in his cup.

"Yes, what is it?"

"You must be from Tennessee."

"What?"

"I *saiiiddd* you must be from Tennessee."

"Huh? No. Why do you think I'm from Tennessee?" I asked, perplexed.

He grabbed his crotch and bent his knees as he started to snicker. " 'Cause baby, you duh only *Ten-I-See.*" He chuckled hard, exposing a few brown teeth as he took the bills from me and counted them for his own satisfaction.

I shook my head and switched inside. I peeked into the ladies' restroom. It wasn't that bad and smelled pretty decent too. I locked myself inside the nearest stall and emptied my bladder for what felt like an entire five minutes. Afterward, I soaped my hands under the flow of warm water, then let them cool down before I dabbed a little on my tired eyes. I felt exhausted after my long drive and was ready for an extended couch break. I hoped Tracee didn't mind if I skipped conversation until later.

I reached over and pulled down on a small black handle on the dispenser, waiting for a paper towel to flow out. When nothing happened, I checked to find it empty. I tried the hand dryer right next to it. That was broken. I looked around, shrugged, then flung my hands in the air. Then I started singing "wave 'em like you just don't care," the hip-hop party anthem like I was back in college. I danced around the floor, feeling silly but it was nice to release some pressure. I continued to flap my arms and sing as I turned around to leave. My eyes met the surprised stare of a middle-aged Hispanic lady who had entered the restroom sometime during my meltdown.

My moves had stopped her dead in her tracks. Her eyes widened, and she backed into the corner behind the door. I must have looked pretty ridiculous, like I had just wigged out in the toilet of a freeway service station. I smiled, gave my hands one final shake, and quipped, "They're out of paper towels, but luckily they still had toilet paper."

It had been fifteen minutes, including my run-in with the homeless comedian and my own restroom routine, since I had spoken with Tracee. So far the people in Houston were a blast. I leaned back in the driver's seat and searched out Tracee's ride. We had exchanged car descriptions like two drivers involved in a fender-bender. She knew where I was parked, too, just in case.

A black Honda Civic with shiny rims that looked more expensive than the car itself moved slowly in my direction. I sat upright as the blaring music grew louder as it neared. The car pulled alongside mine and stopped. I recognized Tracee on the passenger's side, although her hair was much shorter. She had it cut in a cute pixie style and colored a warm burgundy. It complemented her high cheekbones.

I smiled. She smiled and gave me her "hey, girl" greeting. I used the same one out of habit. Then she instructed me to follow them. The driver had kept quiet up until then, only adjusting his dark sunglasses and pulling away. He and Tracee seemed to have very little in common. What favor could he possibly owe her?

I lost track of the signals and turns we made before finally pulling onto a street adjacent to a row of apartment buildings—three to be exact—secluded behind a cluster of bushes and tall dogwood trees with a big wrought-iron fence surrounding everything.

Damn was what came to mind at what the fence kept separated from the general public like a correctional complex. I was no stranger to housing projects since Jackson did have a few. I had driven past them for one reason or another. But this was closer to Cabrini Green on *Good Times*, and I just couldn't believe that Tracee actually lived there. Not my friend-girl who always dressed to the nines and refused to let a fly close to her action.

We drove leisurely through the gate which was almost ripped off its hinges. The sun was still on high beam with a few more hours left before nightfall. Several small groups of people were scattered about in front of the few complexes, each involved in their own politics. One group turned from its game of checkers to watch cautiously as our cars caravanned through. Another group played dominoes on a huge tree stump that had been sanded down and smoothed to perfection. A stratus cloud of gray smoke emerged from a homemade barbecue grill as Zydeco music ridged from a nearby radio. Kids halted on skateboards along the sidewalks, and adults leaned forward from their balconies to get a better view. Old cars, either inoperable or weak possibilities, were draped with shirtless young males clad in sagging pants like idle inmates up to no good. They whispered to one another while they hid their contraband.

Tracee jumped out of the car and screamed. I did the same. She embraced me with her soft scent of freesia. Her big silver hoops clicked my diamond studs as we touched cheeks.

Tracee turned to Honda Man and replied, "I'll hook you up later, when my man gets back, 'kay?"

Honda Man nodded.

"Well, if it isn't Rem'um Lester Compton's baby girl," Tracee turned to me and exclaimed.

"And you must be Clint Ledbetter's? Your head is shaped just like his."

"Girl, you still crazy," she said. We hugged again, giggling like we were back in high school.

"Tracee, I haven't parked in anyone's spot, have I?" I asked as I pulled back from our play and looked around.

"No, you're fine. In fact, you parked so Big Boy over there can watch your car for you," she stated casually.

"Watch it?" I asked.

"Yes. He sits right there all night sometimes. It'll be like having your own private security service."

I looked over at a big guy with a thick goatee and a few tattoos on his massive arms, which were folded across his chest. He must have weighed in at an easy three hundred pounds. His tight, black knit shirt looked two sizes too small. He gave me a reassuring nod. I nodded back at him, afraid not to.

I followed Tracee down the walkway to her apartment. I felt a hundred pairs of eyes glued to me like I was a science experiment. Tracee sashayed on ahead, getting a few greetings from neighbors who kept their eyes focused on me. I was someone she would undoubtedly have to explain later.

The inside of her apartment was small but adequately furnished. It would have probably been a lot nicer if it weren't in the middle of the scene I had rolled up on outside. I looked around. Her quarters were cramped with a navy suede-textured living room set, and an oak entertainment center in the corner held a nineteen-inch color TV. All of it looked fairly new. The bare walls held only one picture, a framed black-and-white of a young man and woman I recognized as Tracee's parents. The rest of the walls were covered with three sizes of small, greasy handprints. And there were three sets of framed school pictures inside the entertainment center, so I assumed she still only had three boys.

Tracee headed toward the kitchen. I followed. The

dining set looked fairly new also—rich oak, just like the entertainment center and pretty striped cloth seats covered in vinyl. I later saw why that was a good idea. She went over to the refrigerator, grabbed a tall can of generic beer, and flopped down in a chair at the table. She sighed and flung one ashy foot in another chair. I suddenly realized how different she was from the person I knew back at Jack Austin High School. For one, she had always been so meticulous about the way she looked and dressed. Although her hair had seen some serious salon attention lately, the body she used to flaunt so proudly was now a little on the thin side. I had noticed how the back pockets of her cutoffs stole kisses from each other when she walked to the refrigerator. I thought she would have some explanation for her living condition and why she never confided in me. Instead, she popped the metal tab on her beer, leaned back in the chair, and lifted both legs to admire the chipped red polish on her toenails.

"Sit down, CeCe. Take a load off," she said, burping her brew.

I looked around at the kitchen suspiciously. Nothing a little imagination and a good cleaning couldn't remedy, I thought. The table was covered with empty potato chip bags, candy wrappers, pieces of dried-up pizza crusts with little half-moon teeth marks, and partially eaten bowls of cereal. I looked down at the chair in front of me. Hard tomato-dried sauce, probably from the pizza, was smeared on the seat.

Alrighty then. I guess I can say good-bye to the ol' Capris, I thought as I sat down on the chair's edge. I slid back, hoping I didn't feel something cool and wet oozing up the crack of my behind.

"Well, Ce, you here," Tracee said rather loudly. Her voice ricocheted off the walls of the apartment, making my heart race. "I can't believe you finally here." She was just going to skip the part where she told me how she had totally misrepresented herself to me as well as the entire state of Mississippi.

"Yes, I actually did it." I told her how I had packed my things and informed Edmond I was leaving all in a span of three hours.

"I just can't believe ol' boy thought he could just skimp on the dicky and you would just stay satisfied. I bet he blew his top when you told him he was out like the Tootsie Roll, huh?" She giggled. "Men just don't always want to believe us when we tell 'em we're fed up."

"Well act—"

"You knucklehead. Why don't I come over there and help you to fall down and break your darn neck next time."

I turned to see which kid she was yelling at. Her youngest had emerged from the back room.

"Javon, did you hear me?"

"Is that the baby, Tracee? He is so much bigger than when I saw him last year."

"Yes, the baby of the three terrors."

"Where are the other two? You didn't leave them here alone, did you?"

"In back, girl. And they were fine. The oldest takes care of the little ones. I never leave them for long, though."

"You know you still have to be careful. I've heard of weird stuff happening in a matter of minutes."

"But boys need to learn responsibility. At least I'm glad they are all boys. Thank the Lord for that. Don't think I could handle no girls. Javon, I'm talking to you, boy."

I thought I would never get used to the noise. I think one of the reasons Edmond and I didn't have kids was because we both liked the quietness.

I dropped my parenting skills lesson for the moment. Javon remained on the table with a long, turquoise beach towel tied around his shoulders. "I'm Rocket Man," he shouted and prepared to perform his grand finale of leaping from the table to the loveseat. He almost didn't make it. Tracee opened her mouth to yell, relented, and waved him off. She took another swig of beer.

"Wow, how do you handle three boys." It was a comment rather than a question to her. I had seen the answer for myself.

"Jaleel, Jaheim, Bring y'all asses in here. I know you're doing something you ain't got no business doing anyway. Get in here, now."

Two older boys emerged from the back. One was just slightly taller than the other. They pushed and shoved each other, name-called under their breath.

"You remember Jaheim," Tracee said, pointing to the taller one. He's nine now. Jaleel there is seven, and Javon over there is four. Boys, you remember Auntie CeCe from Jackson?"

"Hi, boys."

They responded in unison.

"Okay, you can both go and watch TV," she said to Jaheim and Jaleel, then waited until they had left the kitchen and were seated in front of the TV.

"I guess you know who Jaheim's daddy is, don't you?" Tracee whispered.

I gave her a puzzled look and shook my head. "No, I don't think so."

"Yeah, you do. Larry Wilcox from Jackson. You remember him?"

"Oh my goodness. Remember him? Tracee, Larry Wilcox was our high school basketball coach. And wasn't he married to the home economics teacher?"

"Still is."

"Girl, no you didn't."

"I did, girl. He was married, I know, but we got together right after I graduated. Then, again right after I went back to Jackson to see my sick mother. Never told him about Jaheim either. If I had, I would never have gotten rid of him. And what would be the point? You know what a teacher's salary is?" She threw her head back and laughed. I tried to laugh, too, but felt like I was too out of touch with her somehow.

"I'm the baby." Javon ran over to me and signed both of my thighs with little chocolate-coated fingerprints just like the ones tattooed on the walls.

"Brainless, look what you just did to Aunt CeCe's pants." Tracee grabbed a greasy, stained dishtowel and began to wipe down my thighs. The dark chocolate quickly turned to white smears.

"Don't worry about that. There's road crud all over me anyway," I lied.

"You sho are patient with kids. How come you and Edmond never had any?" she asked, getting serious, still viciously wiping down my pants.

"Are you for real? It would have taken too much planning on Edmond's part."

"What? Would he have wanted two-point-five kids four years apart?"

"No. He would want to know how much money he'd spend from conception to graduation first."

Tracee squealed. I laughed, and we high-five.

"Mama, can me and Jaheim have a soda?" Jaleel asked, drawing Tracee's attention away. He had already opened the refrigerator door. I waited for Tracee to correct him but she seemed not to notice.

"Yeah, and give Aunt CeCe one too. Girl, my manners

are on vacation, I guess. These brainless wonders keep my nerves in an uproar all the time."

"There's only one left," Jaleel yelled after examining the empty refrigerator. From what I could see, there was only a half-empty bottle of water, something in a stainless-steel pot, and one can of beer.

"No, Tracee, I'm fine. Let them have that one. I'll run out and get something later."

"I haven't had time to go grocery shopping. Come on, you can run me to the store. I need to pick up a few things for breakfast anyway. That is, if you ain't too tired."

"Sure. I need to pick up a few things myself."

We finished our shopping at a local HEB supermarket, then rounded up the boys who had taken off in three different directions once we hit the store. We headed for one of the express lanes to check out. I'd picked up some Cokes, chips, fruit, Visine, and a map of Houston. I got ahead of Tracee in line. She had a bigger cart than the portable one I had. She had thrown in a more expensive twelve-pack of beer than I had noticed her drinking back at her place, a box of Froot Loops cereal, a loaf of Wonder bread, bacon, eggs, bologna, milk, a large bag of peanut M&Ms, and *Star* and *National Enquirer* magazines. Some of Tracee's choices made me wonder whether she was a good mother.

The boyish-looking, red-faced cashier rang up my items and asked if I had a HEB savings card. I just told her I'd left it at home, mostly because I didn't want her to insist that it only took a few minutes to get one. Although that would be one of the many things I would have to do eventually, if I decided to stay.

"Okay, then your total is fourteen dollars and forty-five cents, please."

I took my wallet from my purse and gave the cashier a

crisp twenty. I noticed Tracee behind me, patting her pockets frantically and thoroughly as a prison guard would.

"What's wrong, Tracee?"

"My wallet! I thought I had it but—"

"You lost it?"

"No. I must have grabbed the wrong one on my way out the door," she said, holding up a small black case that looked to be no larger than a business card holder.

"Don't worry. I'll get it." I turned to the cashier and asked if she could ring Tracee's items up with mine.

"Sure," she replied.

"Thanks."

"Will that be all?" she asked before keying the total again.

"Oh," Tracee responded. "Could you give me two packs of Newports? Filter, please."

5

"Tracee, are you okay living here alone with the kids?" I asked, equally concerned about my stay there for the next two weeks.

We were in her small living room watching TV. I had opted for the floor, sitting on top of a big yellow fluffy pillow that she used to decorate the sofa. Tracee was on the sofa above me, balancing a newly opened beer on one knee while munching on chips. The apartment was quiet for the first time since I had arrived. A hush had fallen over outside except for the occasional scream of a kid who hadn't met his curfew. The boys had been banished to their rooms to snack on M&Ms and three eight-ounce cans of soda. They still had an appetite even after I had treated them each to a Happy Meal, contrary to Tracee's insistence that they didn't eat much meat. I was snacking on salt-and-vinegar chips and a Coke myself while Tracee played along with a show on the Game Show Channel. She answered with the excitement and velocity of actually sitting in that high chair opposite Regis Philbin. If she wasn't watching a rerun, she was quite good, but Tracee had always been good at trivia or any game show for that matter. Back in high school, she always won when we used to play Scrabble, Jeopardy, or Clue. She had that fundamental type intelligence where learning sort of came naturally to her. That was just one of her many talents.

She had also been very popular. As if being pretty and smart with a shapely body wasn't enough, she was also very athletic, a cheerleader as well as a member of the honor society, drama club, and all the things that went along with being well rounded. She was the type who if anyone were going to make it on the most-likely-to-succeed list, she would. She always got the cute guys, too, especially since everyone in school—a few male teachers included—had wanted to date her.

"I don't live alone. I have a man who lives here with me. Name's Streeter."

"Streeter, huh?"

"Yeah." She giggled. "He's outside taking care of some business right now, but you'll meet him later." She spoke of him as if he was a city councilman or representative or something lobbying with his constituents. Like the way I would have bragged about Edmond being a bank president.

"What kind of business is Streeter into?" I asked.

"Well, he's no financial whiz like your Edmond, but he makes ends meet."

"In other words, it's not legal," I said rather sarcastically, remembering the looks of the crowd outside. It wasn't hard to guess his occupation. She gave me a surprised look like I somehow knew some guarded secret.

"CeCe, before you say it, I know things don't look quite the way you expected. I've had some bad breaks, and things are just a little slow right now. I'm gettin' there since I got all the bad niggas out of my life. Streeter is different. He's going somewhere. I just got to hang in there and support him."

"Wait a minute. I'm not judging, sweetie. You don't have to justify your lifestyle to me."

"But I know what you're thinking. I know that I was the one with the big plans about having the mansion and the expensive cars. All that shit that we laughed about and swore we would have when we used to watch *Dynasty,* but this is real life now, Ce, and I don't think *Dynasty* is even in syndication no more. Things just don't come like that these days. I mean, look at you. Hell, you had it all."

"Now wait, Tracee. I never said I lived like the Carringtons."

"Close enough then. And you were still unhappy. So who's to say having it all is the best thing for anyone."

"But having all that money—material things, I mean—isn't what I'm talking about. If that were so, I wouldn't have left Edmond. I'm talking about something you can't buy."

"That's all good, CeCe," she said as she grabbed the remote and began channel surfing and crunching the last of her potato chips, "but that's never paid one bill or put one loaf of bread on my table. I need someone who's down for my needs and my kids. And they don't necessary have to own a bank or half the world."

"Even if it's Mr. Wrong forking over the cash? Tracee, you don't need anyone to pay your bills, especially if he's putting your safety in jeopardy."

"Sometimes you have to swallow your pride and take what you can get."

"And you think Streeter is all you can get?"

"Maybe I'm not as strong as you, CeCe. I never was. If so, I'd probably be in Hollywood by now, getting leading roles opposite the likes of Denzel and Tom Cruise, not having any kids until my late forties, and waking up in a different foreign country every week."

"It's never too late, Tracee. All I'm saying is that if you're unhappy in anything that you're doing or with anything that you have, you're settling for less."

"That's easy for you to say. You were smart. You got out of an unhappy situation before you got trapped. "Now, me," she said, patting her chest, "where am I gon' go with three other mouths to feed beside my own?" She sighed, not waiting for an answer. "Girl, you ever watch these reality shows they be puttin' on TV now?" She switched the subject without missing a beat, and I knew it was time to let my point blow over like a twister in the Delta.

"No, not rea—"

Streeter walked in before I finished my comment. At least I assumed it was Streeter. He'd let himself in without knocking. Streeter looked thirty-five or thirty-six. He was much too old in my opinion to be dressed like a hip-hop gear model. His stiff Sean Johns were pulled inches below his long slim waistline, and a sleeveless T-shirt stretched down over those. Two huge diamond studs were in his ears and his thin neck was heavily accented with a silver linked chain with a fake studded "S" emblem so thick, I thought I could easily hitch it to my SUV and tow it without a problem. He wore his hair braided Allen Iverson style, with a black-and-white bandana studded with a Playboy emblem on the front as a headband, barely leaving his eyes visible.

"Streeter, this is my friend CeCe from Jackson. She's the one I told you about who gon' be staying with us for a while."

"Yeah. Whatup, shorty?" That yo' Lex outside?" he asked, nodding toward the door.

"Hi, Streeter. Yes, that's my car."

"Yeah. Hey, shorty, can I holla at chou?" he said to Tracee.

"Sure, what's up?" She followed him into the bedroom. I turned back to the TV to watch *Fear Factor*. My only hope was that Tracee didn't ask for an update on what she had missed because I wasn't really paying attention. My mind was a little preoccupied with Edmond.

Tracee and Streeter emerged from the bedroom after a few minutes. Tracee reclaimed her spot on the sofa, looking kind of irritated. Streeter took a seat at the kitchen table and started to gesture to her. She cut her eyes at him and after a few more minutes, cleared her throat and spoke.

"CeCe?" She cleared her throat a second time. "Streeter wants to know if he can hold your car for a minute."

Streeter's back was slightly turned to us, and he was hunched over the table, fidgeting with a key ring. I noticed several keys of different shapes and sizes, making him look like the complex's super. I was relieved to know that mine were resting comfortably in my pants pocket.

"My car?"

"Yeah, he says he needs to make a short run to pick up a package, and you know mine is still in the shop. He said it won't take long. You don't have no place to go, do you?"

"No. But Tracee, my car is loaded with my things, and I really need to find a place to stay tonight."

"Find a place? Girl, you know you can stay here. Besides, you can unload your stuff right now. Streeter can help, can't you, boo?"

"Fo' sho," Streeter barked on cue.

I suddenly thought of my clothes being modeled by everyone in the apartment complex, including Streeter, looking like the scene in Eddie Murphy's *Coming to*

America. The thought of seeing him in my navy Zanotti' shoes, humored me.

"No, Tracee. Really. You guys don't need me cramping your style with all of my stuff, and I'll eventually have to get a place anyway. I may as well get it out of the way tonight."

"Girl, you can stay here as long as you need to. Streeter and me have already discussed it. We can clear the boys out and set you up in their room. And the money you would pay a hotel or something, we can shave that price. Streeter says you only have to pay us about five hundred a month. Now that's a hell of a lot cheaper than what you'll get anywhere in Houston."

"Really, I'm okay. I'm prepared to live in one of those efficiency deals or corporate housing for a couple of weeks until I find a permanent place."

"Efficiency? Girl, now why would you want to hole up in a box for two weeks when we were expecting you to hang out here? Besides, the element of the people you meet living in places like that, you'll have a scam ran on you in a New York minute."

As opposed to living with the element of Streeter? I wanted to ask, but let that thought pass.

"I'm serious, Tracee. You guys have your hands full, and with me job hunting, I'll be coming and going all the time, and I don't want to get in anyone's way. Like I said, I'm prepared for this, and I'll be fine."

"Suit yourself, but you know you're family."

I glanced over at Streeter. He was signaling to Tracee that she was up for her lines again, and I waited for the bait.

"Look, Streeter, my girl said no," she said like he'd tested her patience. "Didn't I tell you she don't know you like that? Damn."

"Damn, baby," he said to Tracee. "It's just a short bounce fo' real, and I won't handle her goods atall."

"Streeter, you roll with too many hoodies, and Ce don't want just anybody in her ride."

"It'll be just my potna and me. We'll take care of yo' goods for sho."

Streeter explained. I didn't know if he tried harder to convince Tracee or me.

"To be honest, Streeter, I'm just not comfortable with that. I mean, I know you're Tracee's man and all, but I'm just not big on turning my keys over to strangers. I'm sorry."

"Damn, shorty. How you gon' play us like that? Yo' homey, 'specially after ev'rything she's doing for you. Now you can't even do a brotha a favor. You know, Tracee, this ain't even worth arguing. She wanna act like that, let her find her own place, if not, we charge her six hundred a month to sno' here."

"Excuse me? What exactly have you done for me, Streeter?" I asked, becoming irritated with him. "I don't even know you."

"Now wait, Streeter, CeCe is family. Ain't nobody gon' be rollin' nowhere. Ce, if you don't loan your stuff out, we understand," Tracee interceded.

"Naaww, Tracee, nigga thinks she got it locked. Don't want to help me out, let her go. It's aiight. She'll need us. Bet on that."

"Hold up, Streeter. Now, you don't know CeCe like I do. We go way back, and she ain't like that. Now, Ce, like I said, ain't nobody going nowhere."

That squashed Streeter for the moment but something told me that he and I hadn't exactly bonded. I had been insulted by an over-the-hill, knockoff gangsta about my own damn car. Forget the drama; I had to get out of there. What did I look like, a courtesy cab? Enterprise Rent-a-Car?

"Tracee, I have to go before I say something I'll regret," I said, getting up from the floor. "How do I get to the 610 freeway from here?"

6

I awoke the next morning, utterly confused. Pretty close to nirvana. It took me a minute to get acclimated to the strange hotel room I was in. Then I remembered the six hundred and fifty dollars I had shelled out to stay at the Village Inn for the next two weeks. I thought the price was a bit steep, but given the hour, I didn't have a lot of choices.

It was one of those extended-stay hotels I had found near the 610 freeway after I left Tracee's. I knew it was a downsized version of my living conditions in Jackson when I could almost see the entire room at a glance. A kitchenette equipped with a refrigerator, range, and microwave; a thirty-two-inch color TV with a DVD; a small sitting area (even though the brochure said living area) with a burgundy-and-gold striped sofa that converted to an extra bed—all the mini amenities of home. That's what "extended stay" on the marquee meant, I supposed. I hadn't lived in anything quite so quaint since college. It wasn't home, but it would do.

I thought about calling Edmond, but didn't want to give the impression that I missed being home already.

I pondered the idea for a few minutes. I had promised him one phone call. I owed him that much, if only to let him know that I was safe and where he should forward my mail. I picked up the phone, which was permanently attached to the nightstand so that only the base turned from side to side. Did people actually steal the phones when they could afford to stay here?

"*Geezus,*" I murmured. I thought of Mom. I would have to call her again, but much later. For now, I dialed my old number on Bentley Lane, then I hung up before the first ring, quickly realizing that I wasn't ready to speak to Edmond again so soon.

I got dressed. I needed to grab some breakfast, but decided to skip on the restaurant at the hotel. The food probably tasted like truck stop cuisine anyway.

I jumped into my car and headed down the street. I took note of the kazillion places to eat on both sides of the freeway. An IHOP was actually located within walking distance of the hotel, but the crosswalk had become a temporary home to a cigarette-smoking female and a man seated in a wheelchair stroking a German shepard while holding a sign that announced that they were homeless and to be blessed by giving. I did a U-turn and pulled into the almost vacant parking lot of the IHOP. I checked my purse for cash before getting out. I would need to open a bank account sometime soon, I thought. No matter what my immediate plans were, I still needed a bank. I took the map of Houston that I had bought the night before from the glove compartment and headed into the restaurant, stopping near the entrance to grab a *Chronicle* on the way in.

When it finally arrived, I picked through my breakfast of pancakes, sausages, and scrambled eggs. On my second cup of tea, I flipped to the want ads section of the newspaper and scanned the jobs. I thought I might as well see what the competition was like. I did a quick rundown of my qualifications in my head. I'd held one job worth writing on my résumé, my public relation's position at Jackson Memorial. I matched my qualifications with the several jobs listed but nothing stood out as comparable—until the very last ad which consisted of a quarter-page spot, caught my attention. The salary was certainly enticing. It was at Templeton Advertising Agency, located downtown on Louisiana Street, which was very close to where I was staying. I tore out that section, folded it in half and slipped it inside my purse, then I paid the check and headed back to the hotel.

There was a message waiting for me from Tracee. That surprised me since our conversation had been curt when I had called her the night before to let her know I was safe. I dialed her number anyway. She apologized for being so short with me after I left her place, but that she had argued with Streeter. I was just glad we were still on speaking terms. She told me not to worry about what went down between Streeter and me. She also wanted to get together later in the week, minus Streeter, of course. But the real reason for her call was to let me know that she had gotten a call from Edmond. Her words washed a wave of panic across me. He had tracked down her number from relatives in Jackson just in case I was with her. But I knew his detective work had been nothing short of the strip of paper with Tracee's name and number that I left behind by mistake, along with the last page of directions to her house. Tracee said he would be calling back, so I had to decide if I wanted to talk to him. Reluctant at first, I told her to give him the number to the hotel, then I sat and waited for his call. It came around seven. Even though I was expecting the phone to ring at some point, it frightened me when it finally did.

"Have you finished with this crisis you're going through, and are you ready to come back home?"

"How's Pepper?"

"I gave her to my mother."

"You gave Pepper to your mother? How could you do that, Edmond?"

"I have a bank to run, and I don't have time to be inconvenienced by all the mess you left unfinished."

"But you gave me that *mess* as a Christmas gift. One that I didn't ask for, remember?"

"What did you expect me to do?"

"What about the remaining half of my doll collection? Did you give that away too?"

"Oh, come on, Celia. If you cared at all about me or the damn dog, or anything else, you wouldn't have left the way you did."

"I cared." What I really wanted to say was that Pepper's barking at any and everything had driven me up the wall, not to mention how much she pooped all over the backyard.

"About me or Pepper? And I hope you're aware that you're speaking in past tense."

"You always have to make everything so hard, don't you?"

"Answer my question."

"Which one?"

"When are you coming home?"

"Edmond, you think this can be fixed overnight? Stop trying to confuse my feelings with what you want."

"You know, Celia, I don't understand why you're seeing your life as being so terrible. I mean, the part about me ever hitting you is just ludicrous. And the loan. What's so wrong with a man going to any extent to keep the woman he loves happy?"

"Love, Edmond? You really think that when you shut me out, that's love?" I sighed, then chuckled with that same arrogance he used. "You are in greater denial than I first thought."

"Then why didn't you tell me how you felt, instead of packing up and leaving the way you did? What will people think when they find out you left?"

"I don't care what they think, Edmond. All you've ever cared about is appearance. Is that the only reason you want me around?"

"Celia, you know what I mean. Why did you just up and quit your job? And your friend, Melva, down at the beauty shop, you told her you were leaving, I ran into her. Why did she know before I did? Why didn't you give me that much respect?"

"Edmond, you wouldn't have understood."

"Why didn't you try? Why didn't you sit me down and make me understand?"

"How can I make you understand, Edmond if you don't even see a problem. I'm your wife but you treat me like a stranger. Besides, I knew you would try to talk me out of what I needed to do. The way you're doing now."

"Then why not at least give me the opportunity to understand."

"You can never understand how you've made me feel. I hardly know who I am anymore. I have to decide what I want. I have to find me."

"That is the biggest crock of bullshit if I've ever heard. You sound like one of those fucking Lifetime movies that you watch too much of. The truth is there is something in Houston that's more important than our marriage. Let me take a wild guess. Malachi Douglas?"

That shocked me into temporary silence.

"Mal—" I swallowed the last two syllables of his name. Why had Edmond brought up Malachi? That was supposed to be my little secret. I suddenly needed something to wet the dryness in my throat. "What does an old friend have to do with this?" I finally asked.

"Celia, don't play me cheap, okay? It's quite obvious. Malachi Douglas gets traded to the Texans, and in less than six months you leave me and move to Houston."

"Who told you? How do you know about him?"

"You think all this time I've had my head buried in financial reports? I have my sources."

"How did you find out?" I wasn't going to let him off that easily, especially since he brought up Malachi's name.

"Let's just say your father introduced me to your situation, what, seven years ago?"

"Seven years ago? Are you telling me you knew about Malachi when you and I first met?"

"I'm telling you that our meeting at the bank that day was not altogether coincidence."

"If you're trying to say that my father arranged—"

"What I'm saying is that you were in love with Malachi Douglas then, Celia, and for all I know you still are."

"Edmond, what you're saying is so pathetic I won't even justify it with an answer."

"So, are you denying that he's in Houston?"

"I don't know where he is, Edmond."

"You expect me to believe that?"

"I expect for you to trust me."

"You walked out on our marriage," he pointed out.

"Not because of Malachi." I paused.

"Then who? What? Fucking why? You tell me, Celia."

"You know why. Stop denying what you did."

"I refused counseling. That wasn't the only way."

"Counseling was the least of our problems, Edmond."

"For the last time, are you coming back home?"

"I can't answer that right now."

"You know, Ce...just forget it. I'm done. You know...go ahead and, and, and...go off on your little self-discovery or whatever bullshit label you want to disguise it with. But know this. When you reach the end of your rope and you still haven't found yourself, I won't be here waiting to pull you back in. In fact, why don't you cross me off your list, right fucking now."

"Edmond," I screamed into the phone. I got the sound of his phone being slammed down in my ear. Hard. I dialed my old number again. I let it ring for what seemed like forever before I gave up and rolled over on my pillow.

I closed my eyes and cried until I drifted off into a few hours of tormented sleep. I dreamed of sitting near a stream, much different from the one in Greenwood, Mississippi where Grampy took me fishing. It had crystal-clear water flowing gently over grayish-black stones. I stuck both feet in and let the water flow across and numb my toes. A shimmering pool of solitude turned golden when the sun cast a shining light on top. I sat and gloated in its goodness, where the fish were plentiful. They had faces that looked like men. Some even looked familiar. Like Edmond. They surrounded me, like they understood me. Some rested their heads on my thigh. Others hesitated, teased me, and nibbled at my bait before they swam farther upstream. I continued to fish until I hooked one that was right for my taste. I embellished until I was fulfilled, until all my desires were met, then I slept peacefully on the grassy bank beside the cool water as it continued to flow across my feet.

I had set the alarm out of habit. It sounded and reminded me of the day I left Edmond. I opened my eyes to a pale yellow light gleaming in through the cracks in the mini-blinds. A sunray covered my face, almost blinding me. I managed a smile as I hit the off button, remembering my dream. That drew an even broader smile. I felt more than ready to welcome the start of day three into my new conquest.

7

Malachi *"The Messenger"* Douglas was a star running back for Jackson State University and already a senior when we hooked up. I was still in my junior year. What Malachi didn't know at the time was that I'd had a crush on him forever—since he was fifteen and had moved from Brooklyn to Jackson. The bidding war had started as soon as he hit town, and so did the rumors about his popularity with the opposite sex, but I only knew that he was cute, athletic, and soft-spoken with a northern accent—that same crazysexycoolness to a bunch of southern teenaged girls as Sidney Portier had in my mother's heyday.

I had gotten up the nerve to introduce myself to him one Sunday at Ryan's Steakhouse. We were both on our way back to the university. After reaching for the lettuce tongs at the same time at the salad bar, we laughed, and he graciously filled my plate. We grabbed a booth and later kicked it after class, at weekend frat parties, and finally that spring break in Biloxi, the weekend my parents had relied on their third eye—Tracee's mom—for information about. They'd found out I wasn't really at AstroWorld with Tracee like I'd said.

Malachi said he was threatened; Daddy said it was just a man-to-man discussion. Malachi came around less, then avoided me altogether. He soon went pro, and two months later I met Edmond Cornell Ross.

Edmond felt jilted, was all. I couldn't let his declaration about Malachi and my relationship place me in a position to believe my father could be as deceitful as Edmond. My conscience said Daddy wasn't that way, even if he had always been Edmond's greatest fan. Mom loved Edmond too. That's why I found it hard to even tell them I had left him.

I checked the time. It was eight o'clock. That meant that it was a couple of hours earlier in Atlanta, which was good. I needed to phone Mom and Daddy, they would be up already. Like most southerners, my parents rose with the sun instead of an alarm clock. I wanted to catch them off guard, just as they were about to sit down and have their caffeine and grits.

I pressed the numbers with a sense of urgency, as if not to give them enough time to concoct some lame story like doing what was best for me. *Ha!*

"Mom, where's Daddy?"

"Didn't I teach you to say hello?'

"Mom, where is he?"

"He left already. He had to renew his license at the DMV. What's going on?" I wanted to talk to Daddy. I hadn't expected him to not be there and having to deal with my mother. She would be much tougher to confront. I quickly shifted into a weaker backup plan B.

"How could he do this to me?"

"Do what?"

"Break up Malachi and me by arranging a marriage between me and Edmond."

"Malachi? Arranged marriage? Are you talking about

that hoodlum, Malachi Douglas? Carrie Douglas's boy? Girl, have you been drinking?"

"Geezus."

"Stop using that word."

"Stay on the subject, Mom."

"CeCe, what in this world are you talking about?"

"Come on, Mom. I know everything. You can't keep what Daddy did to me a secret anymore."

"Is that what you think? Girl, you need to lay off the drama. If you think there's some cashed paycheck with your father's signature on it, you better wake up and smell the coffee."

"But Edmond told me—"

"I don't care what Edmond told you," she snapped. "He needs to cap up the highlighters because he's dizzy too. I don't know what kind of problems you and Edmond are having, but if you think they're because of something your father did seven years ago, you're both dead wrong. I won't have you dragging your father's good name in the mud that way."

"But—"

"But nothing. Shut up and listen," she shouted, interrupting me again. She got on a roll when she thought she was right. I wouldn't be able to get a word in edgewise. "The only thing your father is guilty of is caring about you. He loves you and only wants the best for you. Always. And he saw to it that you got it. Now everyone in Jackson, except you, knew that Douglas boy was bad news. Heck, he has enough stray kids there to own a football team. Now yes, your father knew Edmond from doing church business at the bank. And yes, he did make sure that Edmond knew what time you would be at the bank that day, so he could meet you, but everything else was you and Edmond's doing. And I don't remember attending a shotgun wedding. Am I right?"

I took a deep breath and rubbed my face until my thoughts were clear. "You're right, Mom," I finally said. "I'm sorry. I'm just trippin'. Confused. I didn't mean to upset you. And please don't mention any of this to Daddy."

"I won't." Her voice had calmed. "But honey, what's going on with you and Edmond?"

"We're separated."

"Separated? Lord, have mercy. Celia, what in the world is going on?"

"It's complicated, and I don't want to go into it right now."

"But, baby, whatever it is has you upset."

"I'm fine. I just can't go into it right now."

"Well, I'm sure you'll tell us when you're ready. Just remember, whatever you're going through, we'll support you."

"Thanks, Mom. I've gotta go. I'll call you soon."

I hung up the phone, glad that I had gotten that small matter settled, but thinking how I needed to distance myself from all that connected me to Edmond. I spent the next couple of hours contemplating my future over a bowl of Frosted Flakes and a glass of orange juice from the continental breakfast down stairs. I had to go grocery shopping that was for certain. I was doing quite well on my cash flow and could afford to take some time off if I wanted to. But good jobs were scarce even in Houston, so maybe I shouldn't wait too long. I pulled the ad for the Templeton Agency from my purse and dialed the number listed right after the qualifications. Creative Director. I didn't know exactly how that fit into my public relations background. The toughest challenge I'd had on my job ~t the hospital was a press release about the mayor's condition when he had been admitted for chest pains. I did have a minor in marketing that I had never used.

A receptionist who sounded like she'd had too much Starbucks referred me to Gray Tapscott. He sounded really cool. And if my voice profiling was accurate, he also sounded young. We spent the next ten minutes going over tidbits of my job history. The rest he said he would get from the résumé he'd asked me to fax.

I thought Gray Tapscott had given me the brush-off by having me fax my résumé instead of delivering it personally. But then he had wanted to know if I could come in later that day. That would give him time to get familiar with my background, he'd said. I almost panicked. I didn't expect an interview so soon, if at all. He told me to be there around noon and it would be quite informal. I glanced over at the clock on the microwave. It was almost ten-thirty. That didn't give me a lot of time. Regardless of what Gray Tapscott said, I wanted to look professional—suit, heels, attaché, the whole nine yards.

After hanging up the phone, I rushed downstairs, faxed my résumé, then dashed back up to my room to check out my interview suit still hanging in my garment bag. My optimism must have slid off my face like an avalanche once I unzipped the bag. My navy suit had more wrinkles than Methuselah. Mentally, I was toast. As Grampy used to say, I was more nervous than a long-tailed cat in a room full of rockers. Bottom line, I just didn't do well in interviews. And this would be the first where I didn't have to throw Edmond's name in as added security. I inspected my suit again. I would have to use some last-minute handiwork. With no available resources other than a steam iron and a damp washcloth; I pressed it as well as any one-hour cleaners ever could have. And Mom thought I never paid attention to her domestic diva advice.

I hung the cream silk blouse I had chosen to go with the suit above a cute pair of navy Zanottis and pulled out a couple pairs of panty hose in case of any unexpected runs. My nervousness doubled until a thought popped into my head. I pulled a small prescription bottle from my purse. I counted the little white pills that had been prescribed for my anxiety, one of the side effects of trying to cope with my struggling marriage for the last year. Fifteen left, no refills, my therapist had instructed unless Edmond agreed to go the next round of counseling sessions with me. I debated whether to take one before I flushed them all down the toilet. I didn't want to risk it. Templeton probably did pre-employment drug screening anyway. Besides, I was ready to take Houston on, drug-free.

I walked into the Templeton building a little before noon. It hadn't been a difficult place to find, it was located on Louisiana and Milam streets, close to the infamous Enron building.

The receptionist took me to Gray Tapscott's office. My instincts about him had been right. He was young-looking. He had a college-boy face with a pair of round-framed glasses that made him resemble a preppie Clark Kent before he turned into Superman.

"Celia Ross," he said cheerfully, getting up and coming around his desk to shake my hand. He pointed to a small chair. "I'm Gray Tapscott. Feel free to call me Gray. Just like it sounds, I'm just plain old Gray." Dry humor, I suppose, but I didn't laugh.

"It's a pleasure meeting you. And call me CeCe." I gave my intro a second thought. I didn't want to get too informal even though he said the meeting would be.

He sat behind his desk again and pushed up his glasses. His gesture reminded me of Edmond's habit. I glanced around his office. It was nothing special. Didn't speak well of his position at the company. In fact, it looked like he was in the midst of moving in or out. He must have read my thoughts.

"Excuse the mess here. I'm doing a little redecorating." I smiled and nodded before he continued. "So, CeCe, I see here from your résumé you worked in public relations at a hospital in Jackson, Mississippi."

"That's correct."

"How did that work for you?"

"Jackson or the position?" I asked, surprised how relaxed I felt.

He laughed a bit too much. "Both, I guess."

"The job had its moments. Quite honestly, Jackson is a small town, so I can't say my position was demanding."

"Well, we handle some pretty high-profile clients here. We're even thinking of working with a few of the sports celebrities here in Houston. That Malachi Douglas is a hot market."

I tried not to blush.

"Not to say things around here are always that exciting," he continued. "For the most part, it's pretty relaxed. But I'd like to be honest with you if I may."

"Of course."

"This company could really use someone like you. You see, the higher-ups at Templeton like to think we've gotten ahead in technology as well as diversity. Although, I admit we've done well, there are areas we can improve in."

"Such as?"

"Quite frankly, we are underrepresented in the female gender in our top positions."

"So are a lot of firms across the country."

"Yes, but I want to at least make a difference here. Now I see you have a minor in marketing."

"Yes."

"Any supervisory experience?"

"No. I wasn't aware that this position required supervision."

"You're right. There was an assistant, but unfortunately the young man decided to leave. We didn't advertise as such, but later on we plan to replace him. That's just something to think about."

"Oh, that's too bad. Had he been with the firm long?" I asked just to make small talk.

"A few years. But that's our loss. He's a bright young man. Well, now with that said, why don't I show you around?"

Gray gave me the quick walk-through. No introductions and not a lot of details, just the general layout of the place. The generic tour you got like everyone else when no hiring decision had been made. This informal meeting had only been to see what package came with the résumé. Men would never admit to it, but no matter what a woman's work experience looked like, they still wanted a decent face, knockout boobs, and a good pair legs around the office. At least I was a triple threat. Well…maybe two out of the three.

After a few stops, including a local bank located in the supermarket, I made it back to my hotel room a few hours later and had a congratulatory message waiting for me from Gray Tapscott. He wanted to know if I could start at the beginning of the next week.

8

"Ms. Ross?"

The sound of anyone saying my last name seemed distant and strange. Whoever it was said it on the way into my office while simultaneously tapping on the door. I hadn't looked up. I was busy reading the books I'd picked up the evening before at Borders to educate myself. *The Art of Supervision, Common Mistakes for the First-Time Supervisor,* and *Supervision for Dummies* were going to become my work bibles. Gray said I would be getting an assistant soon, and I wanted to be ahead of the game. I was pretending to list different items on my task pad, but was actually jotting down bullet points from the books.

The intruder was still standing there. I had hoped whoever it was would take the hint and leave when I didn't look up. I needed some alone time to get through the first few days of being new on a job. That included everything from finding the closest restroom to stocking my desk with retractable pens and white-out.

"Are you ready for me?"

"Excuse me?"

I finally looked up from my desk into the inquisitive face of a young dark-skinned brother. He was handsome with a fresh smile and smooth skin that was at least two shades darker than mine. His wide eyes and thick eyebrows completed his look. His hair was trimmed neatly and close to his scalp, quite complimentary to his professional dress, but he seemed relaxed in his tailored slacks and a white shirt rolled up at the elbows. His tie hung loosely around his neck. Probably the guy from the mailroom. Gray said he would do a run twice a day.

"Oh, I'm sorry I don't have it ready. Just check back this afternoon."

"What?"

"The mail. I don't have any—"

"I'm sorry to disappoint you, but I'm not from the mailroom," he stated rather sternly. His sparkly brown eyes darted around my office like he might be viewing it for the first time. Then he frowned like my taste in decoration was drab and simple. It probably did look pretty bare compared to my predecessor. I hadn't had time to bring in my own things yet.

"I'm afraid I don't understand." I gave him a puzzled look. "Who are you?"

"You are Celia Ross, aren't you?"

"I am."

"Then I'm your assistant."

"My assistant?"

"Yes, but I can tell you have no idea what I'm talking about, do you?"

"Not a clue. I was told the assistant moved on."

He smiled. A small mole danced below his left eye. He looked a lot more handsome when he smiled, if that was possible. "Well, let me begin again. My name is Tyson Treadwell," he said, still smiling as he extended

his left hand out to me. No ring, no commitment. I
smiled. "And I'm your assistant. Meaning we will share
this part of the building." He had a boyish quality about
him. Maybe even a little roughness, too, when he needed
it. He could probably throw on a pair of sagging FUBU
jeans and no one would be the wiser as to how he made
his living. He was close enough for me to notice a hole
in his left ear for his diamond stud.

Before I could respond, Gray stuck his head inside
my office door. He looked at us both and adjusted his
glasses. He and Tyson's looks suddenly reminded me
how young everyone must be. I hadn't seen anyone yet
who was over thirty in the place.

"I see you two have met," Gray said, turning back
to me. "CeCe, there has been a slight change since your
interview last week." He turned and looked Tyson's way
before going on. "I thought Tyson here would be leaving
us, but fortunately he's decided to stay. I'm sure he will
fill you in on that later. I hope my little oversight doesn't
compromise your accepting the position."

"No. Not at all. We were just getting acquainted."

"Good. I'll let you two get on with that then.
Tyson," Gray said, and nodded in Tyson's direction, who
returned the gesture. "CeCe, again welcome," Gray said
before leaving.

"Thank you, sir," I said warmly as he exited my
office.

"And CeCe, one other thing: We're quite informal
around here. Call me Gray. Sir or Mr. Tapscott make me
sound like my father. And being referred to as him will
really get you on my bad side." He smiled. I smiled and
nodded.

"Okay, Gray."

Tyson waited until Gray was out of earshot. "So, I

guess hearing who I am from the top clears things up."

"It does. And you should also know I wasn't trying to insult you before. I really was expecting someone from the mailroom."

"And I just happened to fit the bill, huh?"

"Look, Tyson, I'm new here. I barely know my office number."

"Ump. Like Gray didn't already school you about me."

"What do you mean?"

"You're part of them. I'd rather not say."

"You make this place sound like a sect or something."

"I have my reasons."

"So if you're not happy, why did you decide to stay?"

"I'll just say I have my reasons for that too."

"But you're not willing to—"

"Look, Ms. Ross."

"Call me CeCe, please."

"Okay, CeCe. Look, I know you're trying to be cordial, but can we just get on with business? Just tell me what you require of me today otherwise I have a deadline. I think we'll both be happy that way. At least I know I will."

Tyson's mood had shifted. He was coming off more bratty than arrogant. Whatever his problem was, he had added the third strike to the two he already had against him. One being he was young, maybe twenty-five, twenty-six, tops, and two, he was my assistant, which I wasn't too keen on having.

"Sure. If you give me a few minutes to get familiar with my role here, I most certainly will," I reiterated. "And you don't have to push so hard either. I'm really happy you decided to stay. I'm not always as slow as I'm pretending to be."

"Yeah, well, I'm not so much pushy as I am anxious."

"So why don't you relieve some of that by showing me what you do around here. Can you handle that?"

"That should be easy since I've been doing it longer than the age of most of the offices themselves. After all, that's part of my job, too, right? To basically do whatever you want me to?"

I followed him through a door that led into his office.

"This is my office. And you just passed the bathroom over there, which we'll share."

Actually our offices were separated from the rest of the firm on the floor just below Gray Tapscott's. We were enclosed behind high-glass partitions with a small reception area. Tyson's office was located just on the other side of mine with a bathroom that connected both offices. Tyson showed me the access door that kind of blended into the wall, except for a small metal handle.

"Co-ed, huh?" I asked.

"Yes, we can both access it from our offices, you just have to make sure you lock both doors; that's how the other knows it's occupied. And don't worry. I'll make sure I leave the seat down." He turned and gave me an ominous stare. "But I don't get coffee, dry cleaning, or lunch, boss."

"Thanks for the quick rundown of your job description," I said, turning to stop just inside of his door, "but I think I should let you in on a little something. First of all, yes, I'm your supervisor. That's the flow of the organizational chart. I supervise, I don't boss. Now, I do like to think of us as a team, but somehow I get the impression that will be difficult for you. What I won't tolerate, though, is backstabbing, disrespect, and most of all that chauvinistic attitude of yours. Now if you have any problems getting with that, I also entertain reference letters. In your case a generic one, being that I'm new." I looked for his expression. He was unfazed. "Well, anyway, that's the brief version of what I do, Mr. Treadwell."

"Point well taken, Ms. Ross. I'll be in my office if you need me." He stood at his door, allowing me to walk through, then he swiftly closed it behind me.

That went well, CeCe, I thought, once back at my desk. This was Tyson territory. I wasn't exactly strong in the advertising arena. I was hired because the timing for change was right. I would definitely need him later.

The morning slipped by with me almost forgetting my first meeting with Tyson. I had also managed to figure out as much on my own as possible. By noon, I was drained and needed some fast energy. I didn't ask Tyson for any suggestions on lunch, afraid he might send me to the local salmonella grill. I grabbed my purse and winged it alone. I jumped on the elevator and pushed the button down from the fourth floor. I would let some blind ambition lead me from the lobby.

The elevator stopped, and I almost step off until I realized it was only at the second floor. A young woman stepped on, rushing like she was already late to be someplace. She gave me a slight smile but I ignored her and thought of Tyson again. I hadn't told him that I was leaving for lunch. I wouldn't make that a habit.

The woman looked over at me and smiled again. I didn't smile back. She was about my age and height, but a little heavier. She had an attractive face, and we must have shared a common taste in clothes. We were wearing similar cream-and-chocolate pinstriped pantsuits, her colors just opposite of where mine were. Nothing made an outfit obsolete faster than to have someone else wear it at the same time, I thought. I had chosen higher heels with mine. I stepped farther back into the elevator. I knew at least one thing about living in a big city. Well, I had heard it from people who had. The takers could smell you like cheap perfume on a windy day, so never appear overly friendly.

"Nice suit," she said, smiling again. I nodded.

She spoke up anyway. "Hey, I thought the people from Jackson, Mississippi, were a lot friendlier. It's okay to smile. Not like I'm going to pick your pockets or something."

My eyes widened. The bell chimed, and the doors opened onto the front lobby.

"How did you—"

"Know you're from Jackson, Mississippi? Girlfriend, I know everything. I'm Jackie Foster from personnel." She stopped, turned, and held out her well-manicured hand.

I couldn't keep from smiling. There was something genuinely warm about her personality that reassured me she was okay.

"CeCe Ross." I gave her a firm handshake.

"Well, I know that too. You're that new head chick in advertising. I need to come by later and get you all processed in. Are you on your way out for lunch?"

"Yes."

"Come with me, sister. I'll show you the hot spots."

We walked out of the Templeton building for about a block before entering the Pennzoil building and a small deli on the bottom floor. Jackie waved at someone she knew seated at a nearby table.

"Heffa," she commented as we slid into one of the vacant booths near a row of windows. We had a view of a small garden with dogwood trees surrounded by a healthy island bed of violas and bluebells. I also recognized some impatiens, cyclamen and a few varieties of hostas mixed in. I knew it had only been a week since I left Jackson but I wondered if my front yard was in full bloom, after all it was April.

"Excuse me?"

"Oh, not you, dear. I mean that witch I just waved to. She gave a friend of mine a bad performance evaluation just to prevent him from getting a promotion. It won't work though. I advised him to grieve her ass all the way to EEOC. You know, except for a few rotten apples sprinkled throughout, this company is otherwise cool. Oh, but, sister don't let me scare you. You'll learn I just go on and on. So tell me, how is your first day at Templeton going?"

I hesitated for a while, not sure if she had finished.

"I'm trying to process everything." I wanted to mention Tyson, but I didn't know how well Jackie knew him."

"And what about Houston? Different from Jackson, I bet."

"Totally. I never imagined living in such a huge place. I'm afraid I'll never learn my way around."

"Nothing to it, sister," she said, taking a sip of the water the waitress had just placed in front of us. I did the same. The chilled spring water felt so refreshing against my dry throat. "You're looking at the same country girl who was in your shoes two and a half years ago."

"Oh, really. And you come by way of?"

"LA."

"Los Angeles?"

She looked around like the tables next to us were bugged. "No. Lower Alabama," she answered with a snicker.

"Get out of here. I didn't even notice the accent."

"Sister, I do have to work on it. Sometimes, when I get real comfortable with a person, it does slip out now and again. See I'm calling you 'sister.' I got that from my mama in 'Bama, I bet yours used to say that." We both laughed, and she grabbed my hand and squeezed.

"Jackie, you are too much."

We continued to chat through the rest of our lunch. She gave me the low down on everyone else who worked at Templeton. She warned me of the O'Jays, her code word for the backstabbers. I thought of asking her where Tyson fit in, but didn't.

After lunch, we walked back to our building and parted ways on the elevator. As the doors closed on Jackie, I knew I had found my second real friend in Houston.

9

Since I had nailed the Creative Director position at Templeton Advertising Agency, I was almost certain that I wasn't returning to Jackson anytime soon. Now I needed a permanent place to live. My extended two weeks stay at the hotel was almost up, so I didn't have much time to waste. But I didn't know what kind of place to look for. If that chore had been left entirely up to me, I would have opted for luxury over safety. Luckily, I had Jackie. She found both.

She recommended a row of condos close to her place. One I could purchase rather than rent. I definitely wanted to start investing in my own future. My condo was a spacious, two-bedroom Victorian-style building, located near an upscale mall called the Galleria. What my realtor, Anita Hunt, referred to as uptown living. She had rattled off the amenities like a walking brochure: good designer lighting, Berber carpet, and ceramic tile flooring in the kitchen, lots of windows, and extra closet space, which I definitely needed. There was also a fitness center, which meant that I could finally get back into my workout routine without any excuses, and a resort-style swimming pool. I added a lot of shelves for my dolls in the smaller bedroom. I had to make sure they had their own space, too, even if the other half of my collection was still in Jackson and I was too chicken to call Edmond to make arrangements to get them.

I loaded the SUV again on the first day in May with the extra boxes I had accumulated since being in Houston; linen, dishes, small appliances, et cetera—basic necessities I hadn't taken from Edmond. But at the same time, I had been careful in controlling my spending. I had nearly ten thousand dollars stashed safely away in my new bank account. Out of fairness to Edmond, I took only the amount I thought I had contributed alone. I didn't expect anything from any investments or stocks we owned. I wouldn't have wanted it anyway. I was planning my future on what I had. The furniture I purchased was nice, but modest, except I did splurge on the couch. I had to have this tomato-colored Zoe with chrome legs from RoomandBoard. Then I got the mustard-and-crimson chair to match, a glass/chrome coffee table, and two end tables. I wanted those same cheerful colors throughout for the dining room and my bedroom, unlike the subtle hues I used in my old place.

I overwhelmed my balcony with lots of colorful flowers and exotic plants. Jackie said I paid too much, but I stayed well within my budget of fifty-five hundred dollars. I did skimp on a computer desk from IKEA for the company-furnished computer. With the basics taken care of, everything else such as the art deco could wait until I got my signing bonus from Templeton. Plus, I still had my severance paycheck coming from my old job in Jackson. From that, I planned to replace the money I'd spent on furniture. Overall, my financial outlook was promising.

"Jackie, what's Tyson's story?"

She had stopped by after work with a pineapple pizza, an order of spicy barbeque wings and a six-pack of soda. Gray had given me a couple of days off to get settled in my condo. We were sitting on the floor around my coffee table. The furniture had been delivered and arranged. A rerun of *Friends* was on TV, picture with no sound, and the radio was tuned in to a local jazz station. I took a bite of pizza still hot from the box.

"Why? Are you interested in him?" she asked curiously.

"No. Are you kidding? I'm just trying to understand his attitude, that's all. Besides, he doesn't like me."

"Why? What did you do to him?"

"We kind of got started on the wrong foot, and I've tried every way I know how to warm up to him, but the more I try, the colder he becomes."

"Just don't push it. From what I know about him, he's a little arrogant but good people. He might have a little something to prove though."

"Prove to whom?"

"Himself, mostly," she said, dunking her wing in ranch dressing then taking a bite.

"Well, I'm new. Why take it out on me?"

"Sister, someone needs to school you."

"School me about what?"

"Tyson will never be fond of you."

"Why?"

"You took his job."

"Come again."

"Tyson had his heart set on the job that you blew in and stole right from under him."

"Stole? I think it was competitive."

"Tyson's young—the youngest in the department. It's kind of like he's fighting some type of inferiority complex."

"Like we all don't have our own cross to bear," I said.

"Try and tell that to someone like Tyson. Look, he's been there for three years and people less qualified than him have moved up. He figured his time had finally come when the creative director's position was announced. Then you happened."

"What ever happened to the best man for the job?"

"Just don't expect instant love from him, alright?"

"Oh, I won't. But at least I know how to deal with him."

"Just be careful. Watch out for the O'Jays. Remember, Tyson hasn't a thing to lose by twisting a knife in your back."

"Sounds like a soap opera," I said, running my hands through my scalp. I thought about when I needed my next perm. I didn't have a hairstylist yet. Jackie's hair always looked nice—cut and layered. Maybe she could recommend someone.

"Welcome to corporate America." Jackie sighed then relaxed.

She gave me the rest of Templeton's history until late into the evening when the pizza had gotten cold enough that the crust had hardened and my open soda had gone flat. We had redirected our conversation and repositioned ourselves on my red couch. Jackie seemed restless and had started to unpack a box near her feet.

"So is this your significant other?" She had picked up a picture of Edmond and me on top of the other items. I had packed it but wasn't sure if I wanted to set it out.

"Yes, that's my husband, Edmond."

"You still refer to him as your husband?"

"That's because he still is. We still have papers."

"What about him?" Jackie asked.

"What about him?"

"You know what I mean. Do the two of you plan on

getting back together?" she asked.

"I don't know. We have a lot of issues. Anyway, it's too soon."

"Was your marriage good?"

"It had its moments."

"So do all marriages, so I hear. If it wasn't all bad, why would you walk away? Isn't that shit from the movies?"

I chuckled at her lighthearted honesty. "Jackie, I don't think I'm the first woman who's left her husband. I just couldn't live with a man who put his job before me."

"That's forgivable, though. I mean, how many women would love to have a man providing for her?"

"If it was only that," I confessed.

"What do you mean," Jackie questioned.

"He was under a lot of pressure. I saw another side of him. I thought he might even hit me the night before I left."

"Whoa. That sounds pretty severe."

"Tell me about it."

"But he never actually hit you did he?"

"No. But Mom always said that you don't wait around to find out if a man will ever hit you. That was close enough."

"So how do you feel about him now?"

"I did love him. I mean do—I do love him. I just don't know if I can ever trust him."

"But you married him. You can get that trust back, don't you think?"

"It's not only trust. I'm afraid. Edmond and I had other issues."

"Like what?"

"Well, Edmond and I had problems, you know, in the bedroom."

"You mean, he's a light-equipment operator?"

"Jackie," I giggled. "No, he is very capable, thank you. He just wasn't skilled in using what he has," I said shyly.

"So it was the sex?" she asked, after gathering her composure.

"What?"

"You left him because sex was boring."

"No. Of course not. That's no reason to leave a marriage."

"Come on now, Ce. You say the man has money, smarts, and the picture says he's gorgeous. The only reason you would leave him is the sex."

"No, it isn't just sex."

"Okay then, good sex."

"Good sex alone doesn't make a relationship."

"But sister, everything can depend on good sex."

I looked at her and snickered. "Maybe you're right."

We let our laughter echo and settled into quietness again.

"So, while you're trying to figure out what you want, are you ready to start checking out the menus? I have some good prospects."

"Jackie! I'm still married. It's a little too soon to be thinking about dating don't you think? And I don't even know if Edmond and I are ready to head down the divorce path yet. Besides, he already thinks I left him for someone else."

"So? Do you honestly think Edmond is sitting in his rocker, waiting for you to decide what you want?"

"Straight-laced Edmond? I don't think he's out there macking anyone either."

"You sound too sure. All men play when given the opportunity."

"Look, I can't worry about what Edmond is doing, but I definitely want to be divorced before I start seeing anyone. Things are less complicated that way."

"Honey, believe me, no one will think twice about whether you're married or not."

"I'll know. Besides, I'm in no hurry to get back into any kind of relationship."

"Suit yourself, but if it were me, I would be living it up."

"Oh? How?"

"Simple. I would start by robbing the first cradle I came across. Some fine stud of a muffin and have him lay it on me so damn good that he would have me screaming the old Kmart slogan."

"Old Kmart slogan, what's that?"

"That's my spot!" She stretched both arms in the air and wriggled her bottom from side to side.

"I had to ask."

"Yes, you did."

Gone fishing. . .

10

"I'm not going," I stated adamantly, switching the cordless phone to my other ear. Jackie had invited me to hang out at one of her "eligible" spots, but I wasn't feeling eligible at all. How could I when I was patiently counting the days Edmond and I had been apart. I felt six weeks was just too soon to start thinking about dating again.

"Why? What's wrong?" Jackie asked.

"Don't have anything to wear." I had been slumping against the doorframe of my closet for the last hour, arms folded across my chest, trying to decide on one outfit that didn't make me look married or like a kindergarten teacher.

"This sounds like an emergency make-over. Don't wash the makeup off your face just yet. I'll be right over."

Jackie arrived, and we went through my closet like two shopaholics at a Foley's Red Apple sale. I frowned at almost every outfit she placed in front of me, including the ones she'd brought from her own closet. Finally, I decided on a sleeveless black dress that was cut deep front and back, which I had somehow overlooked earlier.

Not even that dress would matter when I walked into the Red Cat Jazz Café. How could I feel eligible when inside I still felt like a married woman, period.

The Red Cat was purring. It was a jazz-dinner-bar type atmosphere that I knew Edmond couldn't help but love. It had a New Orleans French Quarters appeal with a sizable dance floor right in front of a stage where the live jazz band was performing. It was a local group called Jazz'um. I looked around at the crowd. Everyone seemed separated by sophistication or extroversion. The latter, seated on the main floor near the band, sipping drinks or nibbling on eats while they grooved to the music. Others occupied the balcony, drinks in hand, under dim lights accented with a train station-like glass atrium. They were all there for the same basic reason—attention—to see and be seen.

Jazz'um played a song called "Chaotic" then "Nappy Funk," neither of which I was familiar with. But their last number had really rapt the crowd as Jackie and I looked on, standing next to the bar. I swayed with the music. I hadn't been listening to that much jazz lately, but I still held on to that small piece of Edmond. He loved jazz because it was the closest thing to the blues, I thought. Blues without the words, he often said.

He had that love-hate relationship with blues for as long as I could remember. It had something to do with his childhood and being raised in Mississippi, the birthplace for the original stuff—Buddy Guy, Robert Johnson, Eddie Cusic, people like that. He had once wanted to become a modern-day B.B., but no one took him seriously. He got laughed at and kicked out of every juke joint and hole-in-the-wall on both sides of the Mississippi. No one would believe that a light-skinned, blue-eyed kid with clean fingernails knew anything about having the blues, let alone singing about them. When his father broke his guitar and handed him a math book, that ended Edmond's dreams.

Jackie waved to a handsome, dark-haired, Italian-looking guy sitting at one of the red-and-black tables near the back corner. He smiled and waved us over like he was expecting us to join him. He pulled out a chair for me to sit next to him. Jackie scooted hers closer on his other side. I hoped this wasn't a set-up.

"I thought you guys weren't coming. You almost missed all the fun," he said to Jackie.

"What fun?" she asked.

He looked around and placed his hands on his chest in self-laudableness. "Me, of course."

Jackie rolled her eyes then broke into hysterical laughter. I smiled. The people at a nearby table turned and smiled at our commotion.

"Marco, this is CeCe Ross, my new pal I was telling you about. She just moved to Houston."

"Oh yeah," Marco said, and nodded my way. He picked up his drink and took a sip. "Welcome to Houston, CeCe."

"Thanks."

Marco drank again and looked around nervously, then he leaned over and whispered in Jackie's ear. They continued that action as I scanned the room, still hoping Marco's being there wasn't about me. But maybe I shouldn't count him out too soon. The "catch" in the Red Cat wasn't exactly what you would call plentiful or appealing at best. As for variety...that I wasn't too familiar with. Jackie had asked me back at my condo about the type of man I preferred. Whether it was the Denzel, Gary Dourdan, Tim McGraw, or the Bernie Mac-type, I had no idea. I only knew the Edmond type.

I spotted Tyson sitting alone at a table in the corner, wearing a don't-bother-me expression. He saw me too. Neither of us acknowledged the other. I looked away first.

Marco asked me something that I couldn't hear over the music. He leaned closer and asked again what I wanted to drink.

"White wine spritzer is fine," I told him.

"Ladies, I'll be back shortly," Marco said before dashing off.

"What?" I asked. Jackie was staring at me giggling.

"Nothing," she stated, still laughing.

"What's up? Did I order something improper?"

"No, girl, you're fine. I'm just glad you're loosening up a bit."

"Jackie, you wouldn't be trying to fix me up with Marco, would you?"

"Now, sister, you know me. Would I do that?"

"I do know you, that's why I asked."

"We're just frontin' for Marco, that's all."

"Come again."

Jackie slid over in Marco's seat closer to me. "You see, Marco has a taste for brown sugar, but he's married."

"Is Marco's girl here?" I asked, looking around.

"Never met her."

"Oh, I thought maybe she worked at Templeton," I said.

"No. You see, Marco works in the building next to us, and I think she works somewhere near him."

"Um, so you're the decoy?"

"Sure, every now and then. He gets me to hang out with him someplace, then she shows up, and he jets. Bet she's here somewhere right now."

"If love's that hard, why bother? Poor wifey."

"It can't be that hard. You'd be surprised at how much office romance goes on."

"Not at Templeton, I'm sure."

"Especially at Templeton."

Well, I certainly didn't have to fret over any office romance. Besides, there weren't even any interesting prospects that I could see. Jackie asked if I wanted to take a bathroom break. I did, but we would have to walk past Tyson, so I declined. Marco was still at the bar, periodically checking out the balcony action. That left me alone at the table. I played off my discomfort. I focused on the band again and tried not to look like I was alone, bobbing my head to the beat of the music. Loneliness was a feeling that would be hard to get used to.

My gaze suddenly fell on the entourage who had filed in through the front entrance. The heavy-set regiment parted, and a familiar face emerged from the center. Malachi Douglas was still fine as hell. He had that same roundness to his face and the big light-brown eyes, long curly eyelashes, and sexy dimples that were deep enough to poke my fingers in, permanently implanted in both cheeks. He sported locks now. I had seen them when he'd done his latest interview with ESPN, right before his trade to the Houston Texans. Dang! He was looking so fine. The kind of fineness that made a girl temporarily misplaced her mind. And that's exactly what I did.

My nerves escalated before my brain had an opportunity to plan my next move, and I started to reminisce on those days gone by—and those hot nights. I got up from my table and walked slowly and seductively in his direction. My curvy hips were swaying from side to side. I held my head high and my shoulders back, making my presence flagrant. My clinging black dress hugged my apple bottom tight, at the same time exposing enough cleavage to turn a few heads along the way. I could feel it riding up my thighs with every determined step that I made. Dang pantyhose. I should have gone bare or tried that new pantyhose-in-a-can stuff. I smoothed my dress down, but not very much. It was just hand simulation to showcase my hips. I entered the circle, stepping on some big guy's foot as I tried to get closer to the main attraction. "'Scuse me," I said. Big Guy didn't seem to mind. He smiled. I guess he was used to that sort of thing happening all the time. I walked right up to Malachi and smiled. His cologne greeted me first. He smelled good, just the way I remembered. He smiled back, revealing his signature gapped teeth.

"Hi, Malachi. It's been a long time. How have you been?"

"Well hello, yourself, shorty."

"I heard you were in Houston," I said.

"Yeah. Look, I'm sorry, but am I suppose to know you?"

My smile froze. I felt my face crack. I collected the shattered pieces before they hit the floor and Big Guy crushed them with his size fourteen Brunos. I scrambled to put my ego back in check.

"Well no, no. I'm just a fan."

"A fine one too! Are you here alone?"

"No, I'm with someone."

"'Nuff said. Hey, if you ever want to travel in the big league, give me a holla. I'm easy to find. Here's my number to help you out." He gave me a business card he pulled from his jacket, then a quick smile and a wink to remind me just how deep his dimples ran.

"Nice meeting you, Malachi."

"Anytime, ma."

● ● ●

"Ms. Ross, I see you do have a life after five o'clock."

Tyson had come up from behind and caught me off guard; otherwise, I had planned to be nice.

"And I see you carry that charm with you twenty-four/seven, Tyson."

"Some women find it sexy, so you never know."

"Some women, huh?"

"So, did you get an autograph?"

"What?"

"I saw you talking to Malachi. You get an autograph?"

"I'm not a groupie."

"No, but I did see you approach him."

"I thought I knew him, okay?"

"Knew him? Look, you either know Malachi Douglas or you don't."

"Look, Tyson, I said I thought I knew him, alright?"

He threw up his hands. "Okay, sorry. I didn't mean to get personal."

"I would prefer that you didn't."

"Anyway, he doesn't seem to be your type."

"What's that suppose to mean?"

He shrugged. "I take it you like a little milk in your coffee."

"And you?"

"I'm just quite selective and very patient."

"Well, I guess that explains why we're both here alone."

"Maybe," he said, then turned and walked away without comment. I just didn't get him at all, and I didn't think I wanted to.

Jackie came back with Marco. They were both laughing.

"CeCe, was that Tyson I just saw leaving the table?" she asked.

"Yes, it was. Him and all of his charm."

"What did he want?" she asked.

"Just to say hello. I think he missed me."

"Yeah, right. Like a hole in the head."

"He seems kinda young, CeCe." That was Marco speaking.

"It's not that way. He works for me."

"So, that's where you get your honey, so they say." He smiled and nudged Jackie.

"I think they say don't get your honey there, so don't twist it, Marco. But younger is cool. I once had a younger boyfriend," Jackie said.

"And you know what they say about older women?" Marco said.

"What's that? I asked.

"Glad as hell, and they never tell."

Jackie made a face. "Oh, you are full of it, you chauvinist Italian," she returned playfully.

"Oh, come on, Jackie. Is it really true about the young ones lasting longer?" Marco teased.

"Forget that shit. I had to wake his tired ass up a time or two, plus they're always looking for you to teach 'em things. Think just because you're older, you can teach," Jackie said.

"So what happened? Did he leave your old ass for someone his own age?" Marco asked.

"Not only that. He used what I taught him on her."

"I love to get you going, Jackie," Marco said after laughing hysterically.

"Forget you, Marco. I gonna kicka ya bagoonies." Her Tony Soprano imitation was horrific. We all cracked up again.

"I don't know, guys. I guess I never really thought much about it before, but age is nothing but a number," I spoke up.

"Spoken like someone who has dated a preschooler," Jackie said, laughing and clinking her glass against Marco's.

"No. It's the other way around. My husband is older."

"Oh. Well, that's cool," Marco said.

"Why? You think it's just being normal when the man has a younger partner?" Jackie asked, looking at him.

"No, just common," he returned.

"You're both cradle robbers. But Ce, go on and do your thing, just keep a copy of nursery rhymes nearby to keep him happy," Jackie said.

I waved her off without a comment.

She giggled and nudged my shoulder with her fist. "Mrs. Robinson."

"Mrs. Robinson?" I asked.

"Yeah, like in that movie *The Graduate*. You know, the older woman, younger man thing."

"Yeah, right. Sure, and I'll just call you dateless."

"Touché," she said making us all laugh again.

Marco glanced up at the balcony and downed his drink. "Well, ladies," he said, "the company's been nice, but love's calling, and I gotta go." Marco pecked us both on the cheek, threw some bills on the table and disappeared through the front door.

"And he's off. Just like you said," I commented.

"I hope for his sake he knows what he's doing," Jackie responded.

"He seems happy. We're the ones sitting here picky and all alone," I said.

"Happy for now, but two weeks, tops and he'll be wishing he'd taken my advice," she said.

"What's that?"

"Don't ever get your honey where you make your money."

11

I was standing in the middle of Tyson's office, feeling halfway between foolish and getting caught. I had rushed in to work still piqued at Malachi for the way he'd dissed me the night before; but ready to spurt venom at Tyson. But Tyson wasn't there. He must've had some errand to run. He hadn't started to keep me informed of his whereabouts.

Well...since I'm already here, I thought, *I might as well take a look around.* I could always use my right as being his supervisor. I smiled. On second thought, what if I lit up a cigarette and gave him the Mrs. Robinson parody like Jackie had mentioned the night before? But that would be admitting that I was paranoid about ever dating a younger man. Not that I was that much older. And why was I even feeling the age thing? Like I was really interested in Tyson, which I wasn't.

Age shouldn't matter anyway, men didn't seem to care. They hooked up with younger women all the time. Like Marco said, it was common. Edmond never thought twice about being ten years older than me. It didn't bother him that he already had a career that consisted of power lunches and boardroom headaches when I was still playing dodge ball and fighting pimples with Clearasil.

My attention turned back to Tyson's office. Things had been changed around. I had intuition like Mom's when I moved anything around in her house. She could point it out right away. I looked over at Tyson's desk. That was it. He used to be able to sit at it and look directly at me, now it was in the opposite corner so his back slightly faced my door. I guess Lamar Street and the Pennzoil Plaza was a better view than I was.

My curiosity drifted to the mirage of framed certificates on the wall—his degree from Texas Southern with honors, the fraternity he pledged. I fast-forwarded to his tenure at Templeton and his accomplishments to date, things no one else would particularly care about that made you look more competent hanging there. Edmond never displayed any of his achievements in that way. He said that he didn't have to prove to anyone where he'd been, that how he ended up was more important. Sometimes I wondered if he believed half of the success BS he expected me to.

Tyson kept a silver-framed picture of an older couple on the corner of his desk. Their blended features made his. They were his parents, no doubt. He must love them dearly. A man devoted to his parents said a lot about him. Made him lovable.

I searched for the obvious, to see if he had a picture of his girl around. I imagined she'd be tall and very sophisticated with upswept hair and jewelry well put together. Her good looks would balance his like most successful men preferred. Maybe she would even be holding a tiny bundle with brightly lit eyes like Tyson's. I saw no lady, no kids.

I mentally processed the information I'd gathered so far about the man who clearly got under my skin. Then my gaze froze above a small credenza on the opposite wall, my lips quivered and my mouth dropped open. Tyson was standing next to Malachi, engaged in a handshake with one arm around Malachi's shoulder. They were both smiling. Malachi was dressed in his Houston Texans uniform; Tyson was wearing a fly dark blue suit. Malachi's autograph was scribbled in the bottom corner of the picture. Geezus. I prayed they didn't travel in the same circle. Not that it mattered when Malachi hadn't even remembered who I was.

I looked back down at the credenza. That was more amazing than the picture above it. Tyson owned a collection of Hot Wheels racecars. There must have been close to a couple hundred, all colors, shapes, and sizes, and some hadn't been removed from their boxes. Rows of glass shelves in a small wooden cabinet next to the credenza contained an overflow of a couple dozen more. I pulled off my jacket, suddenly feeling flushed, as if I was learning too much too soon about Tyson without his knowledge.

I wanted to head for the door, run like a school girl denying her first crush, but my legs wouldn't cooperate. I stood paralyzed, then I got all tingly inside being so close to Tyson's energy, wanting to touch the places he had. I ran my fingers across his desk. I marked my territory across his keyboard, the handle of his phone, across the top of his swivel chair. *Why doesn't Tyson like me?* I wondered, then I went over to his drafting table. *Am I really that hard to get along with?* He was quite the artist. I checked out several sketches for the car ad on which we were working. I traced the outline of the cars that he had sketched. That warm feeling came back. I flipped the pages of his sketch pad and smiled. *How could I get him to like me? Do I even want him to?* Of course I did, otherwise it wouldn't bother me that he didn't. As much as I wanted to deny it, Tyson was in my system.

"Are you checking up on me, Ms. Ross?" He had walked in quietly and stood behind me. My thoughts scattered, played switcheroo with my professional side.

"I was just admiring your work. You have talent."

"I didn't think you noticed."

"I noticed. Plus, Gray has good things to say about you."

"I guess I do aiight."

"So how's the ad coming?"

"You tell me. That's what you were looking at."

"Oh. Very impressive. I almost hate to throw this on you," I said.

"What is it?"

"Gray and I met earlier this morning. He agrees with my change in priorities."

"Oh?"

"We have to shelf the Lexus campaign for about two weeks and finish up with the department store in time for the Fourth of July."

"But I'm almost done with Lexus. I can handle both."

"I'm not doubting that, but I didn't want to put that kind of pressure on you. I thought it would be taking on too much."

"You thought but not enough to ask me?"

"I'm only looking out for you."

"Or yourself?"

"Why would you think that?"

"You don't trust me."

"Trusting you isn't the issue, Tyson."

"Well, then maybe you don't trust yourself," he said.

"What's that's suppose to mean?"

"You're afraid that you might be in over your head."

"Where's that coming from?" I asked.

"Look. I'm not a snoop, and I hate nosy like the next

person, but this is a small office, and your background kind of preceded you."

"And that automatically gave you the impression that I'm incompetent?"

"That's not what I'm saying," he stated with a little tension in his voice.

"Then what are you saying?"

"I'm saying that you could have at least consulted me before making a decision about my schedule."

"I don't have to explain my actions to you. I was hired to do a job, and that's what I intend to do whether or not you feel a need to be consulted."

"Fine, Ms. Ross. I get that you're in charge. I got that from day one. Forget it, okay?"

"Forgotten. And would you do me the favor and drop the Ms. Ross crap?"

"Dropped. Like it's hot."

I couldn't help but smile. Then I looked away. I didn't want him to catch my lighter side. "Okay. I guess we can move on," I said.

"So is that all you needed to see me about?"

"See you about?"

"Yeah. The reason you're standing in the middle of my office."

"The campaign was what I wanted to talk about."

"You sure?"

"Quite sure."

"I mean you were so deep in thought and caressing—"

"Believe me, Tyson, that was it, so save all your creative energy for the next few days."

"Sure, CeCe, you're in charge, and I've got no place else to be. I'm all yours."

12

"Well, we did it," Tyson exclaimed, holding up his Dixie cup in salute.

"Yes, we did, didn't we?" I chimed in.

I was sitting at his walnut-colored desk. He was at his drafting table. We were drinking some sparkling water, the closest thing to champagne that work ethics would allow. We had just wrapped up the ad for Mayfair's department store which we'd been going at for almost ten days straight. It would have taken less time if I hadn't agreed with Tyson's idea to use illustrations instead of live models. Although his way had taken longer, just the rough sketches had already won kudos from the cronies at Mayfair's.

I leaned over the desk, clinked his cup, and watched him sheepishly over mine as I sipped. His eyes remained on me when I glanced away.

"Maybe we should celebrate this properly. What do you say? Dinner? My treat," he said, crushing the paper cup and making the shot into the trashcan. He had rolled his swivel chair closer to me.

"Thanks, but I have plans," I lied. Tyson still made

113

me a little nervous. Sure the past couple of weeks had brought us closer, with no fights and insults or even a hint of arrogance from him. It was as if he had caught a sudden case of the Stockholm syndrome—that breakdown of the mind where a hostage developed rapport with their captive and sympathized with their cause.

"You mind if I ask you something?" he asked.

"Shoot," I said and took a deep breath. I bit down nervously on the pen in my mouth and leaned back in his soft black leather chair. We stared at each other momentarily.

"Is it me, or are you going through a male-hating phase?" he stated, bluntly.

Where had that come from? I took the pen out of my mouth and put it down on the desk, then got up and moved in front of it and folded my arms across my chest. We both were comfortable. I had kicked off my shoes, relaxed down to my stocking feet. My blouse hung loosely outside my pants. Tyson had removed his tie and undone a few buttons on his shirt.

"Just the ones who have a way with words the way you do," I returned.

"My apology. I guess sometimes I can be blunt."

"And arrogant, untactful, offensive, and even down-right obnoxious come to think of it," I reminded him.

"Hey, you can stop anytime. I get your point," he said, putting both hands in front of him. "But seriously, isn't it just a little unfair?"

"What?"

"To judge me by the man who broke your heart. Do I remind you of him that much?"

"Hardly. And I never said anyone broke my heart, did I? How do you know I wasn't the one who did the heartbreaking?"

"Okay, then what is it about me?" he wanted to know.

"I don't follow you."

"What about me don't you like? Really."

"I never said I didn't like you, Tyson."

"But you don't."

"I don't really know you well enough to offer an opinion like that. Not yet anyway."

"Okay, I'll accept that."

"Thank you, 'cause you're making me sound like a tyrant," I said, jokingly.

"I didn't mean to," he said, kind of apologetic.

I tried to finish my water, but found it hard to swallow and not especially from the taste. I had a feeling Tyson wouldn't let the twenty-one questions go.

"So what did he do to you?" He scooted his chair closer, almost touching my legs with his knees. His legs looked so lean and powerful near my short feminine ones. I caught myself thinking how they would feel wrapped around mine. I wondered if his thoughts were similar.

"He?" I asked, shaking my thoughts.

"Your husband."

"How do you know there was a husband?"

"That lighter shade of brown around your ring finger is a tell-tale sign."

"Touché. I suppose I need to tan that, huh?" I said, flashing my left hand and wiggling my fingers. After five years of wearing that ring, six weeks wasn't enough to erase that it was ever there.

"Or stop frontin'."

"You're impossible." I thought I should move away but he was blocking my path.

"So why didn't it work? He didn't agree with a bad hobby of yours or something?" he asked.

"We didn't question each other's hobbies," I said,

really wanting to get off the subject of Edmond.

"Sounds like you two had an understanding."

"The marriage worked while it did."

"And when it didn't?"

"I booked."

"Any kids?"

"No."

"Your decision?"

"You're very personal," I told him.

"You said I was cold. I just wanted to show you I can be sensitive."

"At my expense?"

"No. It works both ways. What is it about me that you want to know?"

"What's up with all the Hot Wheels?" I asked, nodding at his credenza in the corner.

"Anything but that," he said, frowning and scratching the back of his neck. He laughed. I did too.

"Why? I thought we were sharing here."

"You just might think it's immature, that's all."

"I won't as long as you don't think collecting dolls is."

"Yeah. What kind?"

"A little of everything, I guess."

"No. I think that suits you," he remarked.

"My therapist said collecting things might be a substitution for a missing part of me."

"Therapists are just paid sounding boards. We pay them to listen to us answer our own questions."

"You sound like my ex. Edmond thought everything was a waste if it had no immediate financial return, including my collection."

"Sounds like he didn't suit you."

"And what about you?" I suddenly wanted to know what kind of a woman suited him.

"Me?"

"Yes. Does she suit you?"

"Who said there is a 'she'?" he asked, holding up his ring finger.

"So maybe it's not at the marriage stage."

"That would be accurate."

"Your choice or hers?" It was my turn to pry.

"I'd rather not say."

"Oh, I see."

"Let's change the subject, okay?" he said, getting uneasy.

"Okay. To what?"

"I have about two hundred and fifty."

"Huh?" I asked, confused.

"My Hot Wheels. There are about two hundred and fifty cars."

"Oh, cool. How long have you been collecting?"

"Well, my father actually started, then it was kind of passed down to me when I was ten."

"Some of these look really old."

"Some are."

"So why do you keep them here? They look irreplaceable."

"It's kind of a long story, but just say they're safer here for now."

"They must be worth a lot of money."

"Some are pretty rare, but this one is my prized possession." He got up, walked over to the credenza, and moved around a few cars before picking up a little red one to admire it closer. "It's the '69 Beach Bomb. First introduced in 1968, one of only twenty-two ever made. It should be worth somewhere around fifteen hundred dollars now." He paused and searched my reaction. I'm sure I looked interested, but he stopped himself. "Listen at me. I could go on. Now you must think I'm really immature, huh?"

"No, not at all."

"What do you really think of me then?"

"Why is that so important?"

"Maybe I just value your opinion, that's all."

He came back and stood close to me. We had switched positions. I was in his chair while he eased down on the edge of his desk.

"And why is that?"

"You seem like a strong woman. Older."

"So, you think I'm old."

"Older."

"Okay. Thanks for clarifying that. I think," I said, frowning.

"Don't tell me you're hung up on age," he said, and let his leg move closer to brush against my knee. I should have push back but I didn't move.

"I'm not. I happen to think that age doesn't matter, it's the quality of the person," I stated.

"So what qualities do you look for in a man?"

"I'd rather not say. That would be pre-selection, wouldn't it?"

"Do I have any of those qualities?" he asked.

I felt warm. He was much closer than I wanted him to be. I motioned to stand, catch my air. He leaned over and helped me to my feet, while placing his face close to mine. His breath smelled sweet like the cinnamon in the Starbucks we drank earlier. I was reminded of the warm eggnog at Christmas that Granny made from scratch. Tyson's eyes grew warm and fixated as he took my hands into his, turned them palm up and traced my life lines.

A slight tremble rippled through my legs.

One of us had switched on the radio earlier. I couldn't

remember when or which one of us had. It must have been at least two deejays ago. Kasey James was serving up his Quiet Storm.

One of Tyson's hands slid around my waist. My throat tightened as he drew me in closer. I needed to be the sensible one. I would be the one to blame. The supervisor always had the responsibility to not let things get out of hand. I'd read that in my *Supervision 101* book.

Because I didn't seem to mind, Tyson didn't either. Neither of us tried to stop the force that was pulling me to him. Kinetic, magnetic, we were one emotion short of kissing. His hand moved up to my breast and squeezed. Not rough like Edmond, but gentle and considerate. I uttered something useless. I had tried to tell Tyson that we couldn't go down that road. My lips moved but no sound came forth. Only our heavy breathing and Michael Jackson's "Butterflies" drifted through the air. I leaned away and tried to breathe my own air. He pulled me forward, hard into his chest. His Burberry scent smothered me when he wrapped his strong arms around my shoulders. His mouth searched and found my earlobe. He did things there that rendered me helpless while he worked his hand up and down the sensitive part of my back. I tried to object again, but he hushed me with soft, short kisses. He cleared the desktop of the sketches, empty cups, pens, pencils, and paperclips with one sweep, then lowered me down. Then knowing what I might do next, he brought the weight of his body down on top of me.

"Tyson, no," I whispered.

"Ssshh!," he silenced me again, then he ran his tongue along that soft, fleshy spot between my jawline and neck, then down to find my pleasure spot between my breasts. His hips moved with the music until I felt him rise.

"Tyson, let me up," I demanded, bringing my fists to his chest. I was a little embarrassed that I had hesitated too long.

He stopped and looked down into my face. "Are you telling me you don't want it too?"

"I'm still your supervisor."

He tried to kiss me again like those words didn't matter anymore.

"Tyson, I'm serious. Get off." I pressed harder into his chest. I had to reach deep to add some firmness to my voice. "If you don't move right now, I'll fire you so fast, you'll forget how to spell the word *job*," I said, leaving no doubt that I had pulled rank on him.

He looked hurt and didn't speak. He pulled himself away and stood. He started to say something, then changed his mind and grabbed his things before whisking out the door. A part of me wanted to run after him, to comfort and explain that it was my fault, too, but I didn't. I sat upright on the desk until all the blood returned to its proper place. Kasey James's deep, sensuous voice came over the radio and startled me.

"Hey, if you're out there tonight listening, maybe you know someone who's hurting, or you're so lonely and heartbroken that you want to reach out to that special someone, squeeze them and tell them that—"

I hit the off button, then pulled on my jacket and gathered my things. What I was feeling wasn't exactly hurt, but surprised that I was feeling Tyson at all.

13

I had no idea how I would handle Tyson at work the next morning. After all, we had come close to exchanging DNA had I not put the brakes on. But it had been electrifying. Downright riveting! I wanted to deplete those thoughts. My future with Edmond was still too unclear. Not to mention the small fact that Tyson and I shared a supervisor-subordinate relationship.

"Good morning, CeCe."

"Tyson."

He closed my door behind him, then came and stood in front of my desk, setting his attaché on the floor by his feet.

"Can we talk?" he asked, rubbing his chin.

"I suppose we need to, don't we?"

"Not here. Let me buy you breakfast down the street."

"I don't know if we should."

"Come on. No one will even notice. Besides, we'll have meetings together away from here from time to time."

I sighed, feeling convinced. I grabbed my purse and he brought his attaché for appearance. We walked down the street to Café Antoine. It had a breezy patio area with lots of hanging spider plants and Italian music playing, which made it cozy, but that wasn't ideal, so we went inside. The place was completely empty but we got a table right out in the open, trying to make our being there as innocent as possible. Tyson pulled my chair out, then took the one directly in front of me. He ordered light—toast, bacon and a glass of grape juice. I ordered even lighter—bagel with cream cheese, a bowl of fresh fruit and some spicy herb tea. We both knew we weren't really there for the food.

"Now that we can talk freely," he said, taking a sip of water after the waiter left, "I want you to understand that I'm not out to hurt you. I mean, when we first met, I wasn't your biggest fan obviously, but I didn't plan us coming close to having sex last night."

"It shouldn't have happened, Tyson. I can't afford to start off at Templeton on bad terms."

"I understand that, but I have to be honest. CeCe, I don't regret expressing my feeling for you that way."

"We can't go around making out in the office."

"Don't you think I realize that? Listen, I'm not some young high-school kid in love with his teacher, so don't treat me that way."

"Tyson, don't. Let's not go there. That's not what I'm saying."

"What are you saying, CeCe?"

"I have so much going on in my life right now."

"Like what?"

"Things that you wouldn't understand."

"CeCe, we could see each other outside of work. We're both adults. We don't have to bring our personal lives into the office every day."

"You don't really think we can be secret lovers, do you?"

"It's not impossible. You think half of the people at Templeton don't have affairs with each other?"

"Tyson, it wouldn't work. Sooner or later it would show."

"It's not just the fact that you're my supervisor is it?"

"I don't know what you mean."

"Is it the age? The fact that I'm twenty-six?"

"You're not that much younger. That's not an issue."

"How much younger?"

"I'm thirty-one."

"So age isn't the problem. So what is?"

"Tyson, I—I'm still married."

"How married?"

I laughed. "Married is married."

"But you said it was over when you left him. Hell, you don't even wear your ring."

"Just because I left my ring behind on a shelf in my bedroom doesn't change the fact that I'm married on paper."

The waiter interrupted with our food but neither of us felt hungry anymore. I sipped my tea. Tyson stared at me, then tried to wipe the disappointment from his face. I added some sugar and cream and waited for another question. He didn't have one. We remained silent that way for a while, then he picked up a fork and started to share my fruit. I smiled and made him smile. He tried to feed me the rest of my fruit, but I declined. I was too concerned with the sidewalk traffic which had picked up outside, and that sudden flash of bright light through the restaurant's window.

• • •

I dialed my husband in Jackson for only the second time in the month and a half since I'd left. I had purposely waited late into the night to call Edmond, contemplating what I was going to say. Our last conversation hadn't exactly been friendly. We'd argued. He felt I had treated him like yesterday's news, while I thought I was justified in leaving my marriage. Reality check—the marriage I was still in. Even if Tyson was moving into my heart pretty fast, my ties to Edmond were bound, like it or not.

I could have just been flighty. I should have stayed and faced our problems head-on. The line didn't connect. I had punched in the wrong area code. I had forgotten that it changed right before I took off.

I nervously redialed and waited for the ring. I hadn't even decided what I would say right away. I didn't know if I should tell Edmond that my period was a few weeks late, about six weeks, and I could be pregnant. Maybe not just yet, that happened, especially when I got stressed. I would wait at least until I had my annual done the following week and was one hundred percent sure. Edmond would want me to be sure before I told him.

"Hello," a stranger answered.

Still must have been off a digit or two. I told the voice that.

"Who were you trying to reach?" she asked in a most helpful way. She sounded familiar.

"Well, uh, Edmond Ross, but—"

"He's in the back. May I ask who's calling, please?"

My heart dropped, then crawled up and dropped again before I was able to speak.

"His wife," I managed.

"Oh, just a minute, Ce, I'll-I'll get him." She sounded more disappointed than I was.

Hang up the phone, CeCe. Forget about it. Hang up the phone, my womanly intuition said. I had every intention of doing that, but my hand felt glued to the receiver and I held on to fight for my right to know. I wanted Edmond to be a man and tell me what was happening on Bentley Lane.

I held the line while voices mumbled in the background. Sounded like rustling leaves in a windstorm before the phone was finally transferred from her hand to his. I heard him take in a deep breath. He knew that dealing with me would be a battle.

"Hello, Celia. Listen, I know what you must be thinking."

"Oh. Tell me, Edmond, what am I thinking...What? The fact that some bitch is in my house before my scent has even evaporated? It hasn't been that long, you know."

"I know how long it's been. And it's not like that. She's a friend. She only came by to help me out."

"What kind of a friend. A call girl?" I answered angrily.

"Don't get cute."

"Who is she?" I demanded.

"What do you care?" he asked quite arrogantly. "You left me, remember? You walked out. And that didn't entitle you to a marriage on reserve. What the hell did you expect for me to do when you left?"

"Have the decency to at least be discreet," I said coldly.

"Be discreet about what? How do I know what you're up to in Houston or why you even moved there in the first place?" he asked.

"So who is she, Edmond? Someone you picked up in the window of the bank's drive-thru?" Silence. "Answer me, you bastard. Who is the bitch?"

More silence.

"Answer me!" I screamed a second time. Then he said in an almost desperate voice. "It's Ja'Nell from the bank. My assistant."

"Oh, that homely bitch? Your hired help? The skank who doesn't know the fax machine from the copier? So how long after I left did it take the tramp to make her move on you?"

"Celia, can we please stop with the name calling?"

"Excuse me. Oh, now we have feelings for her? Oh, but you do have a knack to do things fast. What a few weeks now and you're in love? Huh? Answer me, Edmond," I screamed.

"Celia, Ja'Nell and I are only friends."

"Friends? Ha. She's hired help."

"Colleagues then."

"Shit. She gets your coffee."

"She only came by to help out with some paperwork for the restaurant, that's it."

"Liar."

"Think what you want."

"What did you say?"

"Nothing. Nothing at all. Look, this is ridiculous, you know. I don't want to fight with you."

"I didn't call to pick a fight with you either, but you know it's kind of hard when I call my own house and some bit—"

"It's not like that, Celia. I keep telling you that. You know me better than that."

"Than what?"

"What do you mean?"

"Why is Ja'Nell in my house?"

"I told you why."

"You're a liar."

"Think what you want, but what if there is something

going on with Ja'Nell? Why are the rules always different for you?"

"What are you talking about?"

"You get to run to the other end of the earth because you're hurting, but what about me? You find comfort; I'm just plain old, boring Edmond. No one ever looks twice at me. Do you think you saved me when you married me, Celia? Do you think that I'm willing to stand by and be mistreated by you because I'm afraid that no one else would ever want me?"

"Where's this going?"

"Maybe there are things that I haven't been completely honest with you about."

"Yeah, try everything."

"Celia, Ja'Nell and I go way back."

"What are you telling me, Edmond?"

"We dated before you, Celia. In fact, we were still dating when I met you, but I chose you because I thought you were the best thing for me. I still believe that, Celia." I remained silent. He couldn't have made me feel worse by adding that. When I didn't comment, he continued. "And there's one other thing. She's also the silent partner with the restaurant business. But not to worry; it's just strictly business between us for now. That's all. But days are lonely and the nights are long. I can't make you any promises."

The room started to spin. My head felt light, I started to sway and grabbed onto the kitchen counter to balance myself. How foolish could I be? To think I was actually feeling guilty and considering working out our problems.

"Business partner? You mean you're going into business with your mistress?"

"Ce—"

"You put us in debt with your bitch! What were you

planning to do, Edmond? Kick me to the curb when the money broke even?"

"It was never that—"

"You know I don't even care."

"Then why did you call?"

"I thought we could have an honest conversation, but I was wrong. Look, I don't need to hear anymore from you. The lies. Everything. You, me, our marriage. One big, fat lie." I slammed the phone down in his ear.

Then I waited.

I paced across the floor and argued with myself, then I got a bottle of wine from the refrigerator, some chardonnay Jackie had brought over and we never opened. I popped the cork, poured myself a glass and drank about half. The rest wouldn't go down. I left it on the counter and went back into the living room. I picked up my laptop and did some quick research on divorces in Mississippi. That information satisfied me for the moment. I stared at a picture of Edmond I had sitting on the table next to the couch. I cursed him, called him a Mississippi raised, workaholic, no-blues-singing, lying, premature-ejaculator, terrible lover, anal compulsive, cheating, two-timing liar, I never should've married him. Liar, liar. I knocked the picture to the floor, picked it up, and threw it against the wall again and again until it shattered. Damn glass was too hard to break. Then I picked up the naked photo that was cut and nicked from the broken glass. It was never one of my favorite pictures anyway. I was looking up at him in it, giving him too much of my power. It was taken the night he was named bank president and we went out to celebrate. I stared at his face and tried to connect the pieces of my life for the last few weeks. For the last five years. Nothing fit. Then my life crumbled right before my eyes. I ripped the picture to shreds and dialed Edmond again.

"Hello," he answered wearily.

"I want a divorce."

"What?"

"You heard me, you ...I said I want a divorce."

"Celia, look, you need to calm down because you're obviously upset. Nothing is going on here. Okay, I admit, I'd love to see you jealous enough to rush back to me, but—. You know how you can become when you're upset, dear. Have you been taking your medication?"

"Go to hell, Edmond."

"You know you get anxious. Before we do anything rash, we need to talk later when things have calmed down, you know, when your head is clear."

"Don't you dare patronize me, you anal, compulsive, arrogant son of a bitch."

"I won't consider a divorce right now. You're too erratic."

"Erratic? Ha." I laughed at him, not caring if I hurt him. Tears trailed. "You want me to show you just how erratic I am?" I asked after I steadied my voice. "If I don't get divorce papers from you within thirty days, I will put your business in the street. I will tell everything."

"Everything? What do you know to tell?"

"I'll make shit up then. Do you hear me? I'll hold a press conference right on the front steps of your precious little bank, if I have to. I will have the entire city of Jackson crawling up your tight ass like they were CSI. Who do you think those old cronies are willing to believe, huh? Especially the part about your live-in secretary. And isn't it a little unethical that she's a partner with you on a loan anyway? One that you borrowed from the bank in your name?"

"You know you wouldn't do that to me, Celia."

"The name is CeCe, and try me."

"Darling, please listen. Don't force my hand this way. I love you."

"Thirty days, Edmond."

I barely remembered the phone slipping from my hand. It hit the floor with a soft thud, right before the tears came again, and the hurt and betrayal slid down my cheeks. The phone rang out again sometime after that. I didn't know for how long. Five, ten, fifteen minutes. My mind didn't allow the sound to register right away, but the piercing rings refused to give up. They kept coming with demand and urgency. *Please, God, don't let it be Edmond.*

"Hello," I said softly, expecting Edmond's voice to return with some apologetic words.

"CeCe, this is Tracee. I need your help. I'm in trouble."

"Trouble?" I blinked. "Tracee, what's wrong? Where are you?" I asked my childhood friend.

"I need you to come right away. I'm in jail."

14

I caught my reflection in the rearview mirror. I was a mess. My red, swollen eyes ogled back at me. My hair was pulled back into a ponytail. I had thrown on an old pair of sweats I had in back of my closet. I didn't want to look attractive nor did I feel that way. I slowed my SUV in search of Travis Avenue. That was the location of the precinct where Tracee was being held. The tiny green street signs looked blurred, the white letters started to run together. I wasn't prepared for this. I was on my way to rescue my friend when I needed saving myself.

I walked into the police station trying to mask the same intimidating look I expected from everyone else there. An overweight officer sat behind the desk talking on the phone. He put his conversation on hold, and I asked about Tracee. I was escorted on the other side of a huge steel gray door. It made a loud echoing noise when it was closed and locked. Three scared faces jerked around to greet me as I entered. They were huddled closely together, seated along a wooden bench. Tracee's baby, Javon, had dried-up tears. The other two just looked relieved. I smiled and cupped Javon's face before rubbing that same comforting hand across the heads of Jaheim, the oldest, and then Jaleel. They were little boys having to grow up too fast.

"When can I see Tracee Ledbetter?" I turned to the female officer and asked.

"Once she's processed. Should be soon."

I slid across the hard wooden bench next to the boys, putting a secure arm around all three. They had snacks beside them from the vending machine. Someone had tried to pacify them with chips, bubblegum, and Oreos. Three cans of soda sat dry and warm looking. Everything remained unopened and untouched. Even at their age they knew that a bullet wound couldn't be soothed with a Band-Aid.

What seemed like fifteen minutes passed with Javon sleeping comfortably in my lap. A steel orange-painted door abruptly swung open, and Tracee rushed in to hug all of her sons at once.

She looked up at me. Her face looked haggard and emotionless, like the first round of her fight had already been lost. I could only imagine what she had gone through. Tears welled up in her eyes, and she looked away, scared and a little embarrassed.

"Tracee, what happened?" I asked, pulling her face toward me before placing a hand on her shoulder.

"Girl, the cops raided my place," she answered, wiping snot from her top lip. She brushed a tear from her cheek. "They said Streeter was under suspicion for selling, but they didn't find much, just a little on him." She then looked around to make sure no one was listening. "They took me, too, thinking I knew something, but I don't. They brought my babies 'cause they couldn't leave them there, and I begged them not to call Child Protective Service. I told them I had family to come and pick them up. CeCe, if I don't get someone responsible to take them until I can get out of here, I'm gon' lose them," she wailed.

"Don't worry about that right now, sweetie. I'll take them home with me. You just concentrate on getting yourself out of here. What else can I do to help?"

"I don't know. These rent-a-cops ain't told me much, yet. Just keep asking all these questions. I think they might just let me go home after a while. They don't have anything to hold me on. Just take my boys out of here, and I'll call if I need you."

"Oh Tracee sweetie," I said, giving her a long, tight embrace. She needed a shower—bad. If she stayed locked up any longer I knew I would have to bring her a care package.

We said good-bye as the stout policewoman led Tracee back to lockup. I reassured Tracee again about the boys, telling her I would watch them as long as I needed to.

I strapped them in the backseat of my Lexus and glanced back as I slid into the driver's seat. They still looked scared. Tracee looked scared. Hell, I was scared.

The boys needed things. I didn't have Tracee's keys. I asked the oldest if they kept a spare someplace.

"We can't go back there tonight, Aunt CeCe," Jaheim said. "The police said so." He was right. I hadn't thought about that. Everything was probably roped off with that hideous yellow tape used in crime scenes. Or did they do that for drug busts? Just as well. It was past midnight, and I was beat down. I would find something close by opened twenty-four/seven with a little bit of everything. I needed to get food as well as clothes for the boys. They literally had only the clothes on their backs.

I pulled into the parking lot of a Wal-Mart near my condo. Thank God, it wasn't crowded. I straightened

my hair as best as I could without a brush and went
inside. I grabbed a cart and headed over to the little
boys section. I looked at the selection. Little boys were
so easy to buy for. I ran my hand over my stomach,
then I asked myself some tough questions about being
someone's mother. I had already failed at being a wife.

I threw in underwear for all three and T-shirts, two
for each of them. They got to choose the colors, which
was probably a mistake because they fought over who
got what. Then I picked out socks, shorts, and PJs, kind
of winging it when it came to their sizes.

"Aunt CeCe, can I go look at the toys?" It was little
Javon. I looked over and hesitated, then thought he
would be okay since I was almost done.

"Okay, as long as Jaleel and Jaheim go with you. Stay
put. I'll meet you there in a little bit," I warned.

They all bolted. I went over to the grocery department
to finish up and got plenty of milk, juice, cereal, those
little microwavable kids' meals, cookies, ice cream, hot
dogs, burgers and all those things that kids don't need
but you buy them anyway when you're spoiling them.
I tossed in a few more junk food items and made a
last stop for toothbrushes and toothpaste. I pushed the
shopping cart over toward the toy department and found
Javon near the shelf lined with action figures.

"Hi," I said to the back of his head.

He turned around with bright eyes and replied, "Hello."
Just like Cosby's Little Bill character. All sweet and
innocent like.

"You like Spiderman, I bet."

"Yeah, I used to."

"Oh?"

"Yeah, 'cept now I like SpongeBob SquarePants again."

"Oh," I said. I admired his intensity on the subject but

I had no clue what he was talking about. I wasn't quite up on all the cartoon characters.

"Where are your brothers?" I asked, looking around.

"Looking at cars."

"Don't try to figure that stuff out, it's a parent trap," a deep voice said.

I turned around to see this tall, handsome, Michael Jordan-looking brother—well kind of. He was bald like Mike, but not as athletically built.

"Well you seem to know. Did that come with a lot of practice?" I asked.

"I have a little brother."

"Mmm, I see."

"By the way, I'm Brady."

"CeCe."

Jaleel and Jaheim's voices started to rise on the other side of the shelf. "Trouble from that way comes," I murmured under my breath.

"And this must be your little man," he continued, running a large hand over Javon's head, releasing a chuckle as Javon pushed his hand away.

"Well, no not—"

"I'm gon' tell on you."

"Go ahead. I don't care, fool!" Jaleel and Jaheim rushed up to me and began screaming snitch tales at the same time.

"Oh, snap. Three. Damn, shorty," Brady said.

"No, I'm just baby-sitting for a friend," I said in my defense.

"Oh. Yeah, right." He laughed doubtfully, looking down at my shopping cart. "Well nice chatting with you, but I gotta go."

I didn't acknowledge him. I was too busy playing referee. I got the boys settled down enough to negotiate one toy each. Javon got an additional one for being the youngest and the quietest. He decided to get both SpongeBob and SpongeBob's best friend, Patrick.

We packed everything into the back of my SUV. I buckled the two youngest in the backseat after settling the argument of who got shotgun. God, I wasn't even sure if Javon still required a car seat. I had no idea of the cut-off age for that, but it was late and I was close to home. I did remind Jaheim of Texas's "Click it or Ticket" law before he snapped his seat belt in place. Once we got home, Jaheim and Jaleel helped me unload everything, then they were sent off to the guest room, each armed with a big plastic shopping bag that separated the things I had bought for them. I prepared sandwiches and milk. After eating seconds, I gave them a warm bath and put them in brand-new underwear and pajamas before tucking them all into my guest room/office's futon. I glanced back at them before turning out the light. Their faces were peaceful but they hadn't fallen asleep. I hope they felt safe enough to drift off soon. I would check on them later. They were certainly a handful. I was just grateful they belonged to Tracee and I was only temporarily watching over them for her.

I checked my messages. There weren't any. I half expected a call from Edmond. I took a shower and turned in. The first cramp hit about fifteen minutes later. I pulled my knees up into my chest until the pain subsided, then got out of bed some time after that to check the moisture forming between my legs. I had gotten my period. False alarm for the pregnancy, but something was definitely topsy-turvy with my body. I made a mental note to speed up my doctor's appointment.

Tyson phoned early the next morning while the kids were still asleep. I was sitting at my kitchen table sipping hot-spiced tea and rubbing the tension of the night before from my forehead. He wanted to see me. He said we could meet on my terms—someplace public but discreet. I had to decline. Without going into detail, I told him I had an emergency with Tracee and would probably be busy with her kids for the weekend. He sounded disappointed, but said he understood.

15

I was staring out of my kitchen window, sipping my morning cup of herbal tea and reevaluating my feelings about Tyson. It had been a month since Tracee's ordeal of spending the night in jail, then released due to insufficient evidence. Just as long since Tyson had phone and asked me to meet him secretively for the first time. Close to three months since I had left Edmond in Jackson.

Aside from work, Tyson and I did continue to share the occasional breakfast and sometimes lunch together. I didn't tell him that I was working on my release from Edmond, and he didn't seem to mind as long as he was in my life at all. But I was careful to keep our relationship on a friends-only level. I didn't trust myself to be alone with him, not until Edmond was a part of my past.

It was a quiet Saturday, and I was sulking over a lot of bad memories with no plans for the day. I thought about calling Jackie. Maybe we could hang out and do some shopping in the Heights. We had talked about doing that. The Heights was a wealthy section of Houston known for exquisite antiques. Or we could make a day of it by driving to Galveston and hitting the shops there near the port. I decided not to call her, mainly since I was in such a melancholy mood. My insides felt like someone was jump roping with my heartstrings. Maybe the third rapture was on its way. But then, that usually came when my life was running smoothly.

The doorbell chimed. For some reason, it wasn't ringing as loud as it should. With what I had paid for the place you would think I could at least get a decent doorbell. When my music was turned up or the TV was going I could barely hear it. I kept forgetting to have someone check it. I peeked out at a tall, dark figure who resembled a delivery guy.

It was Leonard, the hunky Fed Ex man. I recognized him from a few days earlier when he had tried to deliver a package to me by mistake. He had gotten his navigational wires crossed and turned on East Palm instead of West Palm. Leonard had that blue-collar type handsomeness that you remembered. He was someone you would have glanced at twice in his butt-hugging blue shorts if he weren't always in a hurry and didn't have those sweat stains underneath his armpits like a permanent fixture to his uniform. He wasn't in the flirting mood. In fact, I could have sworn he looked at me with a hint of pity, like he knew the secret I would cry over later. Sir Leonard, the bearer of bad news, expedited by King Edmond.

"Afternoon, ma'am. I have a letter for a Ce...Celia Ross."

"Yes, that's me."

"Sign here, please."

I signed my name illegibly on purpose and handed the electronic clipboard back to Leonard. I expected a smile, maybe something suggestive, but I got another pity stare. He handed me the envelope then turned and trotted off to his truck without even giving me a backward glance, like he knew I would have issues for a while. Leonard the Fed Ex man was nothing more than Edmond's flunky anyway.

The letter was from Edmond's attorney in Jackson. Attached to it was the start of a divorce decree, a request from me that Edmond had taken serious. One I didn't think he would. Deep down I wanted him to fight for our marriage and prove that I had meant more to him, I guess. Instead, the notice said that unless I contested, I would have my freedom in a matter of weeks. Thirty days uncontested was all it took. That much I already knew from the Google search on Mississippi divorces the night I had been so angry with him and issued my ultimatum.

I know his response should have exonerated both of us, unloaded the guilt from him and set me free at the same time, healed two broken hearts with one shot. That's what my rational side told me as I scanned over the papers, but then my vulnerable side kicked in, and I was literally sick. I expunged every time he kissed me or touched me, and it was a lie, then I cried, and there was nothing to interrupt my flow. I let the tears come for as long as I needed to. I cried over and over until I was drained of all the pain and betrayal Edmond had put me through, then I went to bed and cried for most of the night. The next morning only brought fresh pain that lasted into Monday morning. I called in sick from work. I couldn't sleep or eat, let alone function. I just wanted to ball myself into a big foolish lump to die.

Tuesday came, and I stayed in bed for another day and called in sick again. It was my own private pity party and I'd cry if I wanted to. My answering machine played receptionist. Jackie, Tracee, someone from Jackson, Edmond, and finally Tyson.

"CeCe, this is Tyson. I'm sorry I missed you but I got both of your messages. You sounded pretty down. Just calling to see if you're alright. Why don't you pick up."

I waited. What in the hell did he want?

"If you don't pick up the phone right now, I'll just keep calling. Maybe the police if I have to because I'm a little worried. I mean it."

"Hello, Tyson. Look, I'm okay, really."

"You don't sound like you're okay. Give me directions to your place, and if you don't, I'm sure I can get them from Jackie."

I didn't have the strength to fight him. The last thing I needed was the office or the police in my business.

He arrived a half hour later. He looked as if worrying about me had aged him a little.

"You look awful." he was quick to point out. I knew he was probably right. I couldn't remember the last time I had eaten, combed my hair, or even taken a bath. I had on the same sweats that I had worn when Tracee called a month earlier.

"Thanks. You don't look all that hot yourself."

"I see whatever is wrong didn't take that sharp tongue of yours away."

"Well, that just goes to show you that sometimes misery does leave you with a little something," I said, looking away before my eyes started to well up again. I choked.

"Now, now, Ce, tell me what's wrong. Let me help." He hugged me, and I rested my head on his strong chest. I tried to tell him, but the words just wouldn't flow. He only held on tighter and refused to let go, and I didn't want him to. I wanted us to remain that way, with him assuring me everything was alright.

"Let me take care of you, CeCe."

He wanted to know where my bathroom was. I pointed it out, and he led me there. I took his hand and followed him. He looked for some bubble bath and ran a warm bath, then he stepped outside the bathroom door and waited until I was completely naked and submerged under the water. He knocked softly waited until I said it was okay to enter. He came to me and rubbed my shoulders and washed my back. His lips felt soft and his breath was warm when he kissed my forehead. I didn't stop him when he continued to do the same to my face and neck. I let him take care of me, then he left me to rest in the tub for a while. He came back with a big, soft peach towel outstretched in his hands. He turned his head politely before wrapping me inside. He gave me space as I switched the towel for my short silk robe hanging behind the bathroom door. I brushed my teeth and met him in the kitchen. Without an utter, he carried me over to the barstool he had placed near the sink. He sat me down and reclined me, so that my head rested near the running water. My peppermint shampoo, conditioner, comb, and a fresh towel waited on the countertop. I hadn't noticed when he took those from the bathroom.

"What are you doing?"

"Sssh," he whispered, continuing his task. He sounded like Grampy Cecil when I talked too much.

Tyson tested the stream of water before taking my head in both hands and placing it underneath. He took the comb and untangled my matted hair. I closed my eyes and relaxed under his touch. The shampoo felt cold as he lathered it through my hair. The scent of peppermint drifted past my nose and woke up my scalp like a morphine injection. He delicately massaged my head like he was handling fine crystal.

Nothing ever felt that wonderful. Not even my

hairstylist Melva, with her hot oil treatments and organic deep-root therapy. I thought she was the best, but Tyson's treatment was sensual and sexy—pure and hypnotic.

"I hope you know that you're spoiling me," I said.

"I mean to."

Tyson worked his same magic with the conditioner. He let it run between his fingers, then pulled it out to the ends of my hair. I relaxed even more. He had put my entire body on erotic alert. When he was done, he wrapped a towel around my head before he raised me up, then I showed him how to blow-dry my hair, section by section. He was a little awkward at first, but quickly caught on. He brushed my hair and caressed it until my eyes grew heavy, my voice faint.

We both stretched out on the bed and hugged each other, face-to-face, before switching positions and spooning. His arms stayed securely wrapped around me all the while. We fell asleep somewhere during the night and slept until early dawn.

16

"Tyson?" I let the syllables of his name roll off my tongue, out into the early morning. I didn't expect him to be there to answer, but wanted to make the night before real. I felt so much stronger. The ringing in my ears had stopped. That pit of hollowness at the base of my stomach wasn't so empty. Damn sure wasn't thinking about Edmond anymore.

I slid out of bed, still tingling from Tyson's TLC. I was starving too. It was close to noon, and Tyson was covering for me at work. He said Gray was away all week, so my absence was cool. I wanted to call to thank him for the previous night, but he was one step ahead of me.

"How's my favorite patient?" he asked when he called a few minutes later.

"Almost fully recovered."

"Did I have that effect?"

"Oh, you certainly did." That greedy side of me contemplated a repeat, but I thanked him instead. "I was in a pretty bad way yesterday, and you didn't have to do what you did. I mean, most guys wouldn't have."

"But I'm not most guys, and it was my pleasure."

"Well thanks for not being most guys."

"Did you find your lunch?"

"My lunch?"

"Yes, I left you a little something on the counter near the phone."

"I'll just have to check and find out what that is."

"You do that."

"Bye, Tyson."

"Good-bye, CeCe."

I hung up the phone and went into the kitchen. I saw a can of chicken noodle soup near a brand-new coffee maker that I'd never used. A note was propped against the soup. Had he found that in my kitchen or had he gone out? The note read: EAT THIS FOR ME, OKAY? YOU KNOW WHAT THEY SAY... IT'S GOOD FOR YOUR SOUL. TYSON. He was corny, but sweet. And thoughtful.

I took another bath, this time a long, hot shower and flat ironed my hair. I applied a little makeup, and put on a pair of jeans and a blue cotton shirt. I walked out of my bedroom, over to the bar and picked up the Fed Ex package that contained my divorce papers and signed them with a little inconspicuous heart at the end of my name that only I knew was there. I didn't even bother to read them, except for the part that said by signing them I was free. I returned the papers that had given Edmond ownership like I was his pedigree. I returned them with the same urgency they had been sent to me.

Then I made a call to Jackie so she wouldn't worry when I didn't show up for work again. First I told her I had some twenty-four-hour virus, then I told her the truth. She wanted to ditch work too. Told me she would use my virus story, come over, and help me celebrate. That made me laugh on the surface, but deep down, I just didn't feel as jubilant about my divorce.

I hung up with Jackie and took control of my loneliness. I broke out some pots and pans that had gone unused since I bought them. Then I made myself a late southern-style breakfast: Grits, Conecuh sausage, bacon, a couple of scrambled eggs, toast, and orange juice. I went the whole nine yards. After breakfast and cleaning my kitchen, I crawled back in bed and cuddle up with some magazines, before watching TV. There was a segment on some talk show about older women dating younger men. I watched that intently until the end, then logged onto Amazon.com and ordered the book How to Love a Younger Man: Tips from an Older Woman. I put a rush on it.

I spent the rest of the day pampering myself, then prepared to turn in early. Tyson phoned, and we chatted until my eyes grew heavy. After that I slept like a baby.

The next day at work, Tyson didn't let up on the attention, but gave me even more by making sure I had everything I needed. He even got me lunch. When I walked back to my office from a bathroom break, there was a huge African violet sitting on my desk.

"When can I see you?" he asked on his way home later that day. I was standing at my desk, fastening the clasps on my briefcase preparing to leave myself.

"Do I have to keep reminding you of the position we're in?"

"All I know is the position I want to be in—with you."

He smiled amorously as he went over to close my door, checking for stragglers, then he came back and began stroking my hair. "I feel really close to you now, you know that? I want to be with you so bad," he said, kissing me hungrily. I moaned when his tongue slipped between my lips and tasted mine. I drew back when his hand moved down my backside and squeezed.

"Soon. I promise," I assured him when we finally came up for air.

"And no later than soon," he warned with another quick peck on the lips before he walked out of the door.

Tyson's kiss slow-burned all the way to my yoga class. My GYN had suggested I sign up to help relieve some stress. I had been willing to try anything after he had informed me of my negative pregnancy test results. Now Tyson had added tension to the tension I was trying to rid. All during class, I lost my concentration and had trouble learning the positions. I would have to try and fit in an extra class to make my time and money there worthwhile. I got home around seven and hit the warm shower. The pressure of the water felt good against my tired muscles. I adjusted the showerhead to full massage before stepping into the force of the spray again.

Tracee and her kids crossed my mind as I dried myself off and slipped on a T-shirt and shorts. It had been a couple weeks since I had last heard from her. I dialed her number but her phone had been disconnected. What was up with her? I rummaged through my purse until I found the number she'd given me to a neighbor. I left a message there, and a few minutes later Tracee returned my call.

"I was worried about you," I said.

"Girl, I'm fine. I've been worried about you. You didn't answer your phone over the weekend," she said.

"I know. I got Edmond's divorce papers."

"Really soon, huh?"

"Yeah, but I did ask. Anyway, how are the boys?"

"These monsters are badder than ever."

"And you? Really, Tracee."

"I'm gettin' it together. I have to now. This was my

wake-up call. Just to think of where I could be right now on some bullshit. Having a dick around ain't worth all that."

"Tracee, I know it wasn't my business, but there was something about Streeter that I didn't trust. I only wish now that I had said something."

"I know, but I was so wide open I wouldn't have believed you no way. That's all behind me now, though. Streeter is outta my life. He'll probably have to do some time, so I'm taking the kids and going back to Jackson for a while."

"Jackson? Tracee, you're leaving?"

"Yeah. I'll find a job and try to give my kids a decent life for a change."

"Tracee, I've been meaning to ask you something."

"What's that?"

"How it got this bad for you. I mean with your education and all, how could you just waste that?"

There was a pregnant pause on the other end.

"CeCe, I don't really know how to say this, but there is no education. No college degree—nothin'."

"What? But you left home. Everyone in Jackson, including your parents, knew you were in college here."

"Everyone thought I was in college. And the leaving home part is the only truth there. I lied to my parents. I dropped outta college the first semester of my freshman year. From then on it was a heap of partyin' or hookin' up with a lot of Streeters while my aunt here covered for me to my parents. I came clean with my dad about everything. Right now he's just excited about having his grandsons around for a while."

"Thank heaven for good parents, huh?"

"Echo that, girl."

"So when are you off to Jackson?"

"Next week."

"That soon?"

"Yeah. Anything you want me to say to your hubbie?"

"Soon-to-be ex. And he's already working on wifey number two."

"That bum. You want me to kick his ass for you when I see him?"

"No. Please, I don't want him to think I'm jealous."

"Well, girl, you just hang on in there. There's plenty of fish in the sea."

"And I hear they're biting too."

"For real, girlfriend."

We said good-bye, and I promised we would get together before she left. I was just glad she was bouncing back stronger after her ordeal. Maybe I could learn a thing or two.

I started sorting through a stack of bills. Two were pink already, which meant they were past due. I supposed that's why Edmond never trusted me to pay the bills. Being on my own certainly hadn't made me responsible yet. I had to get it together so I set up that automated bill-paying program online that my bank harped on so much.

My doorbell rang, and I immediately thought of Tyson. My pulse skyrocketed. A broad grin spread across my face as I imagined him showing up at my door unannounced, leaning against my doorframe, smiling while he waved a bottle of peppermint shampoo in one hand, a brown paper bag with some Chinese take-out in the other. I ran to door and looked out of the peephole, still expecting a treat. It was Jackie. Disappointment must have shown on my face when I let her in.

"You look gloomy," she said and held up a bottle of Sutter's zinfandel. She had some food from the Cajun restaurant called Pappadeaux's in the other.

"I'm starving, that's all." I told her.

"You sure that's it?"

"Yeah. Why?"

"You look disappointed. Like you were expecting someone else."

"No, I'm not expecting anyone. What's in the bag? I hope it's the Pasta Mardi Gras," I said, grabbing it from her and peeking inside. I placed the bag on the counter, then turned back to face her.

"Sister, what's really happening with you?"

"Okay, it's Tyson," I said, sighing.

"What has he done this time?"

"It's what he wants to do."

"Oh. Don't tell me you have gone and tapped into the forbidden?"

"Not yet. But, to be honest, Jackie, I don't know how much longer I can hold out."

"How much longer. Sister, I thought you said you had to hold out. You know, the repercussions of fraternization?"

"I know. But the truth is: I'm not sure if I feel that way any more."

17

"Tyson, what's up?" I said, glancing at the time. Tyson's call had come late—eleven o'clock—at an hour when my jones couldn't be trusted to say no. It had been a week since we shared that steamy kiss in my office. He must have timed his calls that way on purpose.

"It's warm."

"What?"

"The night. I can't sleep when it's warm."

"A cold shower usually helps." I said.

"Not in this case. I need you." When I didn't comment, he continued, "CeCe, I miss you. I know we have to be careful but I want to hold you again."

"I want to hold you too."

"Then if we both agree, why am I on the other end of this phone instead of doing exactly that?"

"Tyson, this isn't the best time to talk about this." The truth was that he was sounding irresistible, and I couldn't think of one excuse for not being with him.

"So, was it my shampoo technique that turned you off?"

"Goodness, no. It was great."

"Then what's wrong? Why are you trying to put me off me every chance you get?"

"I got a copy of my final divorce papers today. I guess it's really over."

"Already? I thought divorces took longer than a couple of weeks?"

"We've been separated for over three months. Besides my ex has connections."

"But as long as it's over right?"

"I guess I can't believe that it really is over."

"What did you expect? It's not like you didn't know it was coming."

"I know, but it still hurts. No matter how much I might have wanted out, seeing my divorce in black and white still affects me. That part of me is gone."

"You're still who you are, CeCe. Whatever little part you might have lost, you no longer wanted anyway. Right?"

"I guess so."

"So?"

"So what?"

"I want to see you tonight."

"Tyson, I don't know."

"What if I don't take no for an answer?"

"What if I don't answer the door?"

"I'm coming over. I'll be there in about thirty minutes. It'll be up to you whether to let me in."

He hung up before I could say anything. A part of me was happy that he did. He was on his way over, and no single reason why I shouldn't let him in came to mind.

I took a quick shower. A long soak in a warm soapy bath scented with cinnamon cream and vanilla would have prepared me more, but he had said he would be here in thirty minutes—twenty, if traffic was light. I hit all the right places on my body and rubbed some Warm Spirits Butter Cream in my skin. I sprayed on a light body mist and slipped on a pair of sexy laced panties. I put on a matching camisole, then I went and unlocked the front door.

How would I greet him? Sit on the bed and look sexy, smiling and all, but then I might look too experienced. Eager. Maybe I could stretch out on the bed with a glass of wine to calm my nerves, but then my breath would reek of alcohol. I exhaled. I was starting to stress like this was high school. I took another deep breath, clasped my hands together, and waited.

I glanced over my place to make sure everything was okay. No souvenirs from my marriage were lying around. Only the scent of my vanilla candles burning in my bedroom mixed with the lavender ones burning in the bathroom, lingered. Both cast a romantic glow over the room. Being in the bedroom was right. I was glad I left the door unlocked too. I wanted to see if Tyson's telepathy was in sync with mine enough to lead him to me in the dark.

I heard the faint sound of a car door slamming. I changed my mind and slipped into the living room. I propped myself on one of the chairs beside the bar, then crossed my legs seductively. I waited for the front door to open and close again making the alarm beep twice. Tyson must have gotten my vibe. He hadn't knocked or rang the doorbell first. I recognized the outline of his body illuminated by the moonlight sifting through the window. He came and stood directly in front of me, swept me up into his arms, and started to kiss me soft and slow without saying a word, then he set me back down on the chair and looked at me. "You're beautiful," he whispered. "I want you, CeCe, here and now."

He slipped out of his shirt and unzipped his pants,

letting them crumple at his feet. He leaned into me, pulling my hips forward. He was more than ready when he lifted my legs around his hips.

"Could you wear protection?" I asked in a low voice. I heard him smile.

"Don't worry, I was going to." He bent and fumbled through his pants pocket, then cracked cellophane. He did what he needed to do to protect us both.

His rhythm started up again, and I arched my back and moaned. He entered me, and my old world exploded. His inward thrusts were hard, slow and gentle at the same time. I threw my head back, closed my eyes and relished in the pleasure he was giving. He brought me to the brink of climaxing, then stopped, scooped me up and carried me into the bedroom. He laid me on the bed under the candlelight and kneeled beside me. I caught a glimpse of his strong physique, his penis swaying in the candlelight like a magic wand. I squirmed with anticipation of his warmness against my skin. He finished undressing me and kissed each part of my body like it was a gift-wrapped blessing. Blood rushed to every spot he touched. I thought I should please him, too, but he wasn't done.

"Tell me what you want, CeCe."

That's what he wanted to know about me, so he could please me more. Before I could answer he started with my face, worked his way downward and nibbled gently at my breasts like he had read my mind. Then his lips ventured further south in search of the warmth, just like birds did during the winter. His skills brought out every erotic bit of emotion I could verbalize. Tyson loved me slow and careful as if his only gratification came from the expression on my face. He eased up when I told him I wanted to watch as I received every inch of him. That made it real for me. "Isn't that a beautiful thing," he whispered as an orgasm surged through my body. It was like...no, I wouldn't go comparing Tyson to anyone else. Not Edmond or Malachi. If I had learned one thing, it was that one man couldn't be expected to measure up to another. It was about the circumstance that had brought us to sex. Be it love, pain, obligation, or physical attraction, that determined the feeling gained from sex itself. Whatever I felt with Tyson, I did so triple fold because I had been so deprived with Edmond. My moans came intensely and frequent as I closed my eyes, and let him love me the way I needed him to, until we were exhausted and satisfied. Then he held me until we both fell asleep.

We slept into early morning. I didn't know if Tyson had planned to stay the night, but the selfish side of me wouldn't have wakened him anyway. I turned my head to see his face. It was peaceful and still. I tapped his leg with my foot once, and he smiled.

"You're full of surprises," I said.

"How's that?"

"First the shampoo, then last night."

"The shampoo just kind of happened. It's not a recurring part of my skills. You were just so sad and I wanted to pamper you."

"That would explain why I never got an encore," I said and stretched to look up at his expression.

"Hmm," he grunted, repositioning his arm. My head had been cradled there for the entire night. His eyes were closed. I shifted the weight of my head. "I guess I'll have to make that up to you," he said, sounding groggy, but still not opening his eyes.

"Just know that I don't forget that easily," I said, turning on my side and sliding my hand, slow and seductively, down his chest. I traced to find his sensitive spots with my fingers. He let me know just where they were by the way he squirmed and moaned. I caressed him back to attention. He was pulling me on top when he stopped suddenly.

"What's that sound?" he asked.

"What sound? I didn't hear anything," I said, stroking him in an attempt to get him back in the mood.

Then the keen sound of a car alarm going off outside my condo broke his concentration again.

"That sounds like my car alarm," he said, sliding me off, then jumping up from the bed. He sprinted, naked, into my living room. I grabbed my robe from behind the bathroom door and followed. He was moving away from the window and fastening his jeans by the time I joined him by the barstool. There was a worried expression on his face, and he didn't answer when I asked what was going on.

The noise level was an octave higher when Tyson opened the front door. He shut the piercing alarm off by clicking his key remote. The morning was quiet again, except for the sound of a few neighbors closing their doors, satisfied that their cars weren't the ones being tampered with. I realized I should have let Tyson park in my garage and was already planning that for the next time.

It was still early enough for the streetlights to flicker in anticipation of dawn. The air was light, not as humid as I expected. Tyson's bare feet slapped against the lukewarm pavement as he trotted toward his Acura. The pitter-patter of my small feet filled in close behind.

He suddenly stopped short of his front fender and because I was looking elsewhere, I didn't notice and bumped right into his back.

"Shit." he said. "Fuck." He threw his hands up and grabbed his head. I hung on to his waist and veered around him to see why he was so upset.

I couldn't completely make it out, but there was something sprinkled all over his car. There was just enough light looming over us to tell that it was a thick white powder. I noticed too, that a piece of paper was stuck under the left wiper blade.

"What is it?" I asked.

"Hell, I don't know, but whatever it is, it's all over my freaking car." He reached out to touch it.

"Be careful, Tyson."

He turned around and gave me a playful look.

"What do you think it is, anthrax?" He grabbed the note and brought it close to his face to read it, then he swore under his breath and balled it up. He started to chunk it but gave that some thought before he stuffed it in his front pants pocket.

"What did the note say?" I asked, curious.

He didn't answer. I shrugged, bit my bottom lip and folded my arms. I looked around the parking lot for some movement. He turned back around to touch the powdery substance anyway, then dabbed at it again and rubbed the goo between two fingers.

"Tyson, please be careful." He continued to ignore my caution as he sniffed his fingers.

"Shit's sticky," he declared.

"What did the note say?" I asked for the second time.

"It said to enjoy my breakfast," he responded.

"Why, what's that stuff suppose to be?"

"Flour and syrup, I think."

"Cute and sick at the same time. Who would do this?"

"You live here. Is your ex in town?"

"Funny."

"Just kidding," he said with a sigh. "I have an idea who it is."

"Significant other?"

"No. Just a mistake I made a long time ago."

"You want to talk about it?"

He looked at his watch and rubbed the tension from his face. "No, don't have time. I'd better finish getting dressed and zip by the car wash and try to take care of this mess. We'll talk later, okay," he said and touched my face.

"Okay."

"I just hope the paint job isn't ruined," he said. "Matter of fact, one person in particular should be hoping that it's not ruined."

18

"Everything go okay with your car?" I asked as I walked into Tyson's office after we'd both gotten to work. I had the urge to kiss him full on the lips. After our interruption that morning, he had finished getting dressed and was out the door before we had the chance for a proper good-bye.

"Everything's cool. There doesn't seem to be any permanent damage."

"So what happened? You know for certain who vandalized it?"

"I have a general idea."

"A jealous girlfriend?"

"Or mistaken identity."

"I'll put my money on the jealous girlfriend."

"First of all, she's not a girlfriend," he said getting up from his desk, coming to stand near me. "The relationship is over, has been for a very long time now. She's the one having problems letting go."

"Tyson, I care about you, a lot. That's why I'm trying not to freak out about this, but I don't want to be caught in the middle of a sequel to The War of the Roses either."

"CeCe, I would never put you in a position like that. Now, I'll take care of my problem, don't worry," he said placing both hands on my shoulders. He made me feel so safe until I would have believed anything he said at that point. I was also thinking about the night before.

"I don't know if I can," I said, taking a deep sigh. "Something tells me she might not be finished."

"Why?"

"Female intuition."

"Well, since your intuition is so accurate, what am I thinking right now?"

"If it's at all like last night, then it's kind of hot."

He smiled. "It's hot." He walked over and closed his door, then embraced me and eased the tip of his tongue between my lips. I kissed him back with the same passion, but glanced back toward the door.

"My lips are over here."

"I know where they are, but someone might walk in. It just looks suspicious with the two of us here with the door closed," I said, pulling away.

"Don't worry, I locked it. Besides, don't you like risks?" He came and embraced me again, nudging my nose with his.

"Yes, but I like my job too."

"Come on, what could they do?"

"You mean short of Gray firing us both?"

"Gray?"

"Yes, remember, our senior vice president?"

"I doubt he would fire us. And besides, I'm sure Tapscott has chased a few honeys around a desk or two."

"You think?"

"I know these things." He looked at me and got a serious look on his face. "You really care about me?"

"I do." I couldn't tell him anything more than that.

"Come here."

He sat us both down in his chair near the drafting table. I was facing him. His warm, strong hand traveled my thigh, then slipped under my skirt. I was glad I had worn it with my garter-style stockings instead of regular pantyhose and a thong. His hand squeezed my backside while he kissed my throat and slid his tongue down tenderly between my breasts. He knew how to control me with his tongue, but being so powerless never felt so good. He used tongue and teeth to undo the buttons on my blouse. Damn. I was glad he'd locked the door when I felt him swell under my hips. He eagerly unzipped his pants.

"No, sweetie. Condom first, remember?" I whispered.

He grimaced at me but complied.

He was inside that familiar place. He crisscrossed his hands behind my back and pulled my hips forward. My legs were strategically placed on the arms of his chair, like a contortionist's. My body heated up and basted in a thin glow of perspiration. His eyes were closed; tiny beads of sweat were popping across his forehead. His chest rose and fell tumultuously as I unbuttoned his shirt and slid my tongue across his pecks. We made love with highly charged passion until I was about to explode with him not far behind, then someone knocked at his door, not with the urgency of business, but more inquisitive. Like they might have suspected what was going on behind closed doors. Instead of panic, thrill charged through me and sent my climax into overdrive. It must have been something about getting caught that made my orgasm multiply. Our lovemaking wound down just as the knocking ceased. We kissed each other down from the high, and I pulled back. I got up and wobbled into the bathroom. He waited and took his turn. When he came back, I was checking myself in his full-length mirror. He came up from behind and kissed me on the back of my neck.

His line buzzed, and I let him answer.

"Tyson Treadwell...Yes. When?... Now?" He glanced at his watch. "Fine. Okay."

He turned and shrugged before giving one last kiss. "I love your lips," he said. I smiled. I liked his too. "I have to run out for a sec."

"Sure."

He opened the door as Jackie walked in my office.

"What's up, Jackie? Personnel got you checking up on us?" Tyson asked, walking past her with his jacket in his hand, keeping his cool composure. I was wondering who had knocked earlier, if not her.

"Hello, Tyson. No, CeCe and I have a lunch date and I thought I would come up to see if you were in one piece. The way your visitor zoomed out of here."

"What visitor?" he asked, still well composed.

"There was someone here to see you earlier. I met her in the hallway. She was pissed because she had knocked on your door and got no response. Guess it was some impatient client."

"Probably so," he said to Jackie, before turning my way. "Look, CeCe can I get you anything while I'm out?"

"No, thanks Tyson, Jackie and I are headed out, also."

Jackie waited until Tyson was completely out of the office.

"Is he alright?" She asked.

"He's fine. Why do you ask?"

"He seems almost nice. He usually insults me."

"I'm assuming that the two of you don't get along."

"He thinks, I'm nosey," she quipped.

"Whatever gave him that idea?" We looked at each other and burst into laughter.

"CeCe, on a serious note, I know that you and Tyson seem a little closer than when you first got here, and that's cool, but be careful."

I grabbed my jacket, and we headed out of my office.

"Careful about what?"

She waited until we were out of the building and headed toward our usual spot for lunch before she answered. "CeCe, the bottom line is that Gray Tapscott hates office romance among other things," Jackie said once we were in the clear of any Templeton ears. "It's why Templeton has this strict fraternization policy in the first place. It goes back with this story about the president who ran Templeton some years ago, falling for his secretary. The wife found out. Then one morning just as the workday started, she burst into the front lobby in her bathroom and curlers, waving a Glock."

"You don't believe that, do you?"

Ask anyone who has worked here long enough and they'll tell you it is."

"So, what does it have to do with Gray?"

"He's has a connection with the story, I hear."

"Jackie, I can assure that Tyson and I are careful."

"Sister, I hope so. I could have easily been Gray Tapscott knocking at Tyson's door, you know."

"You worry too much."

She shrugged and switched to chattering about having to meet Marco after work. My eyes were stinging, which made me wish I hadn't forgotten to put my sunglasses on. I turned my head to escape the brightness. My stare was just slightly on an office building with the revolving doors, just in time to see a well-dressed man and a woman walk through. Not long enough to swear to it that the male figure had been Tyson. The color of the suit was the exact shade that Tyson had worn that morning and my instinct told me it was him. I turned back to ask Jackie if she had seen him, too, but she was still hammering away about Marco needing some serious relationship advice and whether his affair with the mystery girl would last until the end of summer. I decided to keep my suspicion to myself. If I did any confronting, it would be to the horse himself.

⚓ Fish jumped off
da hook!

19

"Women are just colder," Marco said.

Marco and I had met Jackie at her place after work. I was preoccupied with Tyson and the possible other-woman issue from earlier in the day. I had to trust that he was taking care of his past like he said.

Marco and Jackie continued to debate who had less of a conscience walking out of a marriage. I had remained silent. I studied Jackie's place instead. I was always tickled when I went over. I never told her how her condo was almost a replica of my old life—everything arranged so prim and proper and in its own place. She had dual everything. Two white Queen Anne-style sofas with beaded fringe and two whitewood-and-glass coffee tables were sitting side by side. Even the beaded fringe lamp, the painting, and every ornament had a twin. She had enough furniture to easily furnish an additional condo if she wanted. I thought how perfect she and Edmond's life would have been had they met instead.

"Cold?" Jackie repeated, stuffing a chip in her mouth, visibly upset with Marco, who had gotten a refill on the chips and dip before he sat down again on Jackie's couch.

"Yes. When a woman leaves her husband because she is unhappy—no disrespect intended, CeCe—"

"None taken."

"—she is suffocating, right?" he continued. "Finding herself. But a man dealing with the same situation is a low-down, cheating dog. A playa. Now that's unfair."

"Marco, no one is saying that," Jackie said. "I just hope that you're not moving too fast in a relationship with this woman. What about your wife, three kids, and sixteen years of marriage?"

"Kids, marriage, so what? Is that automatically supposed to guarantee my happiness?" Marco shot back. "Look, sure I was married for a very long time, but ask me how many of those years were actually happy."

"Okay," Jackie agreed. "So you were unhappy. And I can even agree with you finding yourself, but do you have to already have someone all lined up and waiting?"

"Gena is not just someone out there waiting. I've asked her to marry me?" he stated matter-of-factly.

Jackie stared at him in disbelief. "Another marriage? Geeezzzz."

"So what if I just happened to find the right person while I was still married? Some might just call it luck."

"Or greed. You're hopeless, you know," Jackie said.

"Greed? How can you say I'm greedy?"

"She's younger, sexier—things you said. Admit it. It's strictly sex."

"Because she's black, and I'm not? You think sex is the only thing we have in common? Well, I happen to love the person she is."

"That wasn't what I meant. I'm saying, had she not come along, you probably wouldn't be leaving your wife."

"You don't know that. If my marriage was that solid,

nothing could have broken it. You feel me?"

"What you are feeling is forty and horny," Jackie continued. You know nothing about this woman. You met her as a client. You slipped around, and the sex was wild and risqué, but there's more to a relationship than that, you know."

"So, now I'm back to my original question. You think I can't have anything in common with her because she's not Italian, right?" Marco asked.

"You're missing the whole point, Marco," Jackie said. "I'm not talking about race. She broke your marriage up, maybe before you were ready, now that's an entire other problem."

"Jackie, shit happens. Feelings don't always dictate who you fall in love with. And if my marriage wasn't ready to be over, Gena could only have helped save it."

"And you really have convinced yourself of that, huh? You know you're impossible. CeCe, could you talk to him? I'm done." Jackie threw up her hands and went off into the kitchen, venting to herself.

Marco looked in my direction, ready to either defend himself or hear my firsthand advice. I hated that people expected me to be a divorce guru now that I was.

"Hey, don't look at me. I don't judge, I said. "Besides, my motives for leaving were entirely different from yours."

"What's that suppose to mean?" Marco asked.

"I didn't leave my marriage because there was some-one on the backburner waiting for me."

"But you weren't happy," he said.

"Not entirely."

"There you go. Like I said before, it's a woman thing. Men are just not looked at the same for leaving their family."

I suddenly needed to relieve my bladder. Marco was making me anxious. Even though Edmond had hurt me, with his lies, I still felt a need to protect him and his image. That made me angry with myself. I shouldn't feel like I owed him anything. I used Jackie's bathroom inside of her bedroom so I could check my phone messages on the way out. Jackie and Marco's voices carried into the bedroom as I sat on her crushed suede chaise with the phone up to my ear. There were only two messages, one from some company congratulating me on winning a cruise and some survey from DirecTV. Nothing from Tyson. I had hoped he would have called me after work. I thought about just calling him instead, but I didn't want to develop a pattern like I was checking up on him. I walked back into the living room to join Jackie and Marco.

"So you're asking me to believe that men can't feel as unfulfilled or unsatisfied in a relationship as women and that it's not always sexual?" Marco continued to argue his side.

"In my opinion, when a man leaves for another woman, it's ninety percent sexual," Jackie threw back.

"And I say you're wrong in my case. Sex was not an issue in my marriage. The fact is that was the only thing that was right. Gena happens to offer me good sex plus a lot more," Marco defended himself.

"So each time the grass looks a little greener, you're ready to jump ship?" Jackie asked. Take it from me; a woman has her way of making things look better on her side until you have to live with her twenty-four/seven."

Marco's cell phone rang, and he took it in the kitchen.

"I just don't know what to do with him. I think he's really making a big mistake to jump so deep into another relationship so soon after his divorce," Jackie said.

"Then let him, Jackie. I might be also, but who's to say? That's one of the chances we take."

Marco returned with a broad smile stretched across his face as he folded the top down on his Sanyo phone.

"I'm assuming that call wasn't from the ex-wife," Jackie said.

"No. That was from my sweetie."

"Oh, Tina, right?" she asked.

"Gena, with an *e*."

"Sorry, I mean Gena with an *e*." We all laughed. "So when do we get to meet her?" Jackie inquired.

"You serious?" Marco asked, excitedly. "You really want to meet her, Jackie?"

"Sure. Besides, if I had the chance to talk with her, I can peep her motives after five minutes of conversation."

"Okay, Miss Cleo, if you're really serious, I'm supposed to meet her in half an hour, but I can have her meet me here, if that's cool."

"On my turf. Perfect."

"You're impossible," Marco teased as he called Gena back. Fifteen minutes later, Jackie's doorbell rang. We waited in anticipation as Marco went to let her in.

She was a knockoff from a true sista. Gena was tall, slim, and pretty alright, but her complexion and hair texture placed her more with Marco's Italian heritage than either Jackie's or mine. They did make a handsome couple as they embraced affectionately before Marco introduced her to us. Jackie wasted no time putting Gena on the hot seat.

"So, Gena, how did you two meet?"

"Actually, I was a client of Marco's."

"Oh, and you needed his services that much afterward?"

Gena laughed, clearly not offended. Jackie had meant for her to be, I thought.

"I think it was destiny that we met. I also worked in the building right next to him and didn't know it."

"Oh, isn't this a thrill? CeCe and I work in the building next to Marco and you're in the building after that. We're all just one happy family," Jackie said rather sarcastically.

"As a matter of fact, CeCe," Gena continued, "I think my girlfriend who also works with me, has a fiancé who works with you."

"Oh," I said, a warm feeling rising inside of me.

"Remember, Marco honey, when you were telling me about Jackie and CeCe and what they did at Templeton and I mentioned Tayla's boyfriend also worked there."

"So, what's his name?" I pushed.

"Ahh, Tyson something. I don't remember the last name."

20

The rain woke me up. There was something peaceful about the melodiousness thumping of it against my window. The sound of the rain freshened my mind like it did the flowers and the grass, cleared out all of the unhappy thoughts about why Tyson wasn't there or why he had taken the last week off. What was really going on with this Tayla person? Was she really his fiancée and the psycho who had tried to make a pancake out of his car? Though Gena had confirmed Tayla as Tyson's fiancée, I still needed to hear Tyson's side.

My anger rose just thinking that if he was engaged, he could still act so suave and lie about it, basically, what Edmond had done. I was angrier with myself for letting sex happen between us too soon. I should have known a young, handsome, and successful man like Tyson wasn't available. I should've listened to what my female intuition was saying. That was usually right on target.

The urgency of the ringing phone interrupted my thoughts as I picked up, half expecting Tyson.

"What's up, my fellow Houstonian?"

"Tracee, is that you? A couple of weeks in Jackson and I hardly recognize you. You sound so...happy."

"All the way and live."

"I can tell that. And early too," I said, checking the time. It was a little after eight.

"Well, you know how we do things in the South. My daddy makes me and my boys get up with the chickens, whether we have anything to do or not."

"Oh, don't remind me. How are you?"

"Just great! You know at first I didn't know how things would be, after not living here for so long, but I said to myself, this is the best thing that I can do for my kids, so I'm looking into this training program for nursing. They'll even pay me to go. Most of all, the kids are happy here."

"Terrific. You really needed a break," I said.

"Speaking of breaks, how are things with you?"

"A few prospects," I uttered.

"How many?" she prodded.

"Just one. How's the fishing in Jackson?"

"A lot of juveniles."

"Haven't I told you about hanging out at Mickey D's?"

"Hey, in case you forgot, Jackson has a limitation on where to meet a good man these days."

"I wouldn't know. I was married, remember?"

"Speaking of being married...guess who I ran into the other day?"

"Don't tell me. Edmond?"

"Sure did. I went in the bank with my daddy to finalize the loan for his new truck, and Edmond had a million questions about you when he found out who I was. Girl, he was begging for info."

"You mean he's not in blitz with his secretary."

"That was probably some mid-life crisis. But now I

think he's missing my girl and that whip appeal you put on him."

"You need to stop it."

We laughed nonstop. We must have covered the entire population of Jackson during our conversation. We talked about others she had bumped into after umpteen years—former classmates; even our old high school coach, Larry Wilcox; Jaheim's father. She said he must have noticed that Jaheim was the spitting image of him, but he hadn't commented. Neither had she. Then we digressed to the commonalities between the folks in a small southern town and a big city like Houston— marriages, divorces, drugs, rehab, more drugs, infidelity, promiscuity, or the ones who had no clue. That was when her father interrupted. He was ready to be driven to wherever he went early on a Saturday morning. She promised to call me soon, and we hung up.

I went into the kitchen and poured a glass of cranberry juice. I checked the time again. It was almost noon. Tracee and I had talked for three and a half hours. I was glad to catch up on how positive her life had turned out. I thought of where mine was headed, feeling a bit jealous.

My phone rang again.

"CeCe, this is Tyson."

"Tyson?"

"You sound a little surprised."

"Just didn't expect to hear from you today, that's all. How are you feeling?"

"Fine. Why do you ask?"

"Well, you took a week of sick leave, remember?"

"Oh, right. Hey, I really need to talk to you. Can we meet someplace?"

"Sure. You know Houston better than I do. Where?"

"How's your handicap?"

"As in golf?"

"Yeah."

"I suppose you're familiar with Tiger Woods, right?"

"Of course."

"Well, I couldn't even carry his golf clubs."

"That bad, huh. Well, I know this miniature golf place right off the Southwest freeway. Nothing elite. It's on the kids' level, so I don't think we'll stand out that much. I know we have to be discreet."

"I know the place, but what about the rain?"

"It stopped almost an hour ago. Say in about another hour then?"

I parted my wooden blinds to look outside. The sun was peeking back at me through the clouds. Most of the wetness on the sidewalks and street was almost completely gone.

"Give me an hour and a half," I said.

Tyson certainly had ensured discretion, I thought as I exited the freeway and pulled into the parking lot of Kiddie Golf Central. It was an amusement place where parents usually took their kids for birthday parties. As I checked out the patrons, there was a slim chance of bumping into anyone we knew over the age of twelve.

He was waiting for me out front by the equipment window. The bright sun shimmering against his fitting white shirt made his smooth chocolate skin tone radiant. He had already purchased the clubs and balls, so we headed straight for the miniature course with no hug or kiss. We acted more like familiar strangers. Tyson teed off first with a serious expression. His body language emitted tension. I got the feeling we were there more for the conversation than for the game itself. He finally spoke without gazing directly at me. When he did look at me, his eyes were tired, older, like he had missed a few nights' sleep.

"CeCe, I know I've been acting distant lately, and I want you to know it has nothing to do with us. I mean it does involve my feelings for you, but not because we made love."

"Yes, you have been distant. I thought things might have happened too fast, especially us making love. I was hoping whatever it was, you would at least tell me."

"Believe me, I wanted to. I just didn't think you would understand, and I didn't know what you would think of me." His voice trailed off, and he went back to the game. Then it was my turn. I purposely held my club awkwardly, though Edmond had shown me how a thousand times. I wanted Tyson to do something appealing like step in close behind and place his hands over mine, tell me all the mistakes I was making. I waited for his body to shadow me. He stood by until I finished up, and we moved on. There was no score-keeping or celebration as we went along. He had me wondering why he had even asked me there.

"Does your asking me here has anything to do with Tayla?" I asked.

He swallowed hard. I almost felt the warm sensation that must have hit the pit of his stomach along with it.

"How do you know her name?"

"From a friend who has a friend who knows about the two of you." I paused briefly to let him take in my firsthand info. "Tayla's roommate, Gena told me."

He looked at me like any argument he might have had was lost. "I should have told you everything up front before we were intimate. But I thought this thing between Tayla and me was over."

"You told me it was over."

"I had every intention of it being over," he said, his voice rising with tension. A small bead of sweat trickled down his temple.

"So you're telling me it's pretty serious between you and her?"

"They were up until about six months ago, then we decided to go our separate ways. It just wasn't working. She said she needed some space, which was cool, then about a month ago we broke it off for good. I hadn't spoken to her since." He sighed like he felt forced to continue. "Then, the same morning I left your place, she called saying we needed to talk." Voices were coming from behind us. We skipped the third hole and continued down the artificial turf to the next one. We were just putting now, forgetting protocol and order. "She went ballistic. And she's not playing fair. She was the one who floured my car, if you haven't guessed by now. I tried to tell her we were finished, and that's when she dropped this scud missile on me, Cc." He stopped and took a deep breath. He blew it out like he was trying to extinguish a hundred birthday candles at once.

"What?" I asked, not really wanting to know. Whatever it was had already come between us.

"She told me that she's pregnant, and the baby is mine."

"You think it is?" I asked after letting the jolt to my system pass over. I thought of my having to remind him to use a condom at least twice.

"I don't know what to think. I mean it's possible even though we took precautions, but I can't take the chance that it is and I'm not there to take care of my kid."

"So what's the next step? Marriage?"

"No. Absolutely not. That would be the worst thing

for us, for the baby. I did promised her that I'll be there for them."

"If not marriage, then how long do you plan to be there?"

"I guess until she's able to go it alone."

"Tayla or the baby?"

"Be serious."

"I am. Tyson, do you think a baby is like some toy, something you can play with until you get tired of it? Whether the baby needs you or not, you're involved with Tayla at least until the kid graduates from high school. The two are not interchangeable like some three-piece suit."

"So what are you telling me about us?"

"Us?"

"Yes, you and me."

"Tyson, there is no us now. It's you and them." Then the whole basis for this little outing hit me like a ton of golf balls. "Wait a minute. Are you asking me to wait around until you plan on ending your parental obligations and then we just pick up where we left off?"

"Just until after the baby comes and Tayla won't need me as much."

"And when will that be? When the baby's potty-trained? Kindergarten? Sixth grade? Tyson, will you listen to yourself? You haven't a clue, do you?"

"About what?"

"That you have been caught up in the oldest web since the invention of hair grease. Girl meets boy, boy no longer wants girl, so girl gets pregnant to keep him. And you fell for it—hard-on and condom-free."

"She knows that I don't love her."

"What does that have to do with it? As long as she has your baby, she has you. And that's your life."

"CeCe, I think I'm in love with you, and you're the only one I want to be with." He let his golf club thump to the ground and grabbed hold of my elbow, pulling me in a little closer until I could smell spearmint on his breath. "Look, I messed up, big time, but I can do this. Just work with me."

"When? In between feedings? Look, Tyson, maybe you can handle this, but I can't. I came to Houston to start my life over, and that doesn't include someone else's family. I'm not blaming you for anything. The timing just wasn't on our side. You go ahead and handle your obligations. I'll be fine."

He let go and turned away, looked back at me, then away again. As he did, I could see the anger boiling inside of him, like a pot of soup when the flame is too high.

"I don't believe this shit. I don't believe you. You talk about not getting hurt, but you don't mind doing the hurting, do you?"

"Come on, Tyson, it's not the same."

"The hell it is," he shouted, getting louder. I checked behind us. No one had made it that far yet. He looked, too, then quickly expelled hot air. He tried to relax. He bit the inside of his lips and shook his head at me. "You know what you are, CeCe? A damn hypocrite. You and every woman who says she wants a man who is honest, who has the balls to tell you what's up."

"Don't you dare blame this on me, Tyson."

"And you call us playas."

"So now I'm a playa?"

"Basically. You leave your husband, find me, tease me, and now it's time to move on. Isn't that the way you do it, CeCe?"

"You know, Tyson, this is crazy. I'm not going to

stand here and listen to this. I know you're upset and confused, but you did this, not me. Don't expect me to stick by you while you make amends with Tayla and your kid. This has nothing, absolutely nothing, to do with me," I spat at him. I was highly pissed for the first time. I threw the club at his feet and hurried toward the exit.

He ran closely behind, trying to catch up. "CeCe, wait."

"Leave me alone, Tyson. Let me go."

21

Jackie and I collapsed on the front steps of my condo after our Saturday morning run. I was bringing her up-to-date on the Tyson and Tayla situation, which I had pondered for the past week.

"Honestly, CeCe. I don't know why you're being so indecisive about Tyson and his problems. Don't you know in any love situation, baby drama wins all the time?"

"I can't just drop him like that. I do care for him. I'm just trying to be as understanding of the situation as I possibly can be."

"Sister, believe me, you're understanding enough. Any more understanding and he'll want the four of you to share a crib like some religious cult in Utah."

"Tyson isn't like that. Maybe she did trap him, but can you blame him for wanting to be there for his kid? And aren't we always dogging the brothers for not being responsible?"

"Responsible? Now that's another thing, CeCe. How careless could he be to let someone he claims he doesn't love get pregnant? With so much information out there these days, I just don't buy the theory that Tayla trapped him."

"Jackie, if you're telling me that Tyson was playing us both and made the fatal mistake of getting Tayla pregnant, I'm sorry, I don't think he's that way."

"Ce, I'm not saying he's a playa. I'm just saying that you should be careful and think this thing through. Don't be too eager to take his word at face value. Come on, you're smart."

"I guess you're right," I said, then sighed and looked into the direction of the park across the street. It was the end of June, but it was at a decent temperature, a beautiful day to be outside. "Want to go antique shopping?"

"Are you serious? Sister, after that workout, I'm down for at least twenty-four hours."

"Slacker."

"I'm not hearing you, CeCe," she said getting up to leave.

"One mile and you need Ben-Gay. That's a sign of old age," I yelled at her back.

"Forget you," she returned and trotted off in the direction of her own condo, waving her hand over her head without looking back. I giggled and went inside.

I had two messages. Both were from Tyson.

I didn't return his calls. The raw morning air I had inhaled had both my nose and eyes running. I took two Benadryl and a long, warm shower, then washed and blow-dried my hair. I sat down at my bathroom vanity table and took extra care in applying my makeup. I had started to use a little more post-Edmond. Not excessive, just a bolder contrast to my eyes and more definition to my lips. I marveled at how I could look on one of my best days. Darn good!

I dressed in some low-riding blue jeans and a sleeveless yellow top, then perched myself on one of my barstools and flipped on the TV. Collins Spencer, the anchorman who reminded me of Edmond, was on CNN. Same distinguished handsomeness and smile, only my bet was that Collins wasn't as anal. Damn Edmond Cornell Ross. He hadn't even bothered to call me since the divorce. It was now obvious that he didn't care how I was affected, even if I had been the one to ask for it. I flipped off the TV and checked my hair again, resigned to being dressed up with no place to go, which was ridiculous since I was in Houston, where something was always going on—rain, snow or shine. I went to the kitchen pantry where I kept at least a week's worth of old newspapers. I grabbed last Sunday's Zest, the section of the *Houston Chronicle* that covered entertainment from A to Z—everything from ethnic street festivals to the latest movie releases.

I thumbed my way through the concert ticket sales. Steppen Wolf, Sheryl Crow, The Who, The Eagles and a Soul Jam Revival featuring the O'Jays, Dramatics, Whispers, and whomever had hooked up and was calling themselves the Temptations were in town. There were some book tours also, but no authors I was interested in meeting. Besides, I hadn't read a good book in ages. There was some mention of a Juneteenth celebration in the park. A free jazz festival it read it bold letters. Free was always interesting. Only, what exactly was Juneteenth? I thought. And as if my question was silently heard, the ad went on to say that Juneteenth was a huge observance in Houston, most of Texas period. On June 19, back in 1865, news reached Galveston that slavery had ended, although it was two and a half years after Lincoln had signed the Emancipation Proclamation.

A little jazz couldn't be all that bad. I smiled as I wrote down the directions to the park. I grabbed my backpack with a supply of water and my car keys and dashed out to my garage. The echoes of my ringing phone were cut off as I closed the door behind me.

I arrived at Eleanor Tinsley Park around noon. Either from a lack of awareness from others or my over-zealousness, I was among the first handful to arrive for the concert. The small exceptions were those manning a couple of large white tents, a few refreshment stands and a face-painting booth. There was also a few other vendors scattered throughout.

Then, I wished I hadn't come. I felt alone and out of place—isolated, like a tiny sparrow in the center of a football field. My spontaneous side told me to stay put and have some fun. I decided that I would grab a beer to loosen up and at least act like I wanted to be there, even if I didn't.

Audio distortion spilled over from the direction of a huge white stage. A man dressed in black pants and black T-shirt was completing his sound check as a crew finished placing folding metal chairs in front. I scoped out his slender but masculine frame. He tapped his mike. *Screeeccchhh!* He frowned and made some additional adjustments.

"Mike testing one, testing two and thrreee." His smooth radio voice floated out into the open air. I paced a little closer, but not enough to appear interested in what he was doing. I was fast becoming bored.

"Mike check." He started up again. Then, "My mike sounds tight, my mike sounds right," he sang or rather to rap. He was hamming it up, maybe for the benefit of his friend on stage who only covered his ears and laughed. I thought he looked my way. I didn't know, but I smiled anyway and shook my head.

Then he waved. I didn't know if it was meant for me, but I waved back. He turned and whispered something to his friend behind him, then jumped off stage and headed in my direction.

"So you look like you didn't enjoy my flow," he said as he stepped up to me. He was slightly out of breath, or maybe his voice was a little nervous. He also wasn't as tall as he'd look on stage, only a few inches taller than my five-foot-six frame.

"I've heard better," I returned, cracking a smile.

"Maybe you can show me better then. If you're with the first band performing, you can change in the trailer behind the bleachers over there," he said, pointing over my shoulder at a long white trailer. I gave him a puzzled look. He frowned. His long, shoulder-length braids glistened in the sun as he moved them out of his face. His thin, black beard made him strikingly handsome.

"Excuse me," I said, shaking my head in confusion.

"You are with the band, right?"

"No. I'm just an overly punctual fan."

"Well then, my bad. I should have known better. Musicians are never on time."

I let go of a quiet laugh. "And are you a musician?"

"Only part-time."

"And the other half?"

"Program Director at a local radio station. I'm Jazz, Jazz Rollins." We shook hands.

"Kind of poetic don't you think? Jazz, music, radio."

"Jazz is my mama-given name. I guess she was the one responsible for determining what my motivation in life would be. I just followed suit."

"I see."

"And what about you? You in the music business or something?"

"Does rotating the music in my CD changer count?"

A quick smile graced his face, revealing a set of white

teeth. "Well, I guess that would depend on what you listen to."

"Oh, I like jazz, the contemporary stuff and all."

"Okay, you're in. I think if you stick around you'll like what you hear."

"I just might do that. Thanks," I said and turned to walk in the direction of the refreshment booth.

"Wait. You didn't tell me your name."

"You didn't ask."

"I'm asking now."

"It's CeCe."

"Just CeCe. That's nothing more than a nickname."

"That's what I give to a stranger."

"Well, CeCe, what would a brotha have to do to get past the stranger phase? I mean how can I track you down?"

"You seem to be a creative person, Jazz. If you really wanted to, I'm sure you could find a way. And if you were meant to, you'll find me."

"Oh, so now you gon' throw that serendipity thing at me? What if I don't find you?"

"Then, you weren't meant to," I said, turning to leave.

"CeCe! Hold on—" He reached for my arm.

"Just remember," I interrupted, "if you do find a way, make it creative and make me laugh. Bye, Jazz."

22

Downtown traffic was light for a Monday morning, but probably normal considering the early hour. It was a quarter past six. I had wanted to get a head start on the campaigns' progress report before my ten o'clock meeting with Gray. Tyson had a meet and greet on the other side of town with some sporting goods client, so that gave me plenty of quiet time to organize my notes.

Jackie drove into the garage behind me and parked beside my car. I waved at her. We both got out and exchanged morning salutations. Jackie clicked the remote to lock her sporty BMW convertible. Maybe I would downsize to something trendier too.

"You're early," I said as she came over and gave me a hug.

"I have some newbies starting work today. What's your excuse?"

"A million things to do and only eight hours."

"Tell me about. So how did you spend the rest of your weekend?"

I told her about meeting Jazz Rollins at Tinsley Park. I said he was a nice guy with a radiant smile, but

I probably wouldn't see him again. I hadn't even given him my number.

"You want to take the elevator up?" she asked. I thought about it for a few seconds. Otherwise, we would have to exit the garage and take the sidewalk to the front of the building.

"Let's walk. I need the fresh air."

Jackie shrugged. She hated spontaneous exercise. "Okay," she said, finally.

We ventured out onto the sidewalk as Jackie continued to scold me for not giving Jazz my number. The streets were deserted that hour of the morning. No one was in a hurry to start their Monday morning sentence. We approached the front entrance to Templeton. I was reaching inside my purse for my keycard when Jackie suddenly stopped me by placing her arm across my chest. She did it in a protective motherly manner like she saw danger lurking.

"What's wrong?" I asked.

"There," she nodded toward the front of the building at a large object that looked like a big, clear plastic bag.

"What is it?" I asked.

"Looks like a garbage bag with stuff inside of it."

"Do you think it might be a bomb? Maybe we should call the police."

"I don't think it's a bomb," she said, moving closer, her arm now interlocked with mine.

We half-stepped the rest of the way, peering and peeping, arm-in-arm like LaVerne and Shirley in their sitcom opener.

We got close enough to recognize it as indeed a garbage bag. There appeared to be a few pieces of clothing and some personal items, a man's razor, toothbrush, bottles of cologne. There was also a bunch of snapshots stuck all over the outside of the bag.

"Who would do this?" Jackie asked. "And look, there's a small bag of crushed CDs on the other side." She kneeled down to get a closer look.

"Probably some pissed-off chick who kicked her man out—"

"Oh, shit. CeCe, shit."

"Jackie, what is it?"

"It's you and Tyson. Look." She pulled one of the pictures off the bag and held it up to me. It was Tyson and me at the mini golf course. I peeled off the rest of the photos and went through them one by one. There was a shot of us in the parking lot at my condo. Tyson was shirtless with his arm around me in my bathrobe on the morning after we first made love. A few more of us as we embraced before going back inside. I looked through the rest. Another one of us coming out of Café Antoine and all the other places we had been together.

"What sick person would do this?" I asked, anxiety creeping up inside of me. Then I immediately thought of Tayla.

"I don't know, but whoever it was, wanted everyone at Templeton to see the two of you together. Come on, let's get this stuff inside. Good thing we got here early."

Jackie helped me take the things up to my office. I stored them out of sight in the bathroom. Jackie calmed me then went to check the rear entrance to make sure there weren't any additional packages left there.

Tyson strolled into my office about 9:25, looking quite fly as usual in a navy pinstriped suit, confident in his masculinity by the soft pink shirt he wore underneath.

"CeCe, we need to talk. It's about business." He took one look at me when I didn't respond and knew something was definitely wrong. "What's up? You look upset."

"Yes, we do need to talk, but not about business," I said, then went into the bathroom and came out with the garbage bags and handed them to him. "Do you recognize this?" He held it up, looked at the contents and took a long breath.

"Where did you get these?"

"They were left outside near the front entrance with these plastered all over." I thrust the snapshots at him. He took them and looked at the first one, then cursed.

"I'm so sorry you are involved in this mess."

"What mess? What's going on, Tyson? Is this from your little girlfriend Tayla?"

"She's not my girlfriend, CeCe. She's pregnant with my child. That's it."

"She's out of control. Do you know what would have happened if someone, anyone here had seen this?"

"I'll handle it, CeCe."

"Then handle it, Tyson. And tell your...the mother of your child to leave me out of this, okay?"

I followed him back into his office, closing the door behind me. I couldn't help but glance over at the swivel chair near his drafting table. Tyson and I had made love there not so long ago.

He caught me looking.

"You said you needed to talk," I said, pacing to calm down again.

"Look, I know I've messed things up between us but I've tried to be honest with you about everything, and you've made it quite clear about the way you feel. Now with this mess left here this morning—"

"I thought this was about business."

"I'm getting there. Just let me say what I have to say."

"Alright."

"As I was saying, you've told me how you feel about my situation with Tayla and I won't press the issue."

"I'm glad. You do understand that things have to go back to being strictly professional between us, right? Now, especially," I stated.

"If that's how you want it. Whatever makes things around here comfortable for you."

"It's about you also."

"But what you want, right?"

"I see it no other way."

"Would me not being here help?"

"What do you mean?"

"Maybe it's time I moved on. You know, make the situation better."

"Tyson, I just need normalcy. I'm not asking you to leave."

"I want to actually."

"So why didn't you just tell me that in the first place? Why put it back on me, like you really care about what I think? Seems like you have it all figured out."

"I do care about your opinion, and nothing is final until it's done. I want you to tell me how you feel."

"What do you want to hear? That I won't be unhappy or that I won't miss you?"

"I want you to say whatever your heart feels. Be honest with me."

"Tyson, you already know the answer. You know how I feel about you. That's not the issue. You want me to be a part of a world I refuse to be a part of. I won't live a lie just to be with you."

He took a step closer and pulled me up against his chest. "Then, I want you to tell me that being without me is going to drive you as crazy as it will me." He kissed my tight lips, then he backed us to his desk and tried to force me into his groin.

"Tyson, stop," I said and pulled away. "Just stop. I can't do this."

"Then, I can't either. Good-bye, CeCe."

He pushed his way past me, grabbed his keys and briefcase, then walked out. I followed in time to see him drop a long white envelope on top of a stack of papers in my in box.

● ● ●

Tyson's resignation consisted of one page, single-spaced on Templeton's letterhead. I didn't read it until later, at home. Somehow I already knew what it was going to say. Of course, it read professionally. He said all of the politically correct things that people say when they resigned without pressure. But between the lines, he had given me choices. Either I could change my mind about risqué office sex and some late-night rendezvous or he was out of my life forever. "I'm sorry, Tyson," I whispered, folding the letter and tucking it away in my upstairs office.

I picked up my ringing phone on the way back downstairs.

"CeCe, thank goodness you're home."

"Jackie, What's up?"

"Sister, do you have your radio on?"

"No, why?"

"You have to hear this guy on 97.6."

"What's he saying?"

"Stop asking questions and turn on the radio."

I ran into my bedroom with the cordless phone held up to my ear. I clicked on the radio sitting on my nightstand with my other hand.

"So, Jazz, in the event that CeCe is listening, let's go

over your request again, okay." It was Greg Anderson. I sometimes listened to his show the *"Afternoon Cruise"* on my way home from work.

"Sure, Greg. I met her at Tinsley Park last weekend and I only know that her name is CeCe."

"Just CeCe?" Greg asked.

"Just CeCe, man, that's all she would tell me," Jazz said, laughing. He sounded good over the radio.

"If that's all she gave you, brotha, then maybe she was scared of you." They both cracked up. "Naw, CeCe, seriously. I can tell you, I know this guy personally, and he's cool. I give you my word on that. So, Jazz, any last words you want to say to this sistarella before you go?"

"Just that I really felt a vibe, and I would like to get to know more than your nickname. If you're interested, I'll be at the Red Cat Jazz Café at eight o'clock tonight. If you don't show, I'll understand."

Greg Anderson stepped in and helped him out. "So, CeCe, if you're hearing this, girl, give the brotha a break so I can get back to my regular announcements. Dude has been camping on the steps of the station for this chance to find you." Jazz laughed out loud in the background. "The place is the Red Cat Jazz Café, on Texas and Congress, downtown. So, for the Jazz Man and his sistarella, CeCe, here's a song to help you find your way to each other. How about some Luther and 'Can I Take You Out Tonight.' Luther's soulful voice cut in, and my heart somersaulted. Jazz had taken the challenge and met it with flying colors.

"CeCe, is that you he's talking about?" I'd forgotten that Jackie was still waiting on the line.

"I guess so. I mean, yes, it's me."

"Girl, who is this man? Sounds too romantic for

me. He's on the radio pining like Gerald Levert. Are you going or what?"

• • •

Jazz was sitting at the bar when I arrived. He had a look on his face like he was already prepared to be let down when I was a no-show. I glanced up at huge black clock shaped like a saxophone on the wall over the bar. I was punctual for a change. I made sure of that. I hoped he liked what I was wearing. I had borrowed a royal-blue dress from Jackie. It hit me mid-thigh and had two narrow, over-the-shoulder straps held in place by rhinestone buckles. I strolled over when he wasn't looking back at the entrance. Jazz turned suddenly; making his long braids whirl before resting in place again on his shoulders.

"Hi." He looked nervous as he stood. I looked him over. Yes, he was definitely going through some type of dark period. He was totally outfitted in black again.

"Hi."

"You look beautiful."

"Thanks."

"So you finally made it."

"Finally? Was I supposed to be here sooner? You said eight, right?"

"Eight, two days ago."

"I'm confused."

"Let's sit first." He led me over to a table and pulled out my chair as I smooth my dress underneath me. I waited for him to continue.

"I made the announcement on the station every day, hoping that you would respond. The station was beginning to think that I made you up. I think they wanted to charge me for an advertising spot."

"So why didn't you give up after the first day?"

"I was hoping you would come. Besides, did Prince Charming give up on Cinderella?"

"Well, personally, I thought that prince was a bit shallow."

He broke into a charismatic laugh. "Why, because he knew what he wanted and wasn't willing to stop until he got it?"

"No. He just thought the woman of his dreams fitted into that one size five shoe, when the truth was, he could have easily found the same happiness with a size eight, if he'd taken the chance."

"So I take it you don't believe in fate."

"There's nothing wrong with a little manipulation when fate doesn't happen."

"So you coming here tonight, was that fate or assignable cause?"

"Let's just say that the shoe might fit, regardless."

He remained silent, staring deep into the red flame of the candle in the center of the our shiny black-and-white lacquered table. He swept his finger across the flame, teasing it.

The lights dimmed, except for the one directly over the stage. Something was about to take place. The scarce crowd seemed to anticipate that also, and prepared accordingly—tranquil mood, refills on the drinks, and little or no conversation. I was the only one who appeared to not be informed.

"It's poetry night. Free flowing, they call it." He still hadn't looked up, but he said it like he'd guessed what I was thinking when I looked around the room.

"I love poetry," I said.

"Yeah, but sometimes the brothas and sistas in here go pretty deep. They act like they want to cut your heart out and examine it for coldness."

"So do you ever free flow?"

"No."

"Why? Can't take criticism?"

"No. My poetry is usually written for my own personal growth. I'm not ready to share it yet."

"Selfishness is not what makes a good poet."

"True, if that's what I was trying to become."

"If not a poet, what do you want to be?"

"I don't know just yet. Sometimes a writer and singer, then at other times I just love what I do behind the scenes, you know like producing. I also do a lot of concert promotions around the city, stuff like that, but I'm sure when that right thing hits me, I'll know."

The waiter came over and took our drink order: white wine for me— nothing too sweet—I told him. Jazz ordered cognac. Smooth, strong, and touch of braise that blended in with the cigar-scented incense haunting the room. It was a scent that reminded me of a cozy, mild winter. We slipped into casual conversation between the poetry sets. Then some heavy sista—a cross between Angie Stone and Erykah Badu—with a strong personality took the stage. She started to praise the strength and uniqueness of her faithful black man, preaching about the things he did for her during her moments of weakness, how he brought her pleasure from her hair follicles right down to her toenails. She ended to a thunder of clapping and a few "go on, sistas."

I turned back to Jazz. I listened as he told me about himself; his southern roots. I really wanted to get to know him. Get absorbed in his fabric to know that he was kind of old fashioned. Liked simple things, ate simple—fish and grits on a slow Sunday morning were his favorites. He was like his mother in that way and got his love for music from his father who had been the lead singer in a local group in Houma, Louisiana, playing everything from weddings receptions to baseball victory parties. As a little boy, Jazz had grown up on the tail end of the microphone, dragged in and out of every juke joint on Bourbon Street. That's where his love for music was conceived. His words came out smooth and crafted, almost like a song.

The last poet came to the stage, sporting an Afro the size of Texas. He was really into his form too—dashiki-inspired linen shirt, wide-legged denims and no shoes. I dubbed him the thinker because he sat on the stool with mike in hand and hesitated at the beginning of each line as if he was giving much thought to his words.

He began in a solemn, almost tranquil mood, but ended in a revolting, militant tone. He was fed up with everything from unemployment to racism. Life in general. He got scattered applause throughout the room, then the poetry set was over for the night. The emcee solicited another round of applause from the audience, then announced the date for the next set.

We ordered dinner—blackened catfish with rice pilaf and steamed vegetables. Jazz ordered a fresh cognac. We talked for another two hours until it was getting late.

Jazz walked me outside. The air was humid and thick. "Where did you park?" He was close to my moist skin.

"Valet," I told him.

"Give me your ticket. I'll have them bring your car around. You warm?" he asked.

"A little."

"Your car should be here soon," he said, handing my ticket to the valet. Jazz didn't request his car, so I assumed he was staying longer.

"So did I follow your rules?"

"Excuse me?"

"When I tracked you down, was I unique, and did I make you laugh?"

"You were quite unique, but more romantic than funny. I liked that more."

"Do I get to see you again?"

"I don't know. Was that part of the challenge?"

"I don't like when you do that."

"Do what?"

"What you're doing. You answered my question with your own question. It tells me you're avoiding being straight with me."

"Sorry."

"So, do I?"

"Do you what?"

"Get to see you again?"

"You want to?"

"I wouldn't have asked if I didn't."

I paused and looked at him. "I suppose that's the least I can do since you went through all this trouble to find me."

"And might I add, I did it with originality and humor and threw in a little style for extra measure."

"Right on all counts."

"And do I get to choose my own consolation prize?"

"Just go easy on me."

"How about another date and I'll call it even. After that, it's up to you."

"I think I can swing that without going broke."

The valet arrived with my car and stopped short of us. He opened the car door, and I slid into the front seat. Jazz closed the door for me.

"So how do I reach you this time without begging over the airwaves?"

I pulled one of my business cards from my purse, grabbed a pen, and scribbled my cellular number on the back. I held it in his direction between my middle and pointer fingers, then pulled away.

23

"That dance floor seems to be having all the fun tonight," Jazz commented.

Jazz and I were hanging out at the Red Cat again after a Frankie Beverly and Maze concert. Jazz had worked their stop in Houston for the Fourth of July weekend. It was our second date in less than a week, and I'd been ignoring him like we were an old married, but estranged couple.

"I'm sorry. I guess my mind was wandering."

"You had fun at the concert?" he asked.

"Well, I guess I did," I said, getting in a playful mood. "That is if I overlook that small oversight."

"Come on now. You're not going holding the cigarette lighter thing against me, are you?"

"I should. I mean, I asked for a small thing like a cigarette lighter, and you let me down. And everyone knows that the one thing you don't forget when attending a Maze concert is a cigarette lighter. That's a no-brainer, for a true-blue fan that is."

"I stand accused and convicted. I throw myself at your mercy, and I'm sorry for not being a big a fan as you. But didn't the backstage pass count for anything?"

"That was sweet of you, and I guess I'll try to forgive you, this time."

"You should."

With that he reached into his pocket, then pulled out his hand again. I couldn't quite make out the lighter at first, until he held it up to the candle. It was fluorescent green. He flicked it on. "Here. I like closure."

"Jazz." I couldn't stop laughing. "Thanks, but I was only playing you.

I told him that I wasn't really upset.

"I like to see you smile. You should do that more often."

"That's because you're crazy. Shall I keep this for our next concert?" I asked, holding up the lighter again.

"If you like, but I'll see if we can make them a part of the ticket sales."

I laughed again. "Are you always that accommodating?"

"I try. Now do I get to know what's on your mind?"

"Would you stop with the questions? Let's go dance."

He smiled and looked away. I still felt anxious, wound up to the edge, and I didn't know why.

"You really want to dance?" he asked.

"Sure."

Dancing cheek to cheek with Jazz calmed me. It felt good being that close to him, his warm skin and toned muscles touching me. He started to hum a Dave Hollister tune in my ear.

I stepped in and slid my chin over his shoulder, drawing him even closer. I shut my eyes momentarily, taking us someplace else where no one knew my truth and what I was feeling. I opened my eyes and blinked to readjust to the black lights, then scanned the room again while Jazz continued to serenade me.

Even in bad lighting, I recognized the brown eyes peering back at me. They were questioning, asking what was going on. Tyson was alone as far as I could tell. I thought he didn't even like hanging out here. Was he following me? I looked away first. The music stopped, and Jazz excused himself toward the bar. He wanted to acknowledge someone he knew.

I headed back to our table. Tyson jumped out of his seat and made a beeline to me before I reached it.

"CeCe, I see it hasn't taken you very long to move on. Are you making that a habit?" he asked sarcastically as I sat down. He sounded much like the old Tyson, before I experienced his intimacy and caring.

"Tyson, I'm really not in the mood for the insults tonight, okay?"

"I'm sorry. Guess that was uncalled for. But you have to understand how I feel, seeing you with someone else."

"How you feel was never in question, Tyson. It was what you wanted me to feel that was the problem."

"I wanted you to give me a little time, that's all."

"You wanted me to play second wheel."

"That's not true, and you know it. I would never play you like that."

"How can I be anything to you, when you're dealing with Tayla and a child?"

Before he could respond, Jazz joined us, then we had that awkward moment when no one knew quite what to say or who should speak first. We all just kind of stood there, three sets of eyes bouncing back and forth in a heated triangle.

I introduced Tyson to Jazz as my friend and vice versa. I could tell by Jazz's expression that he suspected it was more. They didn't shake hands but kind of bumped fists instead, like some kind of pre-war ritual. Men were funny that way sometimes. Jazz carefully examined my old territory, stared him down.

"CeCe, you know where to find me if you change your mind," Tyson said before he retreated.

"Friend, huh?" Jazz spoke up, not moving from his position.

"We know each other."

He had more questions—I saw that in his eyes—but he left it at that.

24

Jazz sent me roses the next day. Not the red velvety ones that you get on Valentine's Day to remind you of a lifeless relationship struggling for survival, but the vibrant yellow ones symbolizing a brand-new relationship full of hope. They were waiting for me on my desk, arranged in a bouquet of gilded splendor when Jackie and I returned from lunch.

"Someone's been naughty," she teased, reaching for the card.

"What?" I grabbed it to check it myself. I'd already guessed who sent them.

"Tyson?"

"I don't think so." I told her the card had no name.

"Oh, the blues guy, then?"

"His name's Jazz."

"Jazz, Blues, Rock and Roll, whatever. Who cares? Your expression said you wanted them to be from Tyson."

"You are always on the right side of wrong. Tyson is history. Ancient history at that."

"Come on, Ce. This is me, Jackie, you're talking to. Girl, you're sprung on Similac baby."

"How can you say that?" I asked, laughing at her name for him.

"For one, you haven't hired another assistant."

"No one's qualified. I told you I need someone with an art background."

"And all fifteen people that I've sent up to see you in the last week don't come close, I assume. You know I hate to say it, but someone has to. You are fast approaching pathetic."

"Then don't say it because you have no idea what you're talking about anyway. I mean, me? CeCe Ross who left Jackson, Mississippi, a husband, a dog, two cars, and a house to start my life from scratch? And I did it all without the least sign of a meltdown. Now I'm going to let some twenty-something-year-old push me over the edge? Pleeeze."

"I hear what you're saying, but you don't have to convince me."

"So why did you bring it up?"

"Only because I love you like a sister, and I don't want you to get hung up on Tyson.

"I'm not even thinking that way, okay?"

"Well, just in case you are."

"Meaning?" I sighed and folded my arms. "Come on, spit it out. What's on your mind?"

"Well, since you pulled it out of me, Marco told me that Gena told him that Tayla, you know Tyson's—"

"I know."

"Whatever. Tayla told Gena that Tyson asked her to marry him." She stopped and caught her breath. "So you see, there had to be more to the story than Tyson led you to believe."

I took a deep one, too, then exhaled.

"Well, to you, Marco, Gena, Tayla, and Tyson, I do

appreciate y'all keeping me up to speed, but I fail to see how it affects me. Like I said before, Tyson is history."

"Fine. Then we have nothing to worry about," she said.

"We never did."

I waited until she left my office to examine my disappointment after hearing that kind of news about Tyson. Then my heart kind of parachuted to the pit of my stomach. It almost felt like that night I called Edmond and Ja'Nell answered my phone.

I dialed Jazz and thanked him for the roses. He sounded glad that I called, and so was I. We decided to meet at his place for dinner later that evening. I was more than excited to be alone with him in his territory for a change. It seemed the more time I spent with him, the less Tyson stayed on my mind. And like water dissolving a sugar cube, soon Tyson would be nothing more than a sweet memory.

I arrived at Jazz's place at around seven. He greeted me at the door wearing black denim shorts and a black wifebeater that simply stated "Music." He showed a little more skin, and that was an improvement.

The night was warm, so Jazz decided to grill dinner outside on his patio. I had made a stop at the neighborhood store on the way over and picked up a few items. Jazz grilled some lamb kabobs with vegetables and prepared steamed wild rice. We munched on a loaf of old Sicilian bread dipped in warm basil pesto while we waited for dinner, then we ate with the stars flickering overhead.

Afterward we cleared the table and moved back inside. I helped him wash and put away the few dishes. I thought Jazz's apartment suited him quite well as my gaze swept it over. It reflected all of what he was about and hadn't yet shared. Everything was made of a similar light-colored wood. African artwork on the walls and an animal-print rug retained the African theme throughout. He owned lots of books that were tightly jammed into a couple of bookcases in the living room. I suspected the dining room served a dual purpose with another bookcase filled to capacity near the window. In fact, he kept that which was important to him nearby between the living room and the dining room. A guitar that looked similar to the guitar George Benson played was in the corner. I wanted to ask Jazz if he played—of course, he probably wouldn't own it if he didn't—but I didn't pry. I didn't want him to feel obligated to play. I hated it when people put me on the spot that way.

Jazz dried the last plate and put that away. I went over to his dining table and admired it by running my hand across the top. "Is this somebody's talent?" I asked. I was fascinated with the craftsmanship. The table had been stained and updated with a bamboo base. He walked up behind me with two glasses of wine. He was close but didn't touch. "Just a piece of my handiwork," he said over my shoulder.

"It's lovely," I told him.

He walked into the living room and set the glasses on the coffee table. I followed. He grabbed a few large, pillows and threw them on the floor around the fireplace. A fluffy flokati rug was underneath those. Instead of a fire, he dimmed the lights and lit an array of aromatherapy candles. Soft music was playing on his stereo. We took off our shoes, then he led me over to the rug where I sat down with both legs tucked underneath me. He sat close and pulled his knees into his chest. He pulled out his CD collection and started to harp on that. I had never doubted that music was his life and love. It showed in the way his face lit up when a particular song came on.

"You like that one?" He was referring to *Fourplay* by 24/7.

"Mmm, that's nice. It's sounds more inspirational though than jazz."

"Yeah. Can you actually close your eyes and feel the sax? Now that's music." He propped himself up on one elbow and got that twinkle in his eyes. "I mean it's one thing to sing what you've experienced, but you have to feel it while you sing. That's the way of the true innovators, like what Marvin did, like what Stevie is still doing today."

"There are a few up-and-comings who are pretty good, don't you think?"

"I agree. They do add their own flavor. Maybe Jill Scott or Alicia Keys. Musiq and Tony Hamilton on the male side. I like that they go for truth in music and feelings as opposed to what just sounds hip."

"You are so deep when it comes to music, aren't you?"

He laughed. "I do get carried away sometimes, I guess. Been that way for as long as I can remember."

"I suppose we all need a passion in life, have to make our time worthwhile."

"So what's yours?"

"Having something that I can feel. A love that I can feel."

He moved in closer. His kisses were slow and careful at first, then stronger. He took my lips into his, nibbling like he was sampling something good.

"Did you feel that?" he whispered gently in my ear. Tag. It was my turn to sample his.

I let him lower me down onto the soft rug. He played

it safe, traveling only the distance that I would allow.
He followed where I led, then I broke my own rules and
tried to take him farther down my path. We were going
beyond my own limitations. That's when he stopped
me.

"What's wrong?" I asked. He sat up and ended the
mood. I sat up and faced him.

"I don't think you're ready for this," he said.

"Ready? What do you mean?"

"To go get to where we were just headed."

"And you're making that assumption based on what?
We were just enjoying each other."

"I get the feeling that I'm enjoying you, but you on
the other hand are someplace else."

"Don't tell me how I feel, okay?"

"That's just it. I can because I feel you. Your vibes.
And they're telling me that you're trying to substitute me
for someone else."

"I don't get you, Jazz. I mean, the wine, dinner, and
music, and now there's a problem. What's the real reason
you stopped? You have something to tell me too. Let
me guess: you're married, engaged, or there's a baby out
there somewhere. Believe me, I've heard it all."

"You must be referring to Tyson, not me, right?"

"What does Tyson have to do with this? I told you
we're just friends. He worked for me once, that's it."

"It was more than friendship, CeCe. And as far as he's
concerned, it still is."

"So you've talked to Tyson? Behind my back, no
doubt." He started to answer but I threw up my hand
to stop him. "You don't have to answer. Why didn't you
ask me if you were confused about something instead of
sneaking around with Tyson, comparing notes?"

"Why are you using me to get next to him?"

"Is that what he said? And you believed him? You know, Jazz, I am so beyond Tyson."

"Are you? Really?"

I stared straight into his big brown eyes. I wanted to push him back down on that wool heap and show him just how over Tyson I was, but there was that shade of doubt that stopped him in the first place. I turned away then turned back to him before I stood. He stood too.

"You know, Jazz, since you rely so heavily upon Tyson as a prime source of information about me, why don't you go ask him."

I had purse in hand and bolted for the front door before he could stop me, giving it a healthy slam. I left him the same as two other men in my life, confused and calling out my name.

• • •

"Now what's gotten you so wound up that you had to drag me out at this hour?" Jackie asked. I had called her up as soon as I got home and she had rushed right over.

"Jazz," I said.

"What about Jazz?" she asked.

"I can't believe him."

"Believe what?" she asked impatiently.

"He and Tyson," I informed her.

"They got a thing?" Jackie asked with a much-too-serious look on her face.

"No, silly."

"Look, back up. Start at the beginning because you're not making sense."

"Jazz invited me to his place for dinner tonight. Things really started to get nice."

"And?"

"He had to ruin it by bringing up Tyson."

"He knows Tyson?"

"Yeah. Kinda. I introduced them at the Red Cat."

"Why on earth would you do a thing like that? Are you crazy?"

"It just kind of happened. Tyson forced himself into the situation, quite honestly."

"So they met. What does that have to do with tonight? Is Tyson stalking you?"

"No. Jazz is convinced that I'm in love with Tyson. It sounded like he and Tyson ended up at the Red Cat together and I became the topic of their conversation."

"Like they compared notes, huh?" She laughed.

"That's not funny, Jackie."

"I just don't see why you're so upset. Let them have their say. You know how men are. They like to compare their tools."

"If I find out that they sat in the Red Cat and discussed me over drinks, like yesterday's headlines," I said slinging throw pillows across the room as Jackie sat laughing at me. "I said, it's not funny. I'm dead serious. That's one act away from betrayal."

"Sorry, but you don't even know for that they even talked. Look, maybe Jazz threw in Tyson's name to confirm his competition."

"So, he could have just asked me."

"It's no more than what we girls do."

"We don't go seeking out their past and have lunch to compare notes on them. At least I wouldn't."

"Maybe not. We just do it in a more spiteful, bitchy way. So every now and then men turn the tables. Don't hate."

"So now you're taking sides with them?"

"There aren't any sides here, Ce, and if there was a conversation, how do you know it was mutual? Don't you think Tyson might have initiated it?"

"I—" The phone cut me off. Jackie checked the caller ID for me.

"It's you-know-who."

"I don't want to talk to Jazz." I let it ring a few more times before it stopped.

"You're going to have to talk to him sooner or later, you know."

"I know, but the later, the better."

"Well, since you dragged me over here, are we gonna watch a movie or what? You know *Claudine* is on TV tonight."

"*Claudine?* I haven't seen that in years."

"Well you need to. If your ass don't straighten up, you're going to end up just like that—six kids and a garbage man."

"Forget you," I said, clicking on the TV. Jackie got up and found some Pop Secret and nuked that in the microwave. She came back a few minutes later with a big bowl of it and two Cokes. The movie was starting when her cell phone rang.

"Shit. Not right when the movie's about to start," she said checking her cell.

"You know you curse too much."

She stuck out her tongue at me as she answered her phone. "Hello... Yes... Can I take a rain check? I'm at my friend's house right now. She's having a kind of rough time, so I'm going to hang out with her for a while. I'll call you later...Me too. Bye."

I was giving her a look when she hung up.

"What?"

"I don't believe you. You come over here and tell me I'm overreacting, that I shouldn't let men get me all worked up, and look at you. You hypocrite. You're just as vulnerable as the rest of us."

"So, my man ain't trippin'. Why should I punish him? You know what your real problem is? You need to stop dating men who travel in the same circle."

"Heifer," I said.

"Shut up and watch the movie," she returned.

My cell rang. I had thought of turning it off until the movie ended.

"You want me to get that, Ce?" Jackie asked.

"No," I said and grabbed the phone from the table to check caller ID. "I don't recognize this number, I said. "Hello."

"I missed Jazz at the Red Cat tonight." It was some female clearly trying to disguise her voice.

"What?"

"Jazz Rollins, he wasn't at the club tonight."

"Who is this?"

"Here's the deal, bitch. You stay away from Tyson and I don't make a play for Jazz, understand?"

"How did you get my number, Tayla?"

"Don't worry. Just remember what I said. And as easy as it was to get your phone number, it'll be just as easy to get a lot more."

I pressed the end call button, shaken.

25

The wings of serendipity had tilted in Jazz's favor to find me, so I was hoping to piggyback on that same luck when I pulled up in front of his favorite hangout, The Red Cat Jazz Cafe.

I was a bit nervous about being on Jazz's playing field again. He was seated in his favorite spot at the bar. I walked up behind him, not sure of how I should get his attention. I almost tapped him lightly on the shoulder, but then I decided to take my chance and slide in the seat right beside him. He turned, looking a little surprised to see me.

"CeCe? What are you doing here?"

"Looking for you. Surprised?"

"Not that you're here. Just the fact that you're sitting next to me."

"Well, I figured coming here was my only way of catching up with you."

"I called you last night. You didn't answer," he said.

"Why didn't you call back?"

"Why didn't you call me? You stormed out. Actually, I had planned to call again tonight, so I guess you saved me a few minutes on my calling plan."

I looked down at my hands, fidgeting with my invisible wedding band, then I looked back at him.

"Can we talk?" I asked him. "That is if you're not waiting for someone."

"Actually, why don't we get a table? It's more private."

He took his drink, and I followed. He pulled out the chair for me.

"So how are things at the station?" I asked.

"The station is fine, CeCe. We're past having to make small talk. I think we both know where we left things." He anticipated where I was going. Jazz didn't like to dance around the truth.

"Yes. I think you were fast accusing me of something that had no merit."

"Even if it came straight from the horse's mouth? Or should I say your boyfriend's?"

"He isn't my boyfriend. And more importantly, what right did you have to go around investigating my past?"

"I didn't. He came to me."

"Who came to whom is really beside the point. You should have come to me if you had doubts."

"And what would you have done? Denied your feelings for this cat or confirmed it as the truth?"

"There's nothing to deny."

"I know. You're just friends, right?"

"Right."

"But he thinks differently. I wonder why."

"Look, Jazz, I don't know exactly why I have to explain myself any more than I have. Maybe Tyson and you should be having this conversation."

He laughed and shook his head.

"You don't have to explain," he said. "You know why?"
He looked up at me, but he didn't want me to answer. "I'll
tell you why, because I've been through enough of these
triangles of me, she, and he to write my own stage play
and shit. When I'm trying to get to know someone, it's a
turnoff to have to wait in line, you know. I'm not down
with that, I thought you knew."

"I wouldn't play you that way, Jazz. Look, is Tyson
here with me now? What more proof do you need?"

"So you can look me in the face and tell me you no
longer have any feelings for this guy?"

"In what way?"

"Don't avoid the question. You know damn well what
I mean. Are you in love with him?"

I couldn't respond. Even though I knew the answer
was a simple no, I didn't feel I needed to say it in order
to satisfy Jazz.

"I take your silence as a yes."

"Does it matter how I feel, when I know Tyson and
I can't work?"

He looked at me, about to respond, but his words
were drowned out as the music started. He swallowed
hard, then wrinkled his forehead. I couldn't tell if he was
more frustrated by the music or me.

"Can we take a drive someplace?" He raised his voice
over the music. I looked around, suddenly uncertain.

"Don't worry. It's not far, and I'll have you safely
back to get your car before closing."

Jazz drove. His ride was a black Hummer H2,
somewhat reflective of what he was made of: strength
with fundamentalism. We got on the 610 and headed
north toward Richmond, and my condo, though he didn't
know exactly where I lived. He was quiet—too quiet,
matter of fact. There was no music, no conversation on

the way, just the whining friction of his monster truck tires against asphalt and the drone of his Hummer's engine. We took the Galleria exit. Surely he wasn't taking me shopping, I thought as he maneuvered through the lot and parked. He got out, and I did the same. We walked toward the south end of the mall. I heard the sound of falling water just ahead. We went a little farther to a small park where there was a lighted fountain. It was beautiful, and I told him so in all honesty.

"I love coming here. The water helps me to think," he said.

"You feel comfortable sharing this with me?"

"Actually, I brought you here to push you in." He grabbed me from behind and faked sending me headlong into the water. His playfulness made me giggle.

"Would that make you feel better?" I asked after he released me.

"Maybe," he said, staring off into the water.

"Then go ahead, feel better."

"Then can we go back to where we were, before Tyson?"

"Is that what you want?" I asked.

"That would satisfy that part of me that doesn't want to end up feeling like a fool," he said.

"I see. It's all good as long as you don't look foolish?"

"Let's just say I know the feeling, and it's not a good one."

"What happened?"

"What always happens when you take your heart out and lay it on a shelf too soon. And this...this particular sista took it, twisted it and gave it back torn and crumpled. She laughed in my face."

"I'm not that sista, Jazz."

"But you're a wonderful woman, and I can react just as fast as I did before."

"But is it fair to judge me by what someone else did?"

"Is it?"

"I'm asking you. You made the comparison."

"Let's just drop it, okay?" He gave me that irritated look again.

"Consider it dropped—like it's hot." I gave him some Tyson parody.

He smiled. "I really should push you in, you know that." This time he faked a fist to my shoulder. I flinched and we both smiled. He turned and looked back toward the fountain, then glanced at me.

"You look cold," he said after a while. "I'll take you back to the club."

"I'm okay."

"CeCe, can I be honest with you, here, right now?"

"I wish you would."

"I really like spending time with you. I want to get to know you, but deep down, I feel something or someone is holding you back. I know about your divorce, and I'm cool with that, but this Tyson cat is fresh on your mind, and I won't try to compete with him."

"So, what are you telling me? You don't want to see me anymore?"

"What I'm saying is that I think you need some time away from our situation."

"And since you're doing all this thinking, how much time do I need?"

"I've got to go to LA for a station promo at an awards show for about two weeks. Now I know that's not giving you a hell of a lot of time, but when I get back, I'd like to know where we stand."

"You can't give me an ultimatum like that."

"You need to be true to your heart, CeCe. It's all or nothing. That's how I deal."

We drove back to the club in the same cloud of silence as on the way over, with as little resolved as before. I stared out of the window for most of the way. Jazz clicked on the radio then clicked it off again. He thought he'd read my feelings about Tyson like he was psychic, and for that I felt anger toward him.

"Remember, CeCe," he said, gently pulling me back by my arm as I opened his passenger door to step out, "two weeks. Either I get an answer from you, or I'm the one who's history."

"Good night, Jazz."

I walked away from his Hummer without looking back. I didn't hear him drive away, and I knew he was sitting there watching me. Maybe for the last time.

26

"CeCe, where are you?" Jackie yelled through her cellular. There was loud music in the background, so I figured she must already be at the Red Cat.

"Still home," I replied.

"Home?" she asked. "Why are you still at home?"

"Jackie, I don't know if I can make it. I don't really feel up to it."

"Come on. It's Friday. We're all here waiting. Pleezzzeeee!"

"Alright." I gave in reluctantly.

Jackie, Marco, and Gena were all waiting at the club. I just wasn't feeling the place anymore. I knew everyone had to have his or her own coming-of-age place. In high school, Tracee and I had the Den; in college, it was Actions. The Red Cat was Jackie's, Marco's, and Jazz's, not mine. I finally agreed because I didn't feel like being alone.

I ran about thirty minutes late. I stood peering around the club until Jackie raised her hand from our usual corner table, and I went over.

"Sorry, I'm late."

"You're always late." That was Marco.

"Hi Gena," I replied, ignoring him.

"Oh, it's like that, huh?"

"It's like that, Marco."

"Hey, we ordered some appetizers, if that's okay with you," Jackie said.

"Absolutely," I said, looking around nervously.

"Don't worry, neither Tyson nor Jazz is here. I already checked," Jackie whispered in my ear.

"That's not why I was looking."

"Right."

Marco made a face and whispered something to Gena before he jetted off to the bar. Jackie leaned over to Gena and started asking her about wedding plans. I sighed. That was the one thing I'd hoped we wouldn't talk about so soon after my divorce.

I checked the faces in the crowd for my own satisfaction. I was leaning toward the small chance of seeing Jazz more than Tyson. Maybe Jazz was still in town. Even so, he was definitely going to give me the space he thought I needed.

I must have focused too long at a table across the way when pure evilness stared back at me. I was used to the behavior of envious women. I dubbed this one Evil Lee the way she eyed me and took out her Mac compact. She applied more lipstick to her already colorful lips. I looked away. Gena noticed the women and waved. Evil Lee stood and headed our way. She actually thought she was moving slow and sensuous in her too-tight, revealing dress, but she just looked more physically impaired than anything. She had blond-streaked hair and too much make up and held her small breasts out when she walked, like she was pushing a heavy load.

"Hey, Gena girl."

"Hey roomie. Jackie, CeCe, this is my roommate—soon-to-be ex-roommate—Tayla."

Shit. Tyson's woman, right here in my face.

"Tayla, Jackie and CeCe," Gena said, pointing each of us out.

"Oh, you're CeCe. Well, I guess we have something in common," Tayla said. She knew darn well who I was, cell number and all. She was going to rub Tyson in my face.

"In common?" I asked, playing her stupid.

"Yeah. My man Tyson used to work for you."

"Oh, so you're Tyson's girl."

"Well, fiancée now. I still have to get used to that."

I quickly checked out her finger. No ring. She stared at me long and cold as if to send a message that she had pussy power, but only because I hadn't put up a fight. If I had, Tyson would be sitting on the other side of that table with me while she struggled with weight gain and swollen ankles.

I didn't comment on her remark. Jackie tapped my foot underneath the table. Tayla gave a quipped "see ya later, Gena" and went back to her friend—high yellow complected with red hair, the lesser of the two evils probably—slid a tall glass of what appeared to be wine closer to Tayla.

"Should your roommate be drinking?" I turned to Gena and asked. "Maybe you should tell her it isn't good for the baby."

Gena gave me a confused look then blinked a few times. "Baby? What baby?"

"Isn't she pregnant?"

"Pregnant? Where did you hear that? Tayla is too selfish for a baby."

"I thought Tyson mentioned that she was, but maybe I misunderstood." I turned and looked over at Tayla. I was giving her the power stare that time, only my victory wasn't coming from quite so low.

• • •

Stars, horoscopes, zodiac signs, incense, lunar, cislunar, translunar—all those things would have made sense to me if I had been the least bit cosmic. Then, I would have noticed on the drive home from the Red Cat that the stars weren't in sync. Jupiter wasn't aligned with Mars. My world was about to split into three equal parts.

I was still vexed from meeting Tayla. If I didn't know better, I would have accused Tyson of purposely having her to show up just to rub their impending parenthood in my face, but I didn't think he would play me that way. And what was there to be jealous of? And what about Gena's admission that Tayla wasn't even pregnant? Tayla was trifling enough to play Tyson that way. But this was Tyson's fight, of which I wanted no part. Besides, in less than two weeks Jazz would be back and in my life again. By then I would have worked Tyson out of my system like a flu virus.

My cell phone chimed in with Chopin's "Chopsticks.' I checked caller ID and recognized Jackie's number. I pulled the retractable earpiece up to my ear and click the talk button on the illuminated dial.

"Yeah, Jackie, what's up?"

"Do you believe the nerve of that heffa?"

"Just staking her claim, I suppose."

"Staking her claim? That wench knew damn well what she was doing. And she knew exactly who you were. She just wanted to get a reaction from you up close."

"Well, if she thought she was going to get one from me—"

"You should have slapped that tight-ass dress right off her, baby or no baby. And you heard it straight from

Gena that there's a greater chance of the latter. Can you believe her?"

"I believe if women are desperate enough, they'll try just about anything to keep what they want."

"How could Tyson not know?"

"Maybe it's true what they say, you know, about love being blind."

"But you know if she's lying, and there's no baby, he'll have to find out sooner rather than later. Why not speed up the process and tell him yourself?"

"I won't do that, Jackie. If he has to find out, it shouldn't be from me."

"You're just afraid."

"Of what?" I asked.

"You know the first thing Tyson will do is run back to your doorstep." Jackie replied.

"But according to you; isn't that what I want?" I reminded her.

"You don't know what you want, CeCe. That's the problem."

"The problem is that I play fair."

"Fair? There's no fairness if you want to win. Baby girl, let me school you."

"I can hardly wait," I said, chuckling.

"No, I'm serious. There's this saying that nothing improves a man's luck like fish that are in a biting mood," Jackie said.

"Meaning?"

"Men like competition, and they like options. You have to give them something to think about," she said.

"Jackie, I'm not about to get out there and fight for Tyson. Now, I refused to do that for Edmond and I was married to him."

"And that got you divorced. It's not about fighting,

honey. It's about letting your feelings be known. How is a man supposed to automatically know what you're thinking?"

"I'll take what you're saying into consideration. Look, I have to hang up. I have to run into the supermarket for a sec."

"Just think about what I said. Maybe if all fails, Tyson being a part-time daddy may not be so bad for you after all."

"But that would also make him a part-time lover, and me back to being a part-time fool. That, my mama didn't raise."

27

I was putting the last of my groceries away when my mother called. I knew she would after she had beeped me in the middle of the supermarket and I had ignored her rings. I was too busy taking my stress-free living to another level by trying to decide if the low-carb chips would taste better than the regular. Besides, I was still debating whether to call Tyson and tell him about my phone call from Tayla and her possibly stalking me at the Red Cat.

Mom's voice sounded urgent, and anytime I heard from my parents on a weekday was extremely rare, especially since they lived by their service plan's weekend rates. Maybe my father's stubbornness to get an annual checkup like men his age, especially black men, had finally caught up with him.

"CeCe, have you lost your mind?" Mom always stated the worst of what she felt was obviously wrong with me first so that any other excuses I gave would be an improvement.

"What are you talking about?" I answered innocently.

"Girl, don't play games with me. You know full well

what I'm talking about. I ran into Edmond's mother here in Atlanta at the Woman Thou Art Loosed conference. I had to find out from her that you and Edmond are divorced. She also told me that he might be shackin' up with his secretary."

"Is that all, Mom? And I don't think they call it shackin' anymore. It's just living together."

"Don't get flip with me, Celia Ross or whatever you're calling yourself now. Why did you lie to me and your father?"

"I didn't lie. I just hadn't told you and Daddy yet because I knew how you would react."

"Probably because you know what you did was wrong and what some of us might consider downright sinful."

"And staying in a marriage when your husband is lying and cheating behind your back isn't?" She didn't respond to that right away.

"Edmond?" she finally asked, clearing her throat. "I had no idea."

"'Cause you never once asked me if I was happy, Mom. You just assumed I was."

"Honey, you know how things are. People just don't poke and pry into other folks' private lives, even if it is their own children's. I just thought that you would come to me if anything was ever wrong."

"And you would have told me to try and stick it out. And that was not what I needed to hear at the time."

"CeCe, I might have, but only because I don't want to see you throw your life away."

"I'm not. Being married to Edmond was not my entire life, Mom. We had some issues. I just did what I needed to do, and that was to move on."

"But baby, your marriage...You and Edmond just

seemed perfect. I don't want to see you rush into something you'll regret later."

"It's too late. We're divorced. I got the final divorce
papers a few weeks ago. Besides, Edmond didn't exactly
put up a fight."

" 'Cause you're both stubborn."

"Look, I know how you and Daddy feel about
Edmond. Don't get me wrong, I'm not painting him
to be a monster, but we just had some problems being
together."

"It's not just that. You're so far away and Houston
is so big. I mean, the news is just full of bad things that
go on there. Are you living in a decent area? What kind
of people are you hanging out with? You know you can
always move to Atlanta with us."

"Mom, Mom, please. I'm fine. I have a job in advertising
here, and I've met a good friend. And yes, I live in a nice
area. You and Daddy can come and see for yourselves."

"Well, alright. As long as you're taking care of
yourself."

"Believe me, I am."

"Are you dating again?"

"Why, Mom?"

"Because Edmond called."

"When?"

"After I talked to his mother."

"Well, what did he want exactly?"

"He wanted your new phone number. He has tried
calling but...you know you've changed the number to
your cell."

"Did you give it to him?"

"You hadn't told me not to. Besides, it's not as if you
had let me know what was really going on."

"What exactly did he say?"

"Why should you care? I thought you were finished with him."

"What did he say to you, Mom?"

"He said he would be out there soon, and he wanted to look you up."

"Coming here? Houston? How soon?"

"Why yes, in two weeks, he said. Houston is where you are, isn't it? What's really going on between you two? Did I do something wrong?"

"No, Mom. You did fine. I'll handle Edmond later."

"Okay, baby. Just remember you might not want to count Edmond out too soon."

"What do you mean?"

"Look, you're not exactly a spring chicken."

"I'm not old either. I'm only thirty-one."

"Thirty-two in a few months, and let's face it, you're not exactly brand new. Your parts are up for recycle."

We both broke out in hysterical laughter. That was my mother. She could be serious, but she was pretty cool at times, too, like my big sister.

"My parts are in mint condition, thank you, Mom."

"Yeah, but they got a few miles on them too. All jokes aside, dear. Even though you're divorce, and maybe feeling a little vulnerable, always remember that you don't have to let anyone play you cheap."

"I'll remember, Mom."

"We love you, dear."

"I love you too. And tell Daddy that for me."

The nerve of Edmond to call now, after he had served me with final divorce papers, when I hadn't heard from him since. The same night Tyson had been there to comfort me. Now Edmond thought he could just reenter my life because he happened to be in town. Did he think I actually wanted to see him again? And what type of business could he possibly have in Houston? He'd never even been there before as far as I knew. He probably had some document that required my signature, so I wouldn't be able to stake a claim later.

Regardless, Jazz was due back in town the same week as Edmond's visit. Maybe I would meet Jazz at the airport, and the two of us just jump in the Hummer and get away from the pressure of everything—Tyson, Edmond, and Houston period. Spend some quality time alone to get to know each other better. Jazz was the only person in my life who made sense. Maybe I could be there for him completely.

28

"CeCe, I think it's time that you made a decision once and for all."

I was in Gray Tapscott's upscale office on the fifth floor of the Templeton Building and he was giving me his overdue opinion about filling Tyson's position. Tyson had been gone for three weeks, and Gray didn't want to waste any more time getting a replacement. I looked around his office. His furnishing had changed since I'd interviewed months before. He was seated behind a huge, circular, glass-top desk with a chrome ball-shaped base. His office was quite powerful looking. The only powerful thing, Gray wasn't that type at all. He was a five-feet-eight, emasculate, slender man with a reputation for hating two things: firing employees for any reason and office romance.

Gray was staring out of his huge glare-proof window. He had a view of a large portion of downtown. From the right angle, he could even see Minute Maid Park where the Astros played their home games. He had taken his glasses off, put them on again, folded his arms, and rubbed his chin during my spiel about which qualifications I preferred in the person I chose to replace Tyson. He looked around his office—things he'd seen a thousand times before—just to avoid eye contact. His body language suggested he wasn't buying my sale. He knew better than anyone that juggling two jobs wasn't getting it and that I was falling behind.

"Besides," Gray said, removing his Polo frame glasses again, "if we continue to contract the graphics service we'll end up paying double the salary for a full-time employee."

"I know. You're right. I've gone over the applications again and again. Quite frankly, they're not the best. Not one meets my prerequisites."

"So have I, and personally I think Harold Hobbs is the better of the picks. Now I agree, he's no gem."

"More like a lump of coal, wouldn't you say?"

"Even so, look what happens to coal when you add a little pressure."

We both laughed.

"Didn't Harold come off a bit strange in the interview to you?" I asked.

"I think you're stalling, CeCe."

"Why would I stall, Gray?"

"CeCe, look." He turned and placed one elbow on his desk then leaned forward. "I don't pay attention to the rumor mill around here, and I certainly don't judge, but let me just say that I think Tyson's leaving was the best thing."

"I don't get what you're saying. Leaving was Tyson's decision, not mine."

"I know, and that's just it. I'm saying that we do have certain policies in place for good reason."

"Policies? Are you insinuating that Tyson and my relationship at work wasn't professional?"

"That's not what I'm saying. As I stated before, the rumor mill has its way of working overtime."

"Do you think about the rumors?"

"I'm not in a position to judge."

"But you brought it up. You must have an opinion."

"Only because...CeCe, look. Do you know why we have a fraternization policy in the first place?"

"Productivity?"

"No." He chuckled. "I mean the history of why it came about?"

"I'm afraid not."

"Well," he said, getting up to stand near the window. He had put his glasses back on and stuffed his hands inside his pants pockets. "Jokes around here will sometimes, refer to it as Tapscott's Law."

"After you?"

"No. My father. He was the employee having the affair with his secretary, and my mother was the gun-welding vigilante."

"Wow. I had no idea. That must have been hard for you."

"I got through it. I guess I remember it more than anyone around here will admit they do. For the most part, I don't think anyone brings it up much." I thought of Jackie telling me the story only a few weeks earlier. "But my point is—and again I'm not judging—I just want you to be careful. You're good, and sometimes personal feelings get caught up in you trying to do the right thing."

"I appreciate that, but I can assure you personal feelings have nothing to do with the decisions I make around here. I'll call Harold Hobbs. He said he was available, so maybe he can start right away."

I got up to leave.

"And CeCe?"

"Yes, Gray?"

"I think Tyson's leaving was for the best."

"But you didn't feel that way a few months ago when I was hired, and you thought he was leaving."

"Situations do change, you know."

"Let me just say that I had nothing to do with his decision to resign."

"Of course. You would have never asked him to leave. Not even if I'd told you that he wasn't being loyal to you."

"What do you mean?"

"Tyson came to me the morning of his resignation and tried to take full credit for the Mayfair's campaign."

"He did what? I asked, my anger rising. "But I gave you a full report earlier that same morning. We worked on it together."

"Easy, now, Gray said, amusingly." He gave me a few to calm down before going on. "CeCe, I knew that. Why do you think I never mentioned it until now. I figured proving himself as more competent than you, was Tyson's last bargaining chip. Look, don't take me telling you this the wrong way. I just want you to know that sometimes we need protecting from the ones we protect. That's the brutality of business."

"You think I may not be cut out for this firm, don't you?"

"You'll do just fine. As I said before, I think Tyson's leaving was a smart decision, whosever idea it was," he said and winked. "I would hate to lose you."

• • •

From what I remembered from Harold Hobbs's interview, he was a thirty-year-old, sweaty guy with a small waistline, broad hips, and a C-cup chest. Unfortunately, he was the better of the three candidates. Since Gray had

already disclosed his suspicions, about Tyson and me, I
didn't want him to get the idea that I was holding out in
hope that Tyson would return. Not that it would happen
since I'd also learned that Tyson had tried to stab me in
the back, big time.

Harold was about fifteen minutes late on his first day.
He was also a hypochondriac. He must have been allergic
to punctuality because he was also late the next two
mornings. It didn't take me long to peep his daily routine
either. That included him rushing in, sweating profusely
like he'd sprung a leak, then he would go into this Jerry
Seinfeld type monologue, detailing the circumstances that
made him late. It would begin with, "You're not gonna
believe what happened to me...." Sometimes he sent
his excuses by e-mail. The computer was one thing he
progressed on quite rapidly. In fact, he thought it was the
only part of his job, even if I hadn't had the opportunity
to brief him on any assignments. I figured as long as what
he did included the computer he would be employee of
the month in no time. Plus, for some strange reason, I
didn't think he was going to last that long.

By day four, I decided to drop in on his action. After
a cup of caffeine, he had gone straight to his computer.
I knew he would remain there until the end of the day.
His mouse started clicking within a few minutes. What
was he doing, personal stuff? I hoped he didn't think he
was hired to free-lance.

I went up to Tyson's old office door and gave it a
gentle tap. I waited for silence then to be invited in. It
surprised me that Harold had the door locked, and it took
a few seconds to open it. The office was exceptionally
warm when I stepped in, but Harold had mentioned that
the air conditioner made him congested. Maybe that's
why he'd turned it off. His thin white cotton shirt was

plastered to his back and armpits. He wasn't wearing anything underneath. Tiny beads of sweat were lined across his upper lip. His eyes looked glassy.

"I really don't know how you function in such a warm office," I said as I drew closer to his desk.

"Believe me, sista, if you had been in and out of the doctor's office with as many flu symptoms as me, you would understand why I keep that baby at eighty degrees no matter what," he replied, nodding at the thermostat.

"Alright." Then a sour smell engulfed me, doing the salsa with my senses. "And also you might want to get housekeeping to clean this office out. I think the last guy may have left some spoiled food lying around." That cover came quickly. I had made it a point to have housekeeping come up the day after Tyson left to clean out any trace of him.

"And, Harold for future reference, please don't call me *sista* or *boss lady,* that bothers the hell out of me. "CeCe" will do just fine."

I had cut my conversation with him shorter than I had intended and left his office gagging. Maybe I would have Gray talked to him, man to man about his hygiene.

I brought up Harold's odd behavior to Jackie later during lunch.

"He seemed fine when he interviewed with me. I mean a lot of people sweat in interviews because they're nervous. Maybe he has a gland problem," Jackie joked.

"I think I have more than a gland problem on my hand. He locks himself in his office like he's working for the CIA or something. He might be doing something weird."

"Weird like what?"

"Porn, internet gambling, drugs," I threw out.

"My dear, you might be overreacting. Are you sure it isn't so much Harold as it is something else?"

"What?"

"He's not Tyson."

"Don't go there, please."

"Alright. Then, I won't bring up the fact that it took forever to even hire Harold."

"Can we change the subject?"

"Okay. You heard from Jazz?"

"Briefly. You know, I think he's taking this ultimatum thing to the limit."

"How so?"

"He called me from LA, right, then he leaves this generic message on my voice mail. Says he's okay, hopes everything is going alright with me, and that he'll call later on with his flight itinerary. But he adds, 'just in case you're still interested.'"

"Sounds to me like he's not going to pressure you."

"That's cool, but he's acting like I'm the one who wrote him off."

"Jazz sounds like a sensible guy. He wants you to be sure of what you want. I would call that considering your feelings."

"I suppose you're right."

"Speaking of feelings, look who just walked in," she said and nodded at the entrance. Tyson was standing there. He headed toward our table.

"Oh no," I mumbled.

"Well you deal with your little bit of pressure, and I'll tell the waitress to prepare my lunch to go. I'll see you back at work unless you need me to stick around," Jackie said.

"No, I'll be fine. I'll see you later."

Jackie got up to leave.

"Hi, Jackie. Look, you don't have to leave. Just wanted to say hello."

"What's up, Tyson?" she returned. "No, I need to get back. Good seeing you though."

Tyson nodded and waited until Jackie was out of hearing range before he spoke. "You mind?" he asked, sitting before I could answer.

"I only have a minute, Tyson."

"How have you been, CeCe?"

"How do you think?"

"I miss you."

"I'm sorry."

"You don't miss me?"

"I haven't really thought about it much."

"That's because you don't allow yourself to."

"Don't tell me what I should allow myself to do."

"Why are you so angry with me?"

"Why are you and your girlfriend in my life?"

"What do you mean?"

"Tayla. She called me, Tyson. She threatened me."

"Threatened you?"

I shot him a cold look. He rolled his eyes and didn't answer, then picked up my glass of water and drank from it. He had developed a habit of sharing my food and drink.

"Look, I'll take care of her. She's a psycho."

"You said you would take care of it before, Tyson."

"Look, I said I will."

Silence. Then I wanted to tell him that Tayla had lied about being pregnant. But then I decided Tyson needed to handle his own business. I might regret it later if I interfered.

"Can I see you tonight? Dinner? Somewhere we can talk in private?"

"Is Tayla in your life?"

"CeCe, you know the situation hasn't changed."

"Then we have nothing to talk about."

"We do." He leaned closer, staring directly into my eyes. "CeCe, I don't want to lose what we have."

"You can't have it both ways."

"Don't make this harder for me than it already is," he pleaded.

"Nothing has to be harder than it is. You made it that way, didn't you? I'll tell you what, Tyson, if you want to be with me, leave Tayla. I mean, be there for her having your baby and by all means, support your baby, but be with me. Leave her and be with me."

"CeCe, you know things aren't that simple."

"But your game sure is." I threw up my hands to stop him when he started to speak. "Relax, you're safe. I have no intention of disturbing your little playhouse with Tayla. You see, unlike you, Tyson, I'm strong. I can walk away from unpleasant and difficult situations. Here, let me show you how it's done."

29

Not being able to shake Tyson out of my life bothered me. I was back at work, sitting at my desk wondering why my feelings for him were anything other than angry. And why hadn't I brought up the fact that I knew he had tried to sabotage my job? Schooling him of that alone was enough to send him packing for good.

It had to be his shampooing skills. The memory stirred a warm feeling inside me like Mom's southern recipe for teacakes. It had me flipping through the yellow pages, reminded that I needed to get my hair done. I put Jackie's stylist on reserve for later and ran my finger down to "B" for beauty salons instead, tried to figure out which shops might have male hairstylists. I needed to know if Tyson had his own magic or if it was something every man possessed. I dialed salon after salon, looking for Tyson's competitor.

"I'm looking for a male stylist," I said in a low, suspicious, almost borderline perverted voice.

"Excuse me?" the female said on the other end.

"You are a beauty salon, aren't you?"

"Yes, but—"

"Then, I want to make an appointment, but I prefer that it's with a male stylist."

"Sure, ah, yes that would be with André. He has an opening today at two-thirty, as a matter of fact. What will you need done?"

"Just a shampoo. And two-thirty is fine." I hung up, then wondered if I should have requested more. Was just a shampoo being too obvious?

I arrived at *Ahead of the Rest* around two-twenty. I asked for André and waited at the receptionist area. The desk looked as though it wasn't being used and was covered with two inches of dust, old magazines, paper, order forms, take-out menus, and business cards. The chair had boxes of products; some had been opened and placed out on the desk. A few other boxes were still sealed and marked *Return,* in red letters. There were several candy jars, most of which were empty. I looked back and forth between three stylists waiting for one to acknowledge me. One finally looked my way and paused from her customer's hair, which she was hot curling. She gave me a quick glance and yelled out André's name. I slid into a chair near the entrance and waited. I only hoped André was worth my time. I was just using him as a sub for Tyson anyway.

Minutes later, André switched directly up to me and proceeded to finger my hair without much of a hello.

"Okay, diva, how can I hook you up today?"

"Just a shampoo."

"Just a shampoo?" He swung a long, slender leg back ninety degrees behind him, eyes widened and threw a hand to his hip in disbelief.

"And you can clip the ends also. And…and maybe a lighter color if you have time," I stammered.

"Come on. Follow me."

I had to jog to keep up with him. I passed near the unfriendly stylist who had summoned André for me. She looked familiar—tall, reddish hair and high-yellow complexion. It was Tayla's friend. Of all the salons in Houston, I had to pick this one. She cut a set of mean eyes over at me; while talking on her cell through her earpiece. I looked down at her nameplate that read Tarsha.

I followed closely behind André until he stopped short and pointed to a vacant vinyl chair underneath a big black shampoo bowl against the wall. Once I was seated, he wrapped a plastic bib around my chest and tied it tightly behind my neck. I placed my purse on the floor between my feet, then picked it up. Mom said that was bad luck. André placed it on the counter for me. He started to move fast. I sat and watched as my black strands gradually changed to a lighter brown. Then, at record speed he adjusted the water temperature and rinsed the color out of my hair. His thin fingers were stiff and swift when he lathered the shampoo, not gentle or sensuous like Tyson's. I opened my eyes and looked at André's expressionless face. He wasn't caring that I wasn't enjoying this. The conditioning process went even faster. He rinsed, squeezed, and wrapped a towel around my head before sitting me up. Instead of my scalp feeling massaged and relaxed, I felt the onset of a steady itch. He clipped, dried, and styled then handed me a mirror for my approval.

"You work fast, André."

"Well, what did you expect, spa day?"

I gave him his charge plus a ten percent tip and thought maybe I should probably consult the rest of the alphabet in the yellow pages. Then again, maybe not. I guess ain't nothing like having the real thing.

● ● ●

I was sitting on the freeway in the middle of a

major traffic delay. My lunch run-in with Tyson plus the disappointment from the André experience had me so wound up until I was craving a cigarette when I didn't even smoke. I adjusted my rearview mirror so I could see myself. The sun streaming through my sunroof made my hair color much lighter than it had appeared back at the salon, but it was attractive on me. About time I did something daring. I wished I could change my feelings for Tyson that fast. He always made me feel like we had unfinished business.

The word *pressure* popped into my head. The opposite of what Jazz was. What Tyson was. What Edmond could be. In a few days I could be sitting on the opposite side of a table from Edmond and be persuaded to take him back into my life. What were the odds of that happening?

Probably the same as getting out of backed-up traffic within the next two hours, I thought, as I pulled out and rubbernecked my way up to the next exit. It was almost five o'clock, and I was starving. I needed something cold to drink.

The street looked familiar but I wasn't sure enough to turn left or right. My cell phone rang as I turned left. It was Tyson. He was unhappy about the way we left things that afternoon and wanted to meet. I agreed. I was too embarrassed to say that I was actually lost.

"Where are you?" he asked.

"Not real sure. I exited from 610 onto Shepherd. I took a left from there."

"Headed south?"

"Yeah, I think."

"I know where you are. There should be a Chili's coming up on your right, I think."

"Yeah, I see it."

"I'll meet you there in about ten, okay?"

"Ty—" He hung up before I could change my mind.

His black Acura pulled beside my car in a little less than ten minutes. I pretended I didn't see him right away.

"Hey," he said to get my attention.

I turned toward him.

"Hi."

"Look at you. You go and change your hair on me. I like."

"Thanks."

"You want to go in?" he asked, nodding at Chili's.

I got out of my car, and we walked in together. We got a table in back of the restaurant. It was still pretty empty. Guess everyone else was stalled in traffic.

The waiter brought over two glasses of water, then he left us to decide on our orders. My throat felt like sandpaper. I drank half of my water in one gulp.

"So, what made you change your mind so fast about seeing me?" Tyson asked.

"I haven't."

"Yet, you're here."

"I'm here, Tyson, but by default." I looked at him. His innocence made me want to renege on what I needed to tell him about Tayla's pregnancy. I looked away then back to him. "To be quite honest, I'm here simply because I'm tired, hungry, and I was lost."

He looked at me and wrinkled his forehead. "I'm confused. What exactly are you talking about?"

"Tyson, after today, I don't plan on seeing you ever again. At least not like this. It has to be over, and I don't like these hide-and-seek games. This is not the type of relationship I want to be involved in, and I don't want to lead you on."

"So is it Jazz? Did he win?"

"This was not a competition."

"Or is it your ex? Is that the reason he's in town next week?"

"And how would you know about that? Are you spying on me now?"

"Jackie told me. I ran into her near your place earlier today, and she let it slip that you were probably still out shopping for your big date with your ex. That means I should back off?"

"It's no secret Edmond will be in Houston."

"She also said maybe I shouldn't bother you and to give you some time. Am I a bother to you, CeCe?"

"I never said that, but backing off may not be a bad idea."

"What if I can't?"

"What if you don't have a choice?"

"I want you in my life, CeCe."

"As a friend. And that's all you can be."

"And love doesn't matter?" I didn't answer. Instead when the waiter interrupted us a second time for our order, I got mine to go. "What if I said love prevents me from being just a friend?"

"And Tayla?"

"Tayla has nothing to do with this."

"And the timing of my ex-husband's visit either I suppose."

"I would have said it regardless of the timing."

"So you love me, Tyson. Where does all of this love leave us?"

"What do you mean?"

"Again, what about—" I didn't say the last word since the image was already making her way towards us. Seeing her startled me to the point that Tyson saw it on my face and followed my stare. Tayla disappeared momentarily behind a thin partition that separated smokers from non-smokers. She reappeared to lock her angry eyes on us, then she rushed up to the table, like a pint-size nuisance of hot air. Tyson leaped up as if to ward off what he knew was inevitable.

"Tayla, what in the hell are you doing here?" Tyson asked through clenched teeth.

"Following your ass. And I should be asking you that same question."

"This is Ce—"

"I know who the bitch is."

"Tayla, this isn't what you think. I used to work for CeCe, and we were just—"

"About to fuck after dessert, I suppose," she said, substituting her own sick version to his reply.

"Look, don't make a scene. You're going to embarrass yourself more than me, okay," he said.

"Embarrass myself." She pointed her long fake nails toward her chest. "Shit," she said, looking away momentarily. "As if sneaking around with this bitch isn't embarrassing enough for you."

"I'll only tell you once about the language, Tayla. You don't own me, and you certainly don't tell me who I can associate with. Now, do you want to walk out of here or should I call the manager?"

"Look, Tyson, why don't I just leave you two alone to discuss whatever you need to?" I said.

"Yeah, why don't you do that, bitch."

I ignored Tayla and got up to leave.

"What is it with you anyway?" she hurled as I walked past her. "You can't find a man in your own league so you sexually harass your subordinates?"

I spun around, not thinking about what I did next. Hot blood had risen too far up into my brain. My hand automatically grabbed her from behind. My fingers aligned perfectly to her windpipe like Wynton placed his on the buttons of his trumpet. The sound that escaped from her mouth was more off key. If I squeezed just slightly, Tayla's rhythm would have been the choking kind.

"Ma'am, you can't do that in here." The manager broke my concentration. "I'm going to have to ask you to leave." He didn't want to be witness to what a woman who is fed up will resort to, what she can be pushed to do when losing her ripple effect can jar her common sense like a chemical imbalance.

"Don't worry. I was leaving anyway. I wouldn't think of leaving a mess like this for you to clean up," I replied. I released Tayla, but not without shoving her into a seat at the next table.

Tyson stepped between us in case I wasn't quite done. He looked from me to Tayla, then he followed me outside, pleading.

"Tyson, I don't need this. Go back inside to your future," I said.

"To hell with her. You don't understand."

"What I do understand is that I'm never going to place myself in a position like that again."

"Just let me follow you away from here, where we can talk."

"You know, Tyson, we always seem to end up this way."

"Like what?"

"Me walking away, and you yelling at my back about how you can fix everything. Well, I'm tired, and you can't fix this."

"What are you saying to me, CeCe?"

"Please leave me alone, and don't ever call me again. It's over, finished."

"You don't really mean that."

"Notice that I don't look back."

• • •

I was back on the jammed freeway, not only craving a cigarette, but feeling like chain smoking. I had come close to having a straight-up chick fight which hadn't happened since high school when this certain gang of girls who hated Tracee and me simply because we thought our shit didn't stink, decided to ambush us. Even then we had managed to walk away without a scratch because of Tracee's street smarts and fake rubber knife.

I wanted to hurt Tayla in the worst way. Not that I even knew whether I cared enough about Tyson to fight for him, but she had made me feel like the other woman. But Tyson hadn't said I was anything to him. I was an intruder struggling for a place in a game that Tayla was an expert at. She had secured it when Tyson thought she was carrying his child. She must have loved him more.

I dialed Jackie's number after I made it home. I almost wished that she didn't answer. I didn't feel like repeating the night's event, but I knew she would never forgive me if I didn't tell her what had gone down.

"No way. Girl, get out here. Are you alright?"

Then she started laughing so hard until I had to hold the receiver away from my ear. I gave it a cynical look as though she could actually see me through the phone. "You're kidding, right?" she finally said once the giggling stopped.

"Jackie, please. I'm calling for support. I can't believe what almost happened tonight."

"Wait a minute. Let me see if I got this right. The minister's daughter from Mississippi grabbed her by the neck? Sister, I definitely should have been there."

"It wasn't that exciting, believe me. More like pathetic."

I rubbed my temple, feeling anxious. "I didn't leave my marriage for this."

"So what did Tyson do?" Jackie wanted to know.

"Just kind of stood there," I said.

"He didn't take your side?"

"It wasn't about taking sides. Tayla just sort of appeared out of nowhere. Neither of us had time to react."

"Ce, what do you mean react? This isn't your problem. You shouldn't have to deal with Tayla."

"What can I do? Tayla has a habit of showing up wherever I am. I don't think it's Tyson's doing."

"Yeah, but knowing Mr. Sex Appeal, I bet he got off on having two women fight over him."

"No, Jackie. I really felt sorry for him. I thought living with Edmond was so terrible, imagine living with the likes of Tayla."

"Why feel sorry for Tyson? He made his own bed."

"We all make our own bed. But I can't help but think that I contributed to Tyson's problems. I should have been able to control my feelings and not lead him on."

"You were human just like the rest of us?"

"What am I going to do, Jackie?"

"What do you want to do, Sister."

"I thought I would find that out when I left Edmond. Now I'm starting to believe that happiness just isn't out there for me. Or am I asking too much?"

"I think—"

Just then my call waiting beeped, and I cut her off.

"Hold on a second. That's my line." I clicked over to answer. It was Tyson. I put him on hold and went back to Jackie.

"Still here," she quipped.

"I have to get this."

"Tyson?"

"No, it's my mother."

"Oh. You want to do breakfast in the morning?"

"Make it dinner. I have some planning to do. Tomorrow is Take Care of Harold day."

30

My plan was to catch Harold red-handed. I had a feeling he was viewing porno. What else would keep him occupied on his computer all day. It didn't matter, anything other than Templeton business was illegal in my book. But I needed to be able to walk right into his office without knocking. I stopped off at *Quik Mart* on my way to work and picked up some of that hard, pink bubblegum in the baseball pouch. I popped a handful in my mouth and chewed it on the way up in the elevator. I had managed to dodge anyone to whom I would have looked absolutely silly. Once in Harold's office, I placed the wad in the catch hole of the doorframe. I smoothed it in real good like I'd seen done in the spy movies. Harold would slam the door like he always did, but if my plan worked, he wouldn't notice when the lock didn't catch.

"Morning, Harold," I said cheerfully when he finally walked in. Harold came in early for the first time since he'd been hired. He had trimmed the usual fifteen minutes off his lateness.

"Morning, boss lady...I mean CeCe," he corrected

himself when I eyed him sternly. "It's been one of those mornings and take your pick of a story because you won't believe the one that happened to me. Let me get some caffeine, and I'll send it to you by e-mail because you have to see it on screen."

"Okay." I said. *Yeah, big boy. Get real comfy and fire up your machine.* Then I waited.

He disappeared into his office and slammed the door between us. There was a muffled bump. I cringed and waited for the door to bounce back open, but it didn't. He didn't notice that it didn't catch either. Silence. Then seconds later, his computer geared up. I breathed a sigh of relief. I gave him a few minutes to warm up, let his guard down and then—as we said in the eighties—cold-busted.

Fifteen minutes later, I actually felt a twinge of excitement as I got up from my desk and tiptoed over to Harold's door. I put my ear to its mahogany finish, careful not to push it open. I could hear his mouse clicking.

I was placing my hand on the doorknob, about to push my way in when someone touched me lightly on the shoulder. I jumped, almost screaming.

"Jackie," I whispered. I led her away from Harold's door, and back into my office. "What are you doing, giving me a heart attack?"

"No. What are you doing?"

"Ssshh. I'm about to catch him looking at porno."

"Who? Harold?"

"Yes. Harold."

"You mean that's what he's in there doing now? At this minute? *Eeewww.*"

"I'm almost sure of it, and I want to catch him in the act. And now that you're here…"

"Oh no. No way."

"Yes way. You're my witness."

"What if he wigs out? Shouldn't we have Big Pete from security in here first?"

"Harold won't. He'll be too embarrassed. Now come on."

We went back over to the door. I listened in again. He was still clicking away at his mouse. I hesitated one last time, looked back at Jackie, and made my move.

Harold's desk was positioned so that his back was facing the door. I had a bird's eye view of his computer. Amateur. He sat with his eyes glued to the screen. He was rocking from side to side like he was keeping time to a music video. I wasn't sure if he heard us come in. The back of his neck looked red and irritated, and his shirt collar was soaked with perspiration. He stopped clicking and moved his hand down between his legs.

What had him hypnotized stopped me so suddenly that I felt Jackie's shoes on the back of my heels. There were naked women in different positions, some leather-clad with whips and chains. He immediately switched to a second screen where a blond with huge breasts sat spread eagle, nothing left to the imagination.

A noise escaped my mouth; then Jackie's. Both were that of disgust.

Harold's head shot around to look back and forth between Jackie and me. He jumped up in total shock, with his pants unzipped and his thin, pale penis protruding in a full erection. I looked down; he did too. He sat back down in his chair again.

"Boss lady, please let me explain," he said, zipping his pants before jumping up again. "I know how this must look."

"Tell me, Harold, what do you think this looks like to me?" I asked.

"Huh?" He swallowed. "The funniest thing happened to me just now."

"Really? Just like it does every morning, right?"

"Well, I sat down, logged onto my computer, and I was pulling up some research material and I hit White House. And lo and behold, this porno site just popped up."

"Unbelievable."

"That's exactly what I said."

"Okay. Harold, you know I can get the girl from computer services up here right now. I can have her pull up your cookies."

"Cookies?"

"Yes, cookies, and not the ones you're thinking of. The cookies that will show me all the websites that you've hit since you were hired."

"Maybe someone else has been accessing sites using my password," he retorted. "Yes, that's it. That would explain why this popped up."

I shook my head at him. "Pack your things, Harold. You're done here."

"Wait a minute. You can't fire me. It was a mistake. Damn. It was a mistake," he screamed. "I need this fucking job."

Jackie, stunned and silent until now, moved in and stood between Harold and me. Told him to calm down. He looked like he might break down and cry but told me again that I'd made a terrible mistake. Our voices started to rise with me telling Harold how much authority I had and him telling me I didn't. I looked back into my office. A few employees had gathered at my door, attracted by all the commotion. Gray rushed in. Someone must have phoned him, he never just happened by. He took off his glasses, and stared between the three of us. For a minute

I thought he might side with Harold without knowing the full story.

"Hey. What's going on? I can hear you guys all the way down...holy shit."

He had spotted Harold's computer screen. I must have really flustered him. He hadn't remembered to shut it down.

"What the hell do you think you're doing, Hobbs? And right here in broad daylight too."

"Sir. Mr. Tapscott, I can explain."

"The only sound I want to hear from you at the moment is that sound of the doorknob hitting your big ass on your way out. You're through."

I had to muffle the snicker that was erupting.

"And shut that garbage off before you leave," Gray yelled as he turned abruptly and walked out.

Harold was cleared out in less than five minutes. I had never seen him move so fast. Gray waited in my office as I explained the entire mess about Harold. He watched as Big Pete escorted Harold out the building, then turned back to me.

"What a loser. How long has this been going on?"

I opened my mouth to answer.

"On second thought," he said stopping me with his hand. "I don't want to know any more than I already do. I'm taking an early lunch. Between you playing detective and Harold's little screen saver, I might just take the rest of the day off."

• • •

I met Jackie after work at one of those formal shops near the Galleria. Marco and Gena's wedding, which we weren't sure would happen was less than a week away. And neither of us had a dress.

I found Jackie flipping the top down on her cellular

and sliding it back inside her purse. She held a periwinkle-colored dress in her other hand. She looked up and smiled. "Hey, Sherlock."

"Watson. Is our dear friend Harold all cleared out?" I asked.

"I will be mailing out what little there is of a last paycheck tomorrow."

"Can you believe him?" I asked.

"Sister, I have seen it all since I came to Templeton," she said, holding the dress up for closer examination.

"That's a cute one. That color will look fierce on you." I told her.

"Hold on to your credit card. That was Marco on the phone. He and Gena had another blow-up. He's meeting us across the street at Starbucks in five minutes."

"Again?" I asked, rolling my eyes.

"Again, sister. You know I think it's safer for Judge Mablean to marry those two on *Divorce Court*." Jackie said.

"He doesn't mind going from the griddle to an inferno, as Mom would say."

"Mmmm." Jackie responded as we headed toward the front of the store with the dress in tow. "Can you hold this one for me? I have a quick emergency and will be returning in about fifteen minutes," Jackie asked a clerk.

"Sure. I'll keep it back here," the salesclerk eagerly replied, like she must have dealt with shopping inter-ruptions countless times.

We walked across the street, into Starbucks and looked for Marco. He was sitting in the middle of the shop staring down into his vente size cup.

"Now you see that face?" Jackie leaned toward me and said. "That's the one that makes me run from the idea of marriage."

"What's up Jackie, CeCe?" Marco said, cupping his head in his hands.

"Hey, Marco." I nodded and took a seat close to Jackie in front of him.

"So, what's the big deal that you had to drag me away from some serious shopping?" Jackie asked.

"I don't know. Gena's trippin' again. You know, just when I think things are going great, bam." he said, smashing a fist into the palm of his other hand. "I get blindsided."

"Why? What happened?" Jackie asked.

"It all started over this family gathering, right. Kind of like a tradition we Gianellis have every year, okay. Now Gena has forbidden me to go."

"Why? She doesn't like your family or something?" Jackie asked.

"She's not invited. Well, to be totally honest, my family hasn't completely accepted Gena yet."

"Why? Because she's not Italian or because she broke up your marriage?" Jackie asked.

"Maybe both. Who knows? I suspect the fact she isn't Italian has a lot to do with it. But to make matters worst, Gena called me a racist for Pete's sake, just because I thought I should still go without her. You believe that?" Marco questioned, searching both of our faces.

"I can."

"CeCe," Jackie exclaimed.

"No, wait a sec," I continued. "Maybe Gena has a point. Not about you being racist, Marco. That's a little extreme on her part, but I've seen a lot of interracial relationships—"

"Yours?" Jackie cut in.

"Funny. Anyway, Marco, as I was saying, I've seen relationships where the African-American side is always the understanding one. I mean when an interracial couple is split down the middle, it seems the African-American side always ends up compromising."

"But they're family. I told her they'll come around eventually."

"So? Gena's your family too. Don't you think it's only fair that you stick it out with her until they do? You have to show your family that your loyalty is to Gena, otherwise, they'll never respect your decision to be with her."

"I understand your point, Ce, but to call me a racist… that put our relationship back to the beginning."

"Marco, Gena is feeling what a lot of interracial couples feel, stress. Believe it or not, just being a few shades darker than my fair-skinned ex, I felt it. I expected Edmond to stand up for me, and he did. Don't assume Gena should be happy with your family's arrangements not to include her."

"But I'm there for her. She knows I've been down since I first met her—the music, the way she dresses, and even that hair thing."

"Hair thing?" Jackie asked, confused.

"Yeah, you know I'd go into the bathroom and half of her hair is lying on the sink and I would go 'Geez, Gena, how come half your hair is out.' "

"Oh, you mean, hair weave?" Jackie asked and smiled at me. We both burst into laughter.

"Yeah, yeah. When she needs it to look fuller or some shit she's saying."

"Okay. But back to being down, Marco," I continued, gaining my composure. "You don't have to change who you are, to say you love her. That's not what she needs. Love her as a person first, black women don't need special handling. We need love just like any other woman."

"Yeah," Jackie chimed in. "Who wrote that stupid book anyway on how to love a black woman?"

"But I do love her," Marco said.

"Then call her. Tell her that," Jackie replied.

"And my family?"

"Put your foot down. As hard as it might be, you have to make a choice between them or Gena. If they don't accept Gena, you have to let them go. That's how you gotta be down, my brother," Jackie quipped.

"Sounds like I have to lose my family to gain a wife," Marco said.

"Not losing. It's called compromising," Jackie returned.

31

Marco's emergency therapy session caused me to get home later than I anticipated. I was expecting Jazz to call, and I wanted to be home when he did so the distractions from driving didn't interfere with our conversation. I wanted to hear everything—all the details of his trip so far—how his promotions gig and the awards ceremony in LA was going; if he'd met P. Diddy, Usher or Mary J. like he expected; whether he had thought about me at all.

Shoot. Why didn't I just call him instead of letting my mind ramble. I dialed the digits for his hotel suite which he had left in his voice mail. I ended up leaving a message. I guess LA was just busy like Jazz had said.

I arrived at my condo, undressed and ran a hot bubble bath and had submerged myself just before my phone buzzed. I jumped out of the tub, dripping water all over the place, panting, thinking it was Jazz returning my call. Instead it was Edmond.

"Celia, I see your old habit of not turning your cell phone on hasn't changed."

"Hello, Edmond."

"Hello, yourself. I've been trying to reach you for the last four hours. You know you rea—"

"You know you really shouldn't care, Edmond. Or did divorcing me suddenly bring out your compassionate side?"

"I've always have a soft spot when it came to you, Cel—CeCe. Still do. And you asked me to divorce you, remember?"

"I don't remember you fighting it."

"I was never perfect, and it might surprise you to know that I make some damn big mistakes. And divorcing you was the biggest."

"That's very flattering, but I'm sure you didn't call to remind me of all your faults."

"Would it surprise you?"

"Nothing surprises me anymore. Why did you call?"

"Well, I can see it's nothing but business with you. I'm sure your mother spoke to you about me being in Houston next week for a few days."

"She did."

"Well, I thought I could see you."

"I don't know, Edmond. I don't think that would be such a good idea."

"Why? Because he might not approve?"

"And she does?"

"There is no she."

"Oh? What happened?"

"What little there was is over."

"So, is that supposed to change anything?"

"No, but I would like to know if you have someone in your life."

"That's none of your business."

"You're right. We are divorced, aren't we?"

"We are."

"Then you have nothing to lose by agreeing to see me."

"Oh, I'm not in fear of losing anything."

"Then have dinner with me."

"I don't think so, Edmond."

"Come on, for old time's sake. Please, chocolate drop."

He had said that little endearment, knowing it would melt my heart. It always did.

"Alright, Edmond," I said after a long sigh. "Dinner, one last time. That's it. And only because you're in town."

"That's all I'm asking."

I grabbed my appointment book from my briefcase and flipped to the weekend. I ran my finger down until I found Saturday. Our meeting would be on my terms. I penciled him in for one hour, regarding him as a business appointment and nothing else.

• • •

The week leading up to dinner with Edmond and Marco and Gena's wedding found me working late almost every night. When Thursday finally rolled around, I had just finished an ad for a local grocery chain. With no new replacement for Harold, I had everything completed except the graphics. I would have to contract that out like before. I was going to take the next day off and breathed a sigh of relief that I had my work taken care of before. I collected my purse and briefcase and took the elevator down, thinking of all the things I still had to get done. That included buying a wedding gift.

The last person I expected to see when the elevator doors flew open was Tyson. His dark eyes caught my reflection by surprise. He spoke up, readjusting his gym bag strap on his shoulder.

"CeCe, burning the evening oil again, I see."

"Hello, Tyson. Yeah, I had some last-minute stuff to take care of before the wedding tomorrow."

"Yeah, Ta—I heard about the wedding. Gena and Marco, right?"

"Right. So what are you doing here?"

"Meeting Ralph from accounting. We still try to work out together next door sometimes."

"He's probably there already. I saw him leaving just ahead of me."

"Okay. Then I'll catch him there, I guess."

"Guess I'll see you at the wedding with Tayla?"

He looked down. I knew I had probably pissed him off by mentioning them as a couple.

"No, CeCe, I probably won't make it."

"Too bad. It's good exposure for when you take your nuptials."

"You're trying to piss me off on purpose. I know that."

"Why would I want to do that?"

"Because you think I've hurt you, but if you would only listen to reason…"

"Look, Tyson, I have a million things to do. I have to go."

"When do you have time? To talk, that is."

"I'm very busy these days. Why don't you try after this whole wedding thing is over."

"Why not tonight? Midnight?"

I laughed in his face before I knew it. He looked hurt then I felt bad.

"Sorry. That sounded more like a booty call than wanting to talk."

"I don't do booty calls. I was only reminding you of our first time together. How easily you've forgotten."

"I have to go."

"I only wanted to ask you something. Things have changed. I know with the way everything went down before I seemed flaky, but I've learned, and I want to be in your life again."

We had made the walk to my car in the parking garage. I placed my day planner and briefcase on top of my car and pulled my keys from my purse but my hand was too shaky to unlock the door. He did it for me.

"Thanks," I said, grabbing my briefcase and getting in.

"You're welcome. So when do I see you?"

"Tyson, don't do this. Now is not the right time."

"Because of Jazz?"

"Jazz has nothing to do with it."

"What then?"

"You know what."

"Do you love this Jazz character? Huh?"

"Our relationship hasn't developed that far yet, but I might want to give it a shot."

"Do you love me?"

"Don't you love Tayla?"

"No, I don't love Tayla. I love you."

"I have to go."

"That's the story of your life, isn't it? 'I have to go.' You are always running when life doesn't suit you."

"That's not fair. I face up to my issues, just like you did. Or have you forgotten that you walked out, not me?"

"Because you didn't want me in your life."

"You're damn right. Not under your terms anyway."

"What about now? There aren't any terms, baby, no restraints. Just me."

"I don't know if I can trust that. I have to know that

as soon as we're happy something else won't come along to ruin it."

"I can promise that. Just give me the opportunity to prove it."

"It's too late. I've gotta go. Take care of yourself."

I sped off toward home as fast as I could to get away from Tyson and that effect he had on me. I was trembling from the emotions he sent through me from being that close to him.

I pulled into my garage, got out, and checked around in the dark to make sure Tyson hadn't followed before securing the garage door. I slipped my key in the door and heard my cordless phone ringing off the hook.

"Hello," I finally managed after making it into the house.

"CeCe, guess who?"

It was Tracee. Damn, I'd forgotten that she would be in Houston already for Streeter's court date.

"Where are you?"

"At a hotel near the jail. They're going to let me see Streeter tonight, then I have to meet with his lawyer early tomorrow before court."

"Do you want me to come pick you up tonight?"

"No, honey, it'll be late when I get done. Just wanted to let you know I was here. I'll see you tomorrow after court."

"Okay, but if you need anything, I'm here."

"Thanks, CeCe. I'll see you tomorrow."

I hoped that I hadn't sounded too overjoyed in not having Tracee's company, but I was exhausted—both physically and mentally—and I still had a pre-wedding dinner with Marco and Gena.

I slipped my skirt and jacket off, hung them in the dry cleaning side of my closet, peeled off my beige silk blouse and looked for another outfit. My doorbell chimed. Who on earth? I pulled on an oversized Jackson State University T-shirt. Maybe Tracee had changed her mind and driven over after all. Probably not though. No way could she have made it that fast in Houston traffic.

I looked out of the peephole. It was Tyson.

I wasn't going to trip in my usual way. I opened the door just enough to fit my body in the crack, glaring into his face with the meanest look I could muster with a few seconds' notice.

He looked me up and down, then a broad grin swept across his face. I looked down to realize that I was wearing only my panties underneath the much-too-short-in-this type-situation T-shirt.

"Does Jackson State know how well you're representing?"

"What are you doing here, Tyson?" I asked, rolling my eyes quickly to show my disinterest.

"I thought you might need this." He held up my black day planner he had concealed behind his back. "You left it on your car and drove off before I could stop you."

"It could have waited."

I looked up just past his shoulder at the sky.

"I'm glad I had the excuse to come over. I wanted to talk to you about something else."

"I'm in a hurry," I said, stepping back to close my door.

He blocked my effort by placing his foot in the space.

"Why do you have to try and be so cold? Huh?" he asked, stroking me playfully on the chin.

Before I could react, he was using his strong, firm body to maneuver me back inside into the living room.

He closed the door behind us with his left foot, all too smooth.

"I didn't invite you in, Tyson."

"You never did. Remember the last time you just left the door unlocked. It was open, so I assumed..."

"You assumed wrong. Now you have to leave."

"You're not my boss anymore. I don't have to listen to you," he said, planting a soft kiss on me. My knees grew weak. He slid his hands under my shirt and rubbed my back, then down between my thighs.

"Don't, Tyson."

"What are you going to do? Reprimand me?"

"Stop it."

"No. I'm not sure if you want me to. Do you?"

He kissed me again. Hard. Then moved me back until we were on the couch. I started to kiss him back. My legs drew up around his hips and pulled him down into me. I wasn't fighting him anymore.

"You want me, CeCe, don't you?"

"Yes."

"I can't hear you."

"Yesss," I said a little louder. Geezus. Damn.

"Say it then. Tell me you want me to stay with you. Say it."

"Let's just enjoy each other for now, okay?"

He pulled away, then he took my face into his hands.

"You're amazing, you know that."

"What's wrong, Tyson?"

"Now who's asking for a booty call? You talk a good game, but listen to yourself." He released me.

"So that's why you came over here, to play games to trap me?"

"I came over because of how I feel. I wanted to give

it one last chance, but you, on the other hand, just want
to see how much you can make me beg. That I refuse to
do, CeCe."

He got up and straightened his clothes, then headed
for the door. He stopped and turned to face me.

"I'm tired of this. I've tried. I am no longer going to
chase someone who doesn't want to be caught. I suppose
you're enjoying your little game of juggling all three of
us."

"You arrogant little...Get the hell out of my house,"
I screamed, running up behind him. "What do you want
me to do, trap you like Tayla did? Would that make you
feel wanted? Why don't you go play house with her and
leave me the hell alone."

"Maybe I will. At least she knows what she wants."

"Get out."

"Gladly. But know one thing. I won't be back.
Obviously, I'm not what you want, so don't expect to
hear from me again."

I screamed and slammed the door at his back, then
kicked it. Who the hell did he think he was, coming
over, getting me worked up and almost ready to give in
to him? To hell with Tyson, I could care less if I saw him
again.

I took a long, warm shower, letting the water flow
into my face to wash away any trace of Tyson's skin
touching mine, his kisses, and the scent of his Burberry
cologne. I dried myself off and slipped into another T-
shirt. I seemed to have a lot of those handy. This one
was a gift from Jazz—a vintage from Maze's concert at
the Essence Music Festival in New Orleans, the year
before.

Just the one thing to calm my woos temporarily,
was Jazz's phone call from LA. He sounded excited and

told me all about the big interviews he'd gotten. He had nabbed one with his home girl Beyoncé to do a plug for the station. Then his voice grew serious. He wanted to talk about us.

"So have you had enough time to consider my request?" he asked.

"It sounded more like an ultimatum than a request. At least it did to me."

"Regardless, you have a decision to make about me."

"And a couple more days, right?"

"My bad. You're absolutely right. I don't want to pressure you."

"So how's LA?" I asked.

"LA is LA, but you can judge for yourself."

"How's that?"

"I could extend my stay here a few days and my suite at the Beverly Hilton."

"Jazz Rollins, would that be an invitation for a rendezvous?"

"I won't lie. It would." He laughed.

"As romantic and as tempting as it sounds, I have too many things going on here at the moment."

"You don't have to do that, CeCe. It was only a suggestion."

"Do what, Jazz?"

"Make excuses."

"I wasn't making excuses. If I had been allowed to finish, I would have told you that I have a wedding this weekend."

"Yours?"

"Very funny. I never knew musicians could have a sense of humor too."

"I tried to tell you what you were missing."

"Oh, I can imagine that you're full of surprises."

"If only you would take the plunge to find out."

"You'll remember to call me with your flight information?" I asked, after some hesitation, to get him off the subject.

"I will. Hey, I'm getting beeped here. Gotta go. I'll see you day after tomorrow, right?"

"Sure thing."

"And CeCe?"

"Yes."

"Ahh..."

"Jazz, what is it?"

"Nothing. Just momentarily trippin', I guess. Enjoy the wedding."

"Thanks. Bye, Jazz."

"So long, CeCe."

Jazz's phone call had left me a little emotional. I got dressed and called my mother on the way to the restaurant to meet Gena and Marco. Talking with my mother always helped when I was feeling blue.

"Hi, Mom."

"Celia? Honey, you sound kind of down. What's wrong?"

"Nothing. I'm sorry. Is it late for you? I just wanted to hear your voice."

"You have man trouble, don't you?"

"What makes you say that?"

"Because I remember all those times you used to call and sound this way, it was money or love. And you haven't needed money since college."

"Whatever, Mom. How's Daddy?"

"Eating or sleeping since he retired. He's already eaten... So back to you. Who is this man, and what has he done to you?"

"Well actually it's two men."

"Two? What kind of job did you take out there in Houston? Is money that tight, dear?" She laughed. So did I.

"Ssh, Mom. You'll wake Dad."

"Maybe I should. What on earth is wrong with you? You know I didn't raise no fluzzy."

"Mom, calm down. I wasn't dating both at the same time. I met Tyson, and things didn't work out. Then I met Jazz. Now Tyson wants to resume the relationship."

"Oh. Girl, you better tell me something. I still don't like the idea of you seeing so many different men that you don't really know."

"Only two, Mom. That's not 'so many.'"

"Obviously too many if you have to decide."

"I wish Grampy was still here. He would understand. I bet he could tell me one of his stories to make everything seem right."

"One of those fishing stories, huh? He was keen when it came to how to make people feel better."

"Yeah. Speaking of fishing, you remember that tackle box he had?"

"You mean the wooden one that he made? You used to sit on it out there by the creek when he took you fishing."

"Yes. Does Daddy still have it?"

"Sure does. He used it a time or two. It's in the garage, I think. Why?"

"I would kind of like to have it. I mean if it's okay with Daddy."

"I'm sure it will be, honey. I'll ask him for you."

"Thank you, Mom."

"Anything else?"

"No, Mom. I won't keep you up. Thanks for the talk."

"Okay, honey. I hope I was some help."

"More than you know. Good night, Mom."

"Night, baby. And CeCe?"

"Yes, Mom."

"Be careful and always go with your heart."

"I will."

32

"Cheers!"

We all bellowed and clinked our tulip-shaped champagne glasses after a celebratory toast to the happy couple on the eve of their wedding. We had hooked up at CoCo's, a sleek restaurant that served wickedly delicious Caribbean cuisine. Only Jackie and I were there for the special occasion.

"I just wish you guys would have let us thrown you a bachelor and bachelorette party," Jackie said after taking a sip of her bubbly.

"Thanks, but I don't think we could have stood being away from each other the night before our wedding, Marco said, smooching on Gena.

"Besides," Gena said, gazing deep in his eyes, "neither one of us will miss the single life. We have all that we need right here and now."

"Oohhh! Isn't that just the biggest bunch of BS that you ever heard?" Jackie remarked. "The truth is that you're too afraid of changing your mind again if you're apart that long."

"No. That's in the past," Marco said, stepping in to

help Gena. "I know things were rocky at first, but we're cool, and everything is solid now."

Marco and Gena sounded so eager to live happily-ever-after. So they thought. Probably thought that marriage was a cure-all for their pre-existing problems too. I know I did after meeting Edmond. I ignored the warning signs when he wasn't very passionate or anxious for intimacy when we were alone. I just assumed marrying him would fix the glitches.

I had rushed home during my senior year at Jackson State and proclaimed that I had met the most wonderful man in the world named Edmond Cornell Ross, and I was ready to marry him right away.

Mom had taken a deep breath, sat me down on her plaid Herculon couch and looked me square in the face. "Are you pregnant, baby?" She asked me honestly.

"No, Mom. I'm in love."

"In love and you just met this man Edmond, huh?"

"Yes, I do love him."

"Well that might be, but what's the rush? CeCe, love has no speedometer."

"What?" I'd asked her, a little confused.

"Look, honey, I'll pass down to you what my mother gave to me as pretty sound advice. Mother was wise, you know."

"What was that, Mom?" I'd asked.

"She said take time to know him. Don't rush into anything. Take time to know him, baby; love isn't an overnight thing. Grandma was wise, huh?"

"Very wise. She was very clever in passing that wisdom on."

Little did Mama know that Grandma was probably in the early stages of Alzheimer at the time and her wisdom actually belonged to those Otis Redding records she liked listening to. Sound advice whether from Otis or Granny that had half convinced me I should wait.

"What's wrong?" Jackie asked when I was quiet for too long. "You look like you just learned that your ex-husband is coming to the same town that your two lovers reside in." She had turned from Gena and Marco and scooted her chair closer to me.

"Quite funny but there aren't any two lovers?" I said, laughing.

"So does that mean Tyson's really out?" Jackie asked.

"He's really out," I said.

"But not out of your mind yet."

"Is it that obvious?"

"Very."

"I don't know, Jackie. I thought I could handle this. I mean, I just have this feeling that Tyson won't let it go. I'm afraid that if I get close to Jazz, Tyson will only try and maneuvered his way back into my life again."

"So, just *womaneuver* his ass out again."

She made me laugh. "I wish it was that simple. Tyson, I can handle. Jazz, on the other hand, made it clear that as long as Tyson is around, he's not."

"I say stop letting these men give you ultimatums for one. If you have to make a choice and you want the truth, your choice is a no-brainer. You know what the issues are with both Edmond and Tyson. Jazz is the only one who seems true blue."

"So you're saying bet on Jazz?"

"I'm saying there's nothing wrong with giving yourself the time to get to know him. As my grandmother would say, take time to know him. Don't rush into anything."

"So was Otis Redding the guru on southern love or what?"

"What?"

"Never mind. I have to go to the bathroom. Hold on to my seat, will you?"

I laughed on my way to the ladies' room, then stopped to check my face in the mirror. I rinsed the alcohol taste out of my mouth. I needed a mint. I opened my purse and popped a Certs, then applied a thin coat of Brown Passion lipstick and dropped the tube back inside my clutch. I gave myself one last mirror check. That's when I saw Evil Lee standing behind me, staring. She had one hand on her hip and the other on her chin.

"Tayla," I said, turning around, "what are you doing here? Stalking?"

"I'm here to support my friend. I have a right," she shot back.

"Do what you want as long as you stay clear of me."

"Don't worry, I wouldn't give you the satisfaction to run and report your lies to Tyson."

"Tyson's smart. He'll figure out what you are all by himself. I could care less about you."

"No, you just want what I have, don't you?"

"I want what you have," I repeated, then chuckled. "What do you have Tayla?"

"You think you're so innocent, don't you? Think you're better than me."

"I'm not a liar, if that's what you mean."

"Whatever. But you're just jealous because I've won."

"Won what? I ask again, Tayla, what is it that you have?" Then, I walked toward her. She cringed. "Let me tell you. You have nothing. Nothing but an empty womb and a prayer that Tyson will screw you again and hopefully validate your lie."

"You don't know anything about me."

"And I don't want to. Because you know what, little girl, what you don't understand is all I have to do is pick up the phone and Tyson is mine. Just like that," I said and snapped my fingers in her face.

She flinched. I turned and walked away as she muttered the "b" word under her breath, then flung her purse into the vanity mirror. In my immature, dirty little southern days, I would have turned back, slipped off my Zanottis and asked her to repeat it, but having grown, I could only smile. I had gotten to her. On the way back to my table, I got a sudden spasm between my thighs at the idea of another woman being threatened by me. I guess that's what it felt like to have pussy power.

33

I slept in the next morning. I figured the wedding must still be on since I hadn't heard anything different within the last twelve hours. I watched TV in bed, munched on fresh fruit and drank hot tea. I caught a little of *Animal Kingdom* and then some TV Land. I loved those old shows— *Andy Griffith, Leave It to Beaver,* and *The Jeffersons.* I laughed for two solid hours before it was time to get dressed.

I frowned at the outfit I was wearing. I didn't particularly care for it. It was a plain strapless baby-blue dress. I had found a long printed scarf of the same color to accessorize it at least. It was the best I could do with all the wedding on-again, then off-again moments. I thought people spent too much on weddings anyway. My parents paid an arm and a leg to make mine nothing less than perfect. That didn't make it last any longer. Next time it was blue jeans, a T-shirt, and a justice of the peace.

I stopped off at Nordstrom's where the couple was registered for wedding gifts. I had ordered mine gift-wrapped to go over the Internet. Later I drove through a double iron gate onto a huge country estate. It belonged to

289

a prominent surgeon friend of a friend to Gena, who had been gracious enough to host the wedding. The wedding itself was very small, only Jackie, a handful of Gena's family, and me. None of Marco's family showed up. His ex-wife also refused to let Marco's kids attend. I assumed that Marco hadn't really expected any of his family to attend anyway.

Soft music played as Gena descended a long spiral staircase decorated with ribbons and white roses. She wore a simple but elegant, ankle-length, off-the-shoulder dress. Her hair was swept up with baby's breath. A nervous Marco wore a black Armani suit. Tayla was Gena's maid of honor and hung out in the background after the ceremony, careful not to come within a foot of me. After a minister said a few words and a prayer for unity, Marco and Gena were joined together as one, at last. After champagne and chocolate banana cream wedding cake, the happy couple was off to Galveston Island to spend the weekend. The real honeymoon would come later.

I had given my gift along with best wishes and was back on the 610 freeway before Tracee phoned. She wanted to meet for a late lunch before she drove back to Jackson. I wanted to change but didn't have time before I met her at the Chat Room at 610 and Richmond around 3:00 p.m.

Tracee looked absolutely fabulous, wearing a really smart tailored blue pantsuit. We screamed in our usual loud fashion after seeing each other, then we embraced. She had gained a few pounds, but they looked good on her.

"Tracee, you look wonderful. Jackson is really agreeing with you."

"Girl, I feel great. Gettin' away was just what I needed. My head is clear, and I am so focused. And you, Miss Thang, you look good yourself. What have you done with your hair? Girl, it's crazy chic."

"Thanks. It's the new me."

"I ain't mad at all. So, whatsup?"

"Problems. Men. Problems. Take your pick."

"Is that right?" She laughed.

"And if things weren't bad enough, Edmond is here."

"What's he doing here? Girl, he wants you back. I told you so."

"I think he's here just to torture me quite frankly," I said.

"They all torture us one way or the other."

"Speaking of torture, how did things go with Streeter?" She gave a smug look. "He's gonna have to do a nickel after all."

"What's a nickel?" I asked, then felt a little naïve.

"Lord, Ce, you are so square. Five years. That's the most the prosecution could get since I wouldn't testify against Streeter. But, still he'll probably get out in about two and a half years."

"And?"

"And what?"

"Will you be waiting for him?" I asked.

"Honey, I'll be in Jackson, or who knows? Don't get me wrong, I owe Streeter a lot for what he did for me, but that part of my life, you know low rent, low living, is in the past. That could have easily been me in jail. I am not spending the next three years doin' jail house visitations on the weekend either or driving fourteen hours round trip to hear a lot of empty promises and how he's found religion."

"And I hear they do find religion fast up in there."

"Okay. Already has. And he wants me to put some money on the books for him. I mean what do I look like, Project C.A.R.E.?"

"So he wants you to sponsor him for ten dollars a month?"

"Can you hear me now?"

"Tracee, you are wild. I'm so happy for you. I just wish you weren't so far away."

"I know, girl, but enough about me. Let's shift the mic back to you. So what were you telling me over the phone about robbing the cradle? And you got a jones for this Jazz man? You know back in the day we had a name for heffas like you."

"Will you stop? It's not like that."

"How is it then?"

"First of all, Tyson is history. Jazz...let's just say Jazz is just beginning."

"And where does that leave Edmond?"

"Maybe not even part of the equation, especially the way he played me with his secretary."

"People make mistakes, Ce. And from what I hear, she did most of the initiating."

"It doesn't matter. Things just got so messed up between us. I think any relationship we had is damaged beyond repair. We couldn't go back to where we were if we tried."

"You might be right. But you know what?"

"What's that?"

"You really don't have to go back to where you were to make it work," she said.

• • •

"Edmond, thanks for bringing these things by, especially the rest of my doll collection," I said, helping him set a brown box on the table in the living room of my condo. There was a smaller box on top. He also had a dozen white roses which he handed to me, then set a large shopping bag down beside the boxes. "It was very thoughtful. And thanks for the beautiful roses."

It was the day after Marco and Gena's wedding and Edmond had called me as soon as he checked into his hotel. All he would tell me over the phone was that he had something he thought I would want to have. I had given him directions to my condo, a bit curious as to what it could be, or whether it was only a ploy to get over to my place.

"Well, Celia, I know how sentimental you are about those dolls, and there are a few other things I knew you would want to have. Anything else that you left remains at the house. You can arrange to get it anytime." He took the boxes off the table and set them in front of the sofa. He stood back up and straightened out the tan suit he was wearing.

"I appreciate that, Edmond." I thought he might want to sit. I asked just in case. He declined. I went off to the kitchen to put the roses in a vase, then brought them out and placed them on a table near the front door.

"So, how have you been?" he asked as I rejoined him near the sofa.

"Good. I've been good. You?"

"You know me. I make the best of a bad situation."

"You always did," I said, looking him over. He was a little thinner but his body was still tight. His hair seemed longer though, but not enough to take away from his refined image. He also had a mustache growing in. He had the kind of look that put a newly divorced man back on the dating market. He caught me staring.

"Is something wrong?" Did I forget to wipe my nose?" He made me laugh. I never remembered him being comical.

"No. I like your different look."

"Probably the mustache," he joked and stroked it.

"It's something more than that."

"I hope in a good way."

"Of course."

"You look good, too, Celia. Cel—he raised his hand. "CeCe, that is. And you've changed your hair too."

"Thanks. Went lighter. I wasn't real sure about the color at first."

"I like it. Matter of fact, you know with you standing there all dressed up in that blue dress, it reminds me of that time you were home from college and I came by your parents' house to take you out."

"Friday night at the Renaissance."

"You wore a cute little blue dress then, and I kept telling you how beautiful you looked."

"You know you were kind of fly in blue yourself."

"And we danced after dinner to that song. What was it?" He snapped his fingers.

"The 'Woo Woo Song' by Jeffrey Osborne," we both said at the same time, bursting into laughter.

"Yes, that was it. And later, I called you my chocolate drop." He got serious again.

"And I called you my vanilla."

"And I asked you to marry me that night. Remember?"

"Of course I remember, Edmond."

He looked at me then at the boxes.

"I brought you something else," he said and picked up the shopping bag from the table.

"What is it?"

"Open it and find out."

I pulled a gift-wrapped box from the shopping bag and tore the paper off in a split second. I was like a little girl at Christmas. I gasped. I was speechless at the content. I couldn't believe my eyes. I was holding the

African-American Millennium Princess Barbie 2000. The one I had searched for months for without any luck. It was the only one missing from my collection. I had even mentioned my disappointment to Edmond, but I didn't think he seemed interested at the time.

"How did you find her?"

"You should know me by now, girl. I get exactly what I want, when I want it." His blue eyes beamed at me, almost casting a spell. I glanced down.

"You shouldn't have, Edmond."

"Shouldn't have brought it or shouldn't have remembered?"

"I don't know, a little of both, I guess. You must have gone through a lot of trouble to get it."

"You're worth it, chocolate drop. I'll do anything for you. Absolutely anything."

I blushed. For a minute, he didn't seem like the man I was once married to, who knew my likes and dislikes, my weaknesses.

"And what is that look for?" he asked.

"You're different."

"How?"

"Sentimental. I just never knew you could be that way."

"I'm not the same person you left if that's what you mean."

"And did the divorce bring that change about?"

"Let's just say I've been a fool. And yes, I guess it did take you leaving for me to realize what you needed from me."

"Maybe I needed more than you could give, Edmond."

"Maybe. But I also wasn't listening to what you needed."

"Did our divorce really give you this revelation or did someone else?"

"That's not important. The fact that I miss you like crazy, is."

"Edmond we can't just wipe away the last few months of our lives. We can't forget what brought us to this point."

"We all make mistakes. I was wrong in believing that giving you the best financially was enough to keep you as my wife. If I had known then, I would have fought harder to save our marriage."

"We hurt each other, Edmond."

"Like I said, we all make mistakes."

"Did you love me?" I asked.

"I've always loved you, CeCe. My problem was showing it."

"Our marriage seemed like so long ago."

"We were happy once. We got married, didn't we? We could try again."

"Edmond—"

"Look, I didn't mean to put you on the spot. I realize things have changed, and we're different people now, but I don't care where we've been." He looked down a little embarrassed. "I thought about the things you said to me the day you left. I've come to terms with a lot of my issues. I'm seeing a doctor—well, a sex therapist. There." He paused before finishing. "At least I can say it now." He chuckled. "I know that one of my problems was that I wasn't passionate, and that had everything to do with me being so career-driven. I wasn't focused on the things that were really important, but I'm getting help."

"I'm glad, Edmond. I know that was a huge step for you. I'm proud of you. But the two of us…I mean, there's been someone else."

"And? There's been someone else in my life. We're divorced. I don't care about what happened in your past, if you can forgive mine."

"It might be too much for either of us to ask, Edmond."
I relaxed as he moved in closer and started to caress my
shoulders. His hands felt so strong. He lifted my chin
and looked deep into my eyes. "I know what you're
thinking. I never cheated on you during our marriage.
I swear to you."

"It's not that. I don't care about Ja'Nell anymore."

"Then what?"

"I could never go back to the way our life was."

"I wouldn't ask you to."

"I just don't want you to get your hopes up, that's
all."

"Oh, darling, was being married to me that bad?"

"I never said it was. You hurt me."

"You could have given me time to work it out. Make
it up to you."

"You wouldn't have changed. You never seemed to
have enough time for me. You were always so wrapped
up in your work."

"I wanted a good life for us, CeCe."

He cupped my face, then he kissed me softly on the
lips. It didn't feel like I was kissing my ex-husband. I was
kissing someone new, and because of that, I didn't feel
scared. It just felt good. I relaxed in his arms, pulled him
closer for more. That surprised me.

"Shall we go to dinner?" he asked, pulling back and
purposely leaving me wanting.

"Sure. Let me grab my purse." I wanted to ask why
he'd cut the kiss short and not taken advantage of the
moment.

We headed for my front door. Edmond opened it. "I
forgot my keys," I called after him. I spun around and
headed back to the kitchen while Edmond waited at the

door. I grabbed my keys right where I'd left them on the kitchen table and returned to find Edmond talking to someone. Whoever it was must have just walked up, I thought. I did a last-minute check in the mirror.

Edmond's back was to me, and I caught a glimpse of a man's face beneath the glow of the overhead light. Tyson leaned around Edmond and gave me a broad, cocky smile. Edmond stepped aside to let Tyson through, although I hadn't invited him in.

"Tyson, what are you doing here?"

"To see you, CeCe."

"Why? And without calling first?"

"I didn't think that I needed to," he said, obviously for Edmond's sake.

"Tyson, this is Edmond Ross. Edmond, Tyson Tread-well."

"Tyson, pleasure to meet you. CeCe failed to mention that we were once married."

"She told me. You're her ex-husband now, right?"

"Newly ex-husband. Quite new," Edmond said, extending his hand to Tyson.

Tyson accepted in a firm handshake. "Yeah, but still the ex no doubt. Good to meet you, man."

"Tyson," I said to lighten the mood, which was fast becoming awkward. "We were just on our way out. Whatever it is, can't it wait until tomorrow?"

"No. I don't think that it can."

"CeCe," Edmond broke in, "we have reservations at eight. If we miss I understand the waiting can be hours."

"Then wait," Tyson snapped at Edmond.

"Look, man. I don't know you—"

"That's right. You don't know me," Tyson interrupted, "so why don't you take your reservations and find someone else to dine with tonight. I'm sure you can handle that."

"You arrogant little punk. Who do you think you are? You have no idea who the fuck you're dealing with, do you?" Edmond said angrily and walked toward Tyson who turned to face him and planted his feet firmly apart. Tyson had his hands balled into fists, ready to defend himself if he had to.

"Edmond Tyson, please. Knock it off, both of you," I turned to Edmond. "Wait in the car. Don't worry. We have plenty of time. Let me give Tyson a few minutes."

"Celia, are you going to let this young punk walk into our—your—living room and demand your time when he sees me standing here? What are you running here, a halfway house for delinquents?"

"Hey, man, you can cut the wise-ass cracks about my age. Don't let the smooth face fool you. I'm old enough, alright?"

"For what? To get her in R. Kelly type trouble?" Edmond said, laughing. I smiled at his sudden looseness, then turned away.

"No. To love her and give her whatever she needs."

"Ha. What she needs, huh? You're looking at seven years of knowing what she needs."

"Yeah, and that's why she left you, right? Look, chief, you had your chance to make her happy, and clearly you failed. It happens to the best of us," Tyson said, giving him a wink.

I screamed Edmond's name as he made a mad dash in Tyson's direction. I stood frozen by the fact that he had Tyson collared and up against the wall. The mirror shifted. Their scuffle had overturned the vase of roses Edmond brought me. Water ran across the glass tabletop and dribbled down onto the tile, making a splattering noise. I was immobilized between picking up the flowers and stopping Edmond.

"Edmond, no. Let him go," I screamed and grabbed his shoulder.

"Stay out of this, CeCe," he said, shaking my hand away. "He wants to handle this like a man, then it's man to man all the way."

"Anytime, partner," Tyson threw back, clasping both of Edmond's hands at the wrists.

"Stop it. Both of you, I mean it. Step off now, or I walk out of here and let the both of you kill each other. I don't care."

Edmond looked at me. He reluctantly released his grip on Tyson, but he remained in his face. Both were snarling like two pit bulls.

"What's it going to be, you two? I'm not kidding. Step off now."

Edmond adjusted his jacket by flexing his shoulders and moved away. Tyson stuck out his chest but went in the opposite direction. I rolled my eyes and drew my breath.

"CeCe, I'm ordering you to send your boy toy on his way and let's go," Edmond said.

Tyson spoke up before I could. "Hey, man, I don't know what you're used to, but whatever, you don't order her to do anything. She's not your servant."

"Then we do agree on one thing. You don't know a damn thing about CeCe and my relationship," Edmond said.

"I know CeCe," Tyson returned.

"So do I, and I know that whatever little phase she's going through with you is only temporary. She will eventually come to her senses and back to where she belongs."

"And is that what you think you know about her, Dixieland?"

"I know what I know."

"Well, let me tell you what you don't know about her, what really pleases her."

Edmond flinched. His left eye twitched like it always did when he was angry. I stepped in to silence Tyson, but he waved me back and continued. "Do you know that she likes to be held and cuddled into the wee hours of the morning, huh, partna?"

"Tyson, that's totally uncalled for," I said.

"Naww. He thinks he knows. Let's see if he does. How about a simple shampoo? Did you know that shampooing her hair drives her mad crazy? Did you know that, brotha?" Tyson stepped forward and raised his hand. "Do you know that one particular spot on her that can be touched ever so passionately to almost send her into paralysis? Well, Edmond, is it? That's what I know. Now you tell me, what it is that you know after, what, seven years?"

The air between the three of us thickened. The fine hairs on my arms stood up as Tyson laid out our most intimate details to Edmond. Then my blood boiled. How could Tyson do that? Did he expect me to be impressed by his outwardly astuteness to my needs? And what about Edmond's feelings? I looked over at Edmond. He burned. He cleared his throat and cocked his head. He was pissed squared by then. Probably hated me too.

"CeCe, I'm not going to stand here and listen to this garbage," Edmond finally said wearily. "I'm telling—asking—you for the last time. Let's go or I'm leaving you to this," he said, gesturing toward Tyson.

"Edmond, I'm sorry. Just go on without me if you want to, please."

"I'm serious. What will it be?"

"I'm not in the mood for dinner now anyway," I said.

"So you're telling me this is what you want?"

"I'm telling you I need to be alone right now."

"Okay, fine, but know that I'll be here until the end of next week. Until then, here's the hotel information," he handed me a card. His room number was scribbled on the back. "Don't expect for me to make another attempt," he said, turning to walk out the door.

"You know, Edmond, fine, I hear you. Good-bye," I said as he gently closed the door behind him without looking back.

"What did you see in that anal retentive—"

"And you leave, too, Tyson," I turned and shouted at him.

"What do you mean? What did I do wrong?"

"What did you do wrong? You have to ask? Coming into my house unannounced and uninvited and disrespecting me and Edmond."

"Edmond?"

"Yeah, Edmond. He was my guest, and you had no right to do that."

"He's your ex-husband."

"And Tayla is your lover, but did I show up at your place disrespecting her that way?"

"Look, baby, I'm sorry. I was running scared when I found out Edmond was in town. I didn't want to risk losing you." He stepped closer with both hands held out. "I wanted to tell you that Tayla lied about being pregnant."

"How did you find out?"

"I showed up at the wedding late and you had already left. Tayla went off in her usual form when she thinks I'm looking for you. Her friend Gena pulled me to the side and told me the truth about Tayla not being pregnant. Gena likes you." He smiled and touched my arm. "Ce, I wanted you to know Tayla is history. Baby, I came to fight for you. Damn."

"Did I ask you to? Hell, I've known Tayla wasn't pregnant longer than you have. Did I rush to get into your business? No. I figured you were smart enough to work things out on your own. I gave you that much credit, Tyson."

"I wanted to let you know how I still feel about you, that's it."

"So you show up and start a bidding war? Did it ever occur to you that having dinner with my ex-husband who just happened to be in town on business could mean only that?"

"Okay. I admit that I screwed up."

"Yes, you did. Royally," I said and picked up my purse and keys from the table, uprighting the vase and the roses. I was too vexed to wipe up the water, so I left it to dry on its own.

"Where are you going? After Edmond?" Tyson yelled from behind me.

"No, Tyson. Right now I need to be as far away from both of you as possible. I have to meet a friend. You can let yourself out." I slammed the door behind me, leaving Tyson standing in the middle of my living room.

34

Delayed flashed beside Jazz's flight number as I stood glancing back and forth between the monitor and my watch. I had decided the last minute to meet him near baggage claim, after I had spent the last couple of hours driving around in my car trying to escape the madness Tyson had put me through earlier.

I had gotten no word from Jazz. No answer from his cell either. So, he wasn't even sure I would be there. Jazz's flight had changed. He'd left an updated version of his schedule while I was at the wedding, but I hadn't called him back to confirm. I was at the airport because I needed to talk with him face-to-face. No more stalling and no games. I wanted to tell him the truth, that I loved someone else. The timing just wasn't right for us. I was being that strong, mature woman he talked about.

His plane was very late. He was arriving by Air West, one of those new airlines still struggling to get their business straight. Impatience gripped me. I blew hot air. I checked my watch again before I searched out the nearest information desk for an update on his flight status.

I waited for the attendant to stop beating up her

keyboard. She looked frustrated, obviously not getting the 411 she needed.

"Yes, may I help you?" she asked.

"The flight from LA. Just how delayed is it?"

"Very."

"When will I be able to find out more?"

"You can wait in the attendants' lounge for further information if you like."

"Attendants' lounge?" She was really trippin'. Now she wanted to isolate me. Did I look like I was related to Al-Qaeda or someone?

"Ma'am—" A message came over the intercom and interrupted her, before she repeated the same useless information she had just given me.

She handed me a red VIP card and pointed me in the direction of the lounge. I really felt like a military wife—don't ask any questions, just hurry up and wait.

The lounge held a handful of people. All of us had that same red card, no clues and lots of unanswered questions. Some stood close to one another, compared notes, and tried to feed on what little knowledge they had. I stood alone. Somehow I didn't belong there. There must have been some dignitary on the plane, so we had to be checked for security reasons. Someone was going to weed me out. Jazz was probably at baggage claim right that minute possibly looking for me.

Finally an aging man came in and positioned himself in front of the group, standing near a United States map. He was that official-looking type, like a cross between an over-dressed pilot and a retiring Army general. He cleared his throat and started to ad-lib from a piece of paper he gripped tightly between his unsteady hands. He paced his words carefully, like we were the blood-thirsty paparazzi standing there with microphones and video cameras. He mentioned Jazz's flight number.

Okay, I was in the right place so far, I thought. But why was he telling me what I already knew. So his flight was delayed. He went on. "At approximately eighteen hundred hours…" He'd used military time. What time was that anyway? He was losing me. Then he said something:"Engine trouble" Oh, dear God…no "…miles outside of Austin." Did he say Austria? Why would he say that?… "No survivors."

Someone was calling me, trying to get my attention. Not by my name, but using that feminine, impersonal title to get through to me. Obviously, the strange lady with the short haircut and pink lipstick didn't know me, but she was helping me to my feet. She gave me some cold chlorine-laced water in a Styrofoam cup. She asked if I was going to be okay. Said I passed out. I looked at her, confused. I'd never passed out in my life. What time was it anyway? I started to look for Jazz, remembered I was in the airport and the sad pieces started to fall into place. I remembered the Army general. The crowd. The bad news.

Barbara. She had told me her name and about the last fifteen years of her life. Nerves, I suspected was Barbara's reason to disclose. She was there to meet someone on that flight too. She said it was an old high school friend whom she hadn't seen in fifteen years. They were to have a reunion. Now they never would.

I couldn't drive. I had to call Jackie. She came right away to rescue me, hugged me and cried though she'd never met Jazz. Then she took me home and stayed through the night. We talked, but I didn't cry. Just felt a lot of emptiness. I thought about calling Mom. Maybe Daddy could tell her something that would be comforting for me. He would know what to say in situations like this.

Comforting was his area of expertise, but he and Mom didn't know Jazz either, and I didn't want Jazz spoken about through secondhand information. No one who really knew me knew him. They didn't have the chance, because chance hadn't given us enough time together.

The radio station, 97.6, did a small tribute to Jazz over the air the next day. They played all of his favorite songs. They said he had family in Louisiana; a mother, two sisters, nieces, nephews, and a host of other relatives and friends. "A host," that's how they would sum up those Jazz knew on paper to honor him. Jazz would be returned to Louisiana and buried in a quiet ceremony. I sent flowers and a small note. I signed it simply "a close friend." I only wished I could have been more was the unwritten line imprinted in my memory.

• • •

Edmond called me to say good-bye the next day, though he said he would stay the week, he had changed his mind and was returning to Jackson early. Since I hadn't contacted him...well, it was good-bye forever. I didn't argue. I saw no reason to give him false hope when my future was so uncertain. I didn't tell him about Jazz either. I figured that part of my life was better left a secret. Tyson called later that same day. He had heard about Jazz on the radio, wanted to know if I was alright and asked if he could come over. I told him I needed to be alone.

I sought out Tinsley Park early that evening. I walked around in its emptiness with only the comfort of nature talking back to me. I remembered that Saturday afternoon in June a month earlier when Jazz and I first met there. Then he had played by the rules of my game to find me again. That helped. I drove past the Red Cat Jazz Cafe. It sat under a gloom of darkness. No lights. No music.

It was closed for the entire day in Jazz's honor. I didn't think I wanted to go inside anyway. I would half-expect him to be there sitting on his favorite barstool, his long, shiny braids twirling as he turned to see me standing in the doorway, that smile he had spread across his face, so reassuring and honest. Maybe I would never go back there. That thought made me sad.

Darkness danced with nightfall as I made it to the fountain at the Galleria. It was dark outside. The hours had flown. It was beautiful there with the reflection of the lights bouncing off the water. That was the place I would want to remember him. It was there that Jazz had given me some time. Then I started to cry for him, for the brief moment I had known him and for not really getting to know him. I probably would never meet another like him, and I never wanted to. Jazz was someone very special. I wanted to hold his love of poetry, music and life and all that was sincere about him right there in my heart. Let his sweet music play on forever.

⚓ The catch
of the day

35

A quiet September settled in and brought with it transition. It had been almost two months since Jazz's death. Even though our relationship hadn't developed enough where I was feeling total loss, I still missed him. I supposed there would always be that question of what might have been.

I was sitting on the balcony of my condo giving my future some serious thought. I had taken time off from Templeton, one month ago when the pressure of trying to balance tragedy in my personal life with holding down a demanding job, had taken its toll. I was actually debating whether I was even going to return. Templeton had become a pitfall for me. Everything that I had come to know while I was there hadn't worked in my favor.

I definitely couldn't go back to Jackson. Though I knew I still loved Edmond, I couldn't pick up the phone and tell him that. I had needed more time to myself than I first realized. But now it was too late; Edmond was moving on with his life, I supposed, just as I was. That thought was prevalent in my mind as I walked upstairs to my home office. I took one look at my doll collection and exhaled proudly. Finally, I had all of them in one place, yet something was missing. I guessed my therapist had been right in saying my collection was a habit to compensate for a missing part of me. I examined the dolls like I was seeing them for the first time. Some had been popular when I was a kid; like the few Barbies, Betsy Wetsy, and Lullaby Baby, but none were even vintage or antique; the closest to that was the Cabbage Patch one. The rest had no real value at all, just pretty and dainty features hand-painted on delicate porcelain.

I spun around on my heels, walked vigorously to the garage and grabbed a few of the boxes I still had left over from my move. I took a roll of packing tape and a Magic Marker from the junk drawer in the kitchen. I tossed an armful of old newspaper from the pantry into one of the boxes. Then once back in my office, one by one, I wrapped and placed each of the dolls securely away. I hesitated when I reached the last one, the millennium princess with which Edmond had surprised me. I quickly tucked it away with the rest of the dolls and taped the top shut. I did the same for each of the boxes and wrote St Luke's Children's Hospital across the top. I felt some recuperating little girl could better benefit from them than I could. I carried each of the boxes down to the garage, and stacked them neatly in a corner. I would arrange to have them delivered later.

I went back inside to my phone ringing. It was my cell. Edmond was calling me from Bush Intercontinental Airport. Although I didn't expect him back in Houston, it surprised me more that he would call me. I think I had tried his patience during his last visit when Tyson showed up, uninvited, at my condo. Edmond probably wanted to severe any ties we had once and for all. Unlike me,

Edmond left no business unfinished. I agreed to meet him.
It was fast approaching noon and I still had my PJs on.
   I was in my bedroom changing when Tyson phoned.
   "How are you, CeCe?"
   "Fine. And you?"
   "I was thinking of you. I wanted to call but I
understood when you asked for some time to yourself...
you know, after Jazz's death."
   "Yes. Thanks for respecting that."
   "I'm only calling now because you were the only one
that I could think of to share my news with."
   "News? What news?"
   "I don't want to tell you over the phone. I want to
show you. Can you meet me at the Park Place building
across from the Toyota Center?"
   "Toyota Center? That's the stadium for the Rockets,
right?"
   "Yes. I'll be on the fourth floor, suite 205. Say in about
an hour?"
   "Tyson, I really can't. I have somewhere to be."
   "You can just say no, CeCe. I'll understand."
   "It's Edmond. He's back in Houston, and he called a
few minutes before you did." There was a long stretch of
silence between us. "Are you still there?"
   "I'm here. So did the two of you work things out?"
   "Things are the same. He just needs to see me this
last time, I hope."
   "And of course, you're there for him."
   "Tyson, I already promised him."
   "Then, by all means keep your promise. Good-bye,
CeCe."
   "Ty—" He had already hung up.
   I dressed comfortably, there wouldn't be any blue
dress this time, or anything similar that might start a

new tradition for Edmond and me. Instead, I slipped on some brown slacks and a matching sheer, printed top, which Edmond would think was too revealing. I thought it was perfect.

Instead of going immediately to Edmond's hotel, I exited 610 to I-45 north, then took Polk Street to downtown. It was almost two o'clock in the afternoon and I wasn't meeting Edmond until four. I was headed for the Park Place building that sat on the corner facing the Toyota Center. That was the address Tyson had given me. Hopefully, he would still be there, I thought, as I drove underneath to the parking garage. I had to convince the attendant of the reason why I didn't have a permit and Tyson Treadwell had asked me there. I guess my name still held some kind of magic because he waved me through after phoning someone.

With my purse in tow, I secured my car and caught the elevator up. The door to suite 205 opened onto a lavishly decorated reception area, high-class and high-tech. The receptionist sat multitasking while she spoke into a Janet Jackson-type headset. Big gold letters on the wall behind her informed visitors that this was the advertising firm of Treadwell and Williams, but left enough room below them for another name if need be.

I mouthed the name Tyson Treadwell to a young, Anglo girl; professional-looking with a cute, short haircut and braces. She understood and pointed me toward a big mahogany double door. Behind that were some additional offices. Tyson's was first and his door was slightly ajar. I tapped on it gently.

He whirled around in his chair and smiled while talking on the phone. He pointed to a chair just in front of his desk before he wrapped up his conversation.

"Well, if you're here for the mail, we're not quite

open for business. Why don't you come back in a few days?"

"Touché."

"Couldn't resist. Give me a hug."

We hugged briefly with me pulling away first.

"I'm glad you decided to come," Tyson said.

"You said you had good news to share. I didn't want to disappoint you," I said, looking around.

"What about Dixieland?"

"He'll keep."

"So, what do you think?"

"Just from the walk in, I'm impressed. You did quite well for yourself, Tyson."

"Thank you."

I checked out his office again. He had started to decorate—a few pictures, but not the one with Malachi. I was glad of that. It was a huge office, bright and lots of glass window overlooking a view of the Toyota Center. "I must say you've really moved up."

"I like to think so." He glanced out of his window, then turned back to me with thought. "You know there's another vacant office around the corner. It's the same size as this one with the same view."

"Are you asking me to work for you?"

"No. Not for me, but as a partner. There's room for one more."

"And you think that would work?"

"What do you mean?"

"I don't know, the last time we worked together…"

"This would be different. We would be partners, equal shares in the business, fifty-fifty decision-making."

"We have a history in working together, you know?"

"But we wouldn't have any fraternization rules this time." He gave me his infamous smile. The one he had given me the day we first met where his upper lip curled up on one side and made him look immature and cocky then.

I looked away. "That wasn't quite what I meant, Tyson," I said turning back to him. "Gray told me about the Mayfair's campaign. He said you tried to take all the credit. Edge me out."

"CeCe, I hope you know I was a different person then. Look, I had been passed up and over on the job Tapscott hired you for without even knowing you. I—"

"You were looking out for you. Believe me, I understand."

"I hope you don't hold that against me. You know I wouldn't purposely do anything to hurt you."

"Oh, I'm not angry with you. It wasn't a big deal when I found out and I've since moved on."

"But you're bringing it up now."

"Just thought I would mention it, you know, in the event that we do become partners, we need everything out in the open." I replied.

"So, you will consider my offer to partner?"

"I'll need time to think about it."

"That's fair. Why don't you let me take you to an early dinner and we can go over my proposal. Then you can give me your answer when you're ready."

"Sounds tempting, but I'm meeting Edmond later."

"So things have changed between the two of you," he stated.

"We'll always be friends, Tyson. If that's what you mean."

"And us."

"Was there ever us?"

"You call what we had together, nothing?"

"We had sex, Tyson. Now I realized that was probably

because I felt rejected by my husband. And let's face it, you couldn't really call what we had a relationship."

"That's just the way you look at it because of what happened with Tayla. But we had more than just sex. Believe me there was more."

"I'll still need time to think about your job offer." I said standing up to leave.

"Sure, we can get together later. I'll call you. Take care of yourself, okay?"

"I will. You take care, too, Tyson."

• • •

Forty-five minutes and a couple of traffic jams later, I arrived at the bar in the Airport Hilton to meet Edmond. He hadn't made it down from his room, so I took a seat and ordered a glass of water.

"Hi, beautiful. You come here often?" he whispered in my ear some minutes later. I turned around to find him smiling. I smiled back.

"Only if I'm meeting Edmond Ross," I said, to play along.

"That's good to know."

We got the greetings and the compliments out of the way. I felt his eyes quietly scan my outfit but he didn't comment. He didn't look displeased either.

"So why are you back in Houston?" I asked, as he slid atop the stool next to me. His mood was certainly upbeat if he was here to give me the ole kiss-off.

"I just had some unfinished business to wrap up, and I thought I should tell you since it's almost a done deal. But first thing first," he stated, patting the front of his sports jacket like he was searching for something. "Before I get to that...He reached inside and pulled out a letter-size, brown envelope, then handed it to me.

"What's this?" I asked, staring down at the envelope, but I didn't attempt to open it.

"Well, it's your share from the sale of the house and a few investments and stocks we owned. I know you didn't ask for anything in the divorce. But I wanted to make sure I was fair."

"Edmond, I don't know what to say."

"Well, say it after you've opened it. Go ahead, you know you want to. You never liked presents or the secrecy of things all wrapped up."

I laughed. "You're right," I said, ripping it open. I removed the check made out to me. Just right of my name, were three numbers followed by a set of triple zeros. My eyes widened and my mouth fell open. Edmond had been generous all right, three hundred and fifty thousand dollars worth. "Edmond. I hate to sound redundant, but I really don't know what to say." Then I leaned over and hugged him.

"You don't have to say anything," he said, after leaning back from our embrace. "Besides, better now than later when you bring the IRS and some hot-shot lawyer after me."

"You know I wouldn't do that."

"Oh, I'm sure you could be vicious if you put your mind to it."

I looked down, laughing, and wiped away a tear. I put the check in my purse. "So you had some news to tell me?"

"Right," he sighed. "Well, I've been working on a business venture for the last couple months. One of the reasons I've been back and forth to Houston. I'm opening a restaurant here. A jazz club/restaurant combination, rather."

"Jazz club? Really?"

"It's for real, Ce—CeCe."

"But, what about the bank?"

"They already have my notice."

"Wow. Edmond this is a major step. What about the restaurant in Jackson?"

"Booming. That's why I'm so excited about opening this one. The people in Jackson were so receptive to this kind of hangout; I'm trying my luck here. If all goes well...next stop New Orleans."

"I would say you were really serious about this."

"I thought about what you said. Well, you and my therapist, of course, about me being so career-driven. Sure, I worked hard down at that bank, but I've never really been happy with where I am."

"You're president. Isn't that where you've always wanted to be?"

"But, being president didn't make you happy. I mean, my whole reason for working so hard was you. I wanted to take care of you. Make sure you never wanted for anything. In the end, I gained a lot career wise, but I lost you."

"Edmond, there was more to blame for the breakdown of our marriage than your work. I didn't—"

"Come on CeCe, I'm trying to do some soul-searching here, help me out."

"Sorry," I said, laughing. "Tell me about this jazz club of yours."

"Oh, yes. It's a cozy little club, downtown Houston. It's near the Theater District, so it's prime location. It's called the Red Cat."

A hot feeling leapt up and grabbed my heart. "Red Cat?"

"Yes. You heard of it?"

"Yes, I've heard of it."

"I would really like it if you went with me tonight. I

need to hear your opinion on some of my suggestions for the club. I have a few ideas like maybe put a few beds in there too. Did you know that putting beds in night clubs is becoming very popular?"

"Edmond, I don't know."

"Just dinner and a drink. Please? I promise not to keep you long if you have other plans for later."

"It's not that, Edmond."

"Then what?"

"I have some history with the Red Cat that you don't know about."

"What kind of history?"

Edmond ordered a drink. I took a sip from the glass of spring water sitting in front of me, then slowly began to tell him about Jazz.

• • •

I awoke in Edmond's lavishly-decorated, rented hotel room near the airport. He was heading back to Jackson later on that day, then he was returning to Houston permanently in a few weeks.

I had a smile on my face the size of the nearby landing strip. Not because all of Edmond's and my problems had been miraculously solved overnight, but I had just dreamt about Grampy Cecil. We were sitting along the bank of his favorite fishing spot at Mills Creek. I was seated on his tackle box. The fish were jumping as the sun baked a deeper shade to his copper penny-colored skin. The tiny lines on his face ran deep to define the wisdom that he'd shared with me so often. He smiled down at me, as I hummed and prepped my catch for home just like he had shown me. He spat out a stream of brown liquid from his mouth, then repositioned the big wad of tobacco in his jaw using his tongue. He pitched his last catch for the day back into the water.

"Grampy, why did you throw it back?"

"Because," he said, fanning the bothersome gnats from his eyes. I came to know later that he gave me those short or one-word answers just to make me pumped him for knowledge.

"Because, why?"

"Well, baby girl. You might be too young to understand this now, but later on you'll find that fishing is a lot like life and falling in love. You see, you don't have to keep the one you catch if it don't quite suit you."

"I don't. Well, what do I do with it?"

"The way I figure, you have some choices."

"What's that?"

"You can keep it or you can throw it back. You know— take the chance on catching a better one. Or you risk catching one worse than what you already had. You might even catch the same one."

My dreams of Grampy had brought me full circle. My heart raced with anticipation of good things to come. How could he have known back then that his wisdom would some day play such an intricate role in the decisions I would make?

I was resting on my side—clad in Edmond's silk pajamas' top while he wore the matching pants. Edmond had taken me back to my condo to change before we went to the Red Cat. That black halter-top dress now across the room, draped neatly over the back of the chair. My strapless shoes, one resting on its side, were almost underneath. Edmond's beige slacks and matching crewneck silk shirt had been placed nearby in an almost protective way. Silver-dome covered plates scattered with leftover shrimp and scraps of buttered bread were on the table. A small tray with a few strawberries dipped in melted chocolate next to that. A half-bottle of wine was beside two half-empty wine glasses on a smaller table near the window.

Car horns blasted from below, amid sirens from an ambulance and a fire engine zooming by. Planes taking off and landing registered noisily in the background. How could he sleep through all of that? I glanced back at him still sleeping innocently by my side. We were in a spooning position, close but not actually touching. I felt like waking him with my kisses to let him know I was still there. He'd had too much wine after we made it back to his room, and didn't want me to drive alone at 3 A.M. He had insisted I stay, but probably expected me to run off before day break. I thought he might have even hidden my keys to make sure I didn't.

I kicked his leg, just firm enough to wake him. He nudged closer until he found my neck. Maybe he was dreaming when he searched for my lips, and kissed them softly.

"Good morning," he said, and bit the sensitive part of my neck, making me squirm. "You didn't leave."

"I didn't. Besides you hid my keys."

He chuckled and nudged me again. "You smell nice in the morning."

"That's because we didn't get to bed until morning," I said.

"That's true. But we had a good time, didn't we?"

"We did. Good food and conversation. I don't think we've ever talked as much. How did you enjoy the music?" I asked him.

"I really got into it, even though it wasn't jazz. Who was that guy singing at the club, again?"

"Jaheim. I keep telling you that," I said.

"I should remember that. That's your friend Tracee's oldest son's name isn't it?"

"Uh, huh."

"Maybe I'll think about getting him to sing at the club again."

"That would be nice?" I said.

"So, you think this club is really going to work?"

"Are you kidding? When you, Edmond Ross, are behind it?"

"Thanks for the vote of confidence."

"You're welcome."

He moved in closer and placed his arm across my waist, then caressed my stomach.

"Now what?" he asked.

"What do you mean?" I replied.

"You shared my bed all night. That has to mean something."

"That you had too much to drink and couldn't drive me home, and I didn't want to sleep in a chair."

"It was hard for me, you know."

"What? Keeping your hands off me?"

"That too."

"Naughty. But you managed."

"Can I ask you a question?"

"Sure. What?" I said.

"What would be the one fantasy you would want to live out?"

"Ooh. I've never been asked that before."

"But you must have one. We all do," he stated.

"Then what's yours?"

"I asked first."

"Alright. If you really must know, it would involve me being completely naked in a big open, grassy field. And oh, there's a downpour of rain. Satisifed?"

"A little splendor in the grass, huh? So who else is in this fantasy?"

"I don't know. His face isn't clear."

"So if I check the weather for the next few days; and rain is in the forecast, you think it could be my face?"

"I think anything's possible."

Edmond took me in his arms and kissed me tenderly. All my unpromising thoughts from the last few months started to fade. Was this the man I'd been searching for to fill this void inside me? Jeffrey Osborne's song lyric: *takes separation to bring appreciation,* probably said it best, as it played softly in the background. Edmond and I were at a good point. I loved him and he loved me back. Whether we could ever fall *in love* again? Well...that we were building on. Slowly, though. I had learned not to expect too much too fast as Edmond had learned not to rush things. He took his time. So much that he didn't seem to care that hotel check-out was at noon, and the morning had slipped way past then. He also didn't seem to care that he was going to miss his flight back to Jackson.